teach me
like that

Copyright

Extras

Teach Me Like That Playlist
Cover Design: Essen-tial Designs
Photographer: Jim Cauthen
Cover Model: Justin James Cadwell

Dedication

Just FYI, Renee Hoffard claims Kegan Cole as hers! (But I won't tell if you want to keep him for yourself!)

Prologue
Kegan

"I need you." Kadin's broken voice echoes in my head as if on a continuous loop since the phone call ten minutes ago. He's never one to ask for help, and I can't even hide the pride I feel when my older brother reaches out for me.

His wife London had gone into labor just after midnight. She's full-term, so that isn't the issue. Kadin explained that they went to the hospital, and everything was normal. This is their third child, so they're pretty much pros by this point. They weren't even going to call family until morning time, but there have been some complications.

I couldn't get much from Kadin other than the baby's heart rate dropped, and London was rushed in for an emergency C-section. Since they didn't have time to prep her, she'd been completely sedated, and Kadin wasn't allowed in the room.

He's frightened and terrified he's going to lose his wife, again. That pain is heightened by the signs of distress the baby was showing when everything went completely haywire in the delivery room.

Since I'm only a few miles from the hospital, I'm walking into the waiting room to meet Kadin within twenty minutes of the call. Hell, I was half-dressed before he even hung up. He refused to let me call our parents and give them an update because they were at the house with the girls. As far as they know, everything is completely normal, and there are no problems.

My brother stands from the hard plastic chair the second he sees me. Without care, he wraps me in a hug. I squeeze him back, knowing he must be completely distressed if he's not worried about looking manly and just handing over one of his usual brotherly 'rough pat on the back' hugs.

"Has there been any news?" I ask as we break apart.

He shakes his head but doesn't verbalize anything.

I know he's terrified. His first wife Savannah was killed in a car accident years ago. He was nearly at the end of his rope when fate intervened and threw London into his life. This man has suffered more loss than anyone else I know, and I'm certain he wouldn't handle more grief very well.

Unsure of what to do, I just sit beside him, hoping he takes comfort in my presence. I'm not going to placate him with false assurances or promises of a positive outcome. How can I? I have hardly any information to go on, other than my normally stoic brother seems to be falling apart before my eyes again.

I don't know what he saw in that delivery room or what comments were made by hospital staff, but it can't be good if he's sitting here like his world has already ended.

"Mr. Cole?" We both hear the voice from a door on the other side of the room.

We stand and walk toward the smiling nurse.

"Mr. Cole?" she says again looking between us.

"Yes," we both answer.

Kadin looks over at me like I'm a fucking idiot.

"Sorry," I murmur, clearly out of touch a bit with reality as well.

"How's my wife? My son?" Kadin asks. His voice isn't any stronger than it was on the phone call he placed just over an hour ago.

"Both are doing very well. They're in recovery, and you can go back to see them soon." The nurse gives him a reassuring smile.

Relief washes over me as I clasp his shoulder with my hand at the good news. I feel the tension in his muscles ease a bit, but not completely. I know he won't settle completely until his entire family is home and safe.

My head is throbbing more than usual. Watching my mother try to wrangle Anastyn and Lennox is like suffering a hangover without the reward of the fun night before the pain hits. They've been limiting visitors while London recovers from her surgery, so I've been in the waiting room with my mother, father, and the girls for the last couple of hours. I never should've called them.

I knew Kadin would be hard pressed to pull himself away from London's side once he was able to go back and see her. We've received texts and pictures from the bowels of the hospital where the other Coles are located, but I haven't seen my brother's face since he walked through the double doors to see his wife and son.

I honestly can't believe the hospital staff hasn't kicked the girls out yet. They're like banshees or feral cats, bouncing all over, squealing like pigs. I don't know how London and Kadin deal with this on a regular basis.

Thankfully, after what feels like an eternity, Kadin emerges, appearing more put together than he did a bit ago. Seems all is well in that branch of the Cole family tree.

The girls begin squawking even louder when they see their father. If this is how normal five and six-year-olds act, you can count me out. I'd be in jail for gagging them and locking them in a closet; I'm certain of it. Knowing I'm going to get to see my nephew, the first male to be born since my gorgeous mug made it into the world, is the only thing that has kept me in this hospital.

I won't admit it out loud, but having another man in the family is something I've been looking forward to since the piñata popped at Sunday dinner a few months back and London and Kadin were covered in blue confetti.

I love being an uncle to the girls, from afar... very, very far away. Women confuse the hell out of me, but little girls make me want to curl up in the fetal position and hide in the corner until their parents come home.

I'm certain being an uncle to a boy is going to be so much more rewarding than tea parties with no alcohol and plastic crowns that dig into my scalp. Once he's past the awkward toddler stage, it's going to be nothing but hunting, camping, and fishing; man things that will never include the colors pink and purple or dining with fake food with stuffed animals.

If I had to wager by the glint in Kadin's eyes when he bends down to hug the girls, he's looking forward to the manly stuff as well. His smile covers the entire expanse of his face. He was born for this, made to be a dad. I'm happy for him and proud to have him as my older brother.

His life? Settling down with one woman and making tiny little replicas of ourselves? No thanks. There are way too many women in the world, too much variety to just settle down and pick one.

Chapter 1

Kegan

The last thing I need after a wild night of partying and an even more entertaining couple of hours with Sasha... Sarah? Shasta? It doesn't matter. We had a great time. *Back on track*. My phone ringing at six in the morning is not the wake-up call I need. The perfect wake-up? A tight mouth wrapped around my...

The phone continuing its demand breaks me from my thoughts. I reach over to my bedside table without even opening my eyes.

"Hello," I grumble into the phone that has interrupted my very limited rest time.

"You awake?" my brother asks with too much cheer in his voice.

"Do I fucking sound awake to you?"

His chuckle makes me want to hang up on his ass.

"I need a favor."

I sit up in bed and wipe the sleep from my eyes. It's rare that he calls me for help, especially before the sun is fully over the horizon.

"Whatever you need, man."

"I need you to come to the house and take the girls to school," he says.

"Except that," I complain.

He pulls the phone from his ear and speaks to London.

"What about mom?" I ask. It's not that I don't want to help him, but those girls scare the shit out of me. They team up and become unstoppable. There's a real chance they'll hit me over the head, steal my truck and credit cards, and head to the nearest toy store. I cringe every time I think about being alone with them. The last time I watched them, I somehow ended up locked in the closet for an hour while they drank chocolate syrup from the damn bottle.

"She and dad are on a long weekend," he explains.

"And why do you need me?" I know I sound like an asshole. I know he never really asks much of me. I know I should be a better brother. Those girls, though.

"Easton isn't feeling well," he begins.

I stand from the bed and head to the bathroom.

"What's wrong with my boy?" I ask as I load my toothbrush up and turn on the shower.

"He's cranky and has a low-grade fever. He's just turned six months old, so I'm sure he's just teething or something, but London is freaking out. I don't want her to have to take him to the doctor alone. The only appointment they have available is first thing this morning. It's only the first week of school, and I don't want the girls to be late," Kadin says. I can tell he's distracted because he keeps pulling the phone away from his mouth and speaking to others in the room with him. "This is the only time we can get him in. If we don't make this appointment, she's going to carry him to the emergency room, and there's no sense in that."

"I'm your man," I tell him around my toothbrush. I'll be there in just a bit.

"I owe you big time, Kegan."

"Don't worry, big brother. I'm keeping a running tab."

I can't really complain about Kadin calling so early. My alarm went off while I was in the shower. I lost maybe fifteen minutes of sleep; no big deal. The mere three hours I got before the phone rang? Status quo for me. My mind is clear, and my body is sated and loose, but a couple hours between the sheets with a no-strings-attached woman is enough to keep me going *almost* all week long.

I go out a lot. I love to have a good time with several of the guys on my crew. It's been the norm for us for years.

A beer or two and going home with a beautiful woman? That's my idea of a perfect night. With alcoholism running rampant in my family, I never take my consumption to an extreme. Plus, I can't drive myself home if I'm drunk. I always go to their place or a hotel, since not being able to escape is not a situation I ever want to be in, not after that one time in college.

I pull up to Kadin's country house just a little after seven. Pudge, Kadin's dog, thumps his tail loudly on the porch as I walk up. I reach down and scratch his head. He's just as exhausted as I would be having to deal with Anastyn and Lennox day in and day out. He licks my hand in thanks and goes back to snoozing.

The door swings open before my knuckles can make contact with the wood.

"Hey, man," Kadin says taking a step away from the door.

I smirk at his jeans and t-shirt. My brother is the CEO of Cole International, our family's company. He took over quite some time ago, but has just recently in the last five or six years started acting like the powerful businessman we've always known him to be. I'm lucky enough to actually be able to get out into the field and work with my hands building the custom log cabins we've become the go-to company for.

Kadin despised his 'promotion' in the beginning, but I think he's pretty grateful for it now that he's a serious family man. I'm not saying corporate tasks and shit are easy, but they don't compare physically to the work my crew and I do. He'd never be able to get the upper hand on the girls if he was exhausted from working in the sun all damn day.

"You'll need to put their booster seats in your truck," Kadin says walking away and heading into the kitchen. "We have an extra set in the hall closet," he says over his shoulder.

I leave him to help the girls finish breakfast and grab the little pink car seats from the closet.

Just what I need in my jacked up Dodge pickup; girly as fuck car seats. They match perfectly with the heated leather seats and mud tires.

By the time I have the cock-blocking pink seats in my truck and turn around, Lennox and Anastyn are barreling down the front steps and jumping into the truck. I turn and give Kadin a look of despair.

"Where am I taking them?" I ask closing the door once the last little plaid skirt settles into her seat.

"Edgewood Academy," Kadin responds.

I cock an eyebrow at him, giving my head a little shake to get more information out of him.

"Seriously? You went there with me last year when we were looking at schools for the girls."

"Got no clue, man."

"Pretty sure you banged the headmistress," he says with a smirk.

I narrow my eyes at him, my recollection failing me this time.

"T&A?" he says quietly, looking over his shoulder to make sure London isn't within earshot. I grin at him. He's completely dedicated to his beautiful wife, but the man still has eyes in his head. "Blonde?"

"Ah," I exclaim with my eyes widening and a smile spreading across my face. "Super nice tits. Thick ass. Hell yeah!" I say rounding my truck as Kadin chuckles and turns to go back inside.

I'm not one of those guys that does the hit it and quit thing. If a woman is great in bed and doesn't get those romantic stars in her eyes, if she doesn't set off any 'need for commitment' bells, I'm known to give her a second ride in my truck.

The headmistress at Edgewood Academy, from what I remember of her, was very… enthusiastic, but wasn't interested in anything but my cock the couple of times we hooked up. The perfect woman as far as I'm concerned.

Before I can pull out of the driveway, Kadin comes running to the truck with two handfuls of bright purple fabric bags.

"What the—" I look in the rearview mirror and smile when Anastyn narrows her eyes at me, daring me to finish the sentence.

I roll down my window even though I know what he wants.

"London reminded me that these need to go to the classroom with the girls," Kadin says handing over the bags.

"How in the world are they going to carry them to class after I drop them off?" I ask situating them on the passenger seat. "They weigh a good twenty pounds."

"You have to walk them into their class, Kegan. This is a private school. You don't just drop them off down the block and wish them luck. They're in kindergarten, not flipping middle school."

"Amateur," Anastyn's sweet voice says from the back. Kadin bites his lip to keep from smiling. Six years old and that girl has a mouth on her many people can't seem to control.

"Two different classes?" I ask pulling my death glare from Anastyn.

"Same class," Kadin says. "Anastyn's birthday was after the fall cutoff. Since they're only ten months apart, they're in the same class."

I nod in understanding, immediately feeling sorry for their teacher. One on one the girls really aren't that hard to handle. Together? Well, let's just say, Mary freaking Poppins would walk out on her first day!

We aren't even out of the driveway before Anastyn begins talking. "Guess what, Uncle Kegan?"

"What's that?" I say looking at her in the rearview mirror.

"We're getting a cat!" Lennox interrupts.

I shake my head. "No way. Your dad is allergic to cats; that's why you have Pudge."

"Yes way," Anastyn argues. "We heard daddy telling mommy how perfect her kitty was."

A quick glance back finds Lennox nodding in agreement with her older sister.

"I think they're hiding it until Anastyn's birthday in a few weeks."

"How about some music?" I ask turning on the radio while trying to divert their attention. London and Kadin need to seriously watch what they're saying or sound proof their room. I shouldn't have to suffer through conversations like this.

Twenty minutes later I'm pulling into the parking area at the private school. I check my ears in the rearview mirror. Much to my surprise, I don't have blood flowing from them. I was certain after listening to a kid bop station on the radio during the drive in would have done some damage.

I instruct the girls that they will lose every toy they ever wanted if they do not file out of the truck on the same side and hold each other's hands as they walk across the narrow driveway into the school. They may be complete heathens, but I'll be damned if they get hurt on my watch. Surprisingly, they comply.

I file threats of toy loss into my mind to use again at a later date.

Lennox holds my hand, and Anastyn holds her other one as we walk in a line to the front of the school. The bright purple bags on my arms make me feel like a complete douche, but it is what it is, right?

I ignore, mostly, the looks from all the soccer moms as I clear the front door of the school. You'd think rich women would have enough couth to not openly gawk at me while standing in little clusters giggling like damn teenagers, especially with the huge rocks of their wedding rings shining in the damn morning sunlight.

I may have enough notches in my bed post that I'm surprised it's still standing and hasn't been relegated to sawdust, but married women are something I don't even touch. Ever.

"This way," Lennox says tugging my hand down a wide hallway.

I increase my speed. The sooner I get out of here, the sooner I can get rid of the girly ass bags dangling from my arm. I'm not anti-female anything. I love all kinds of women, especially very feminine women, but carrying these bags makes me want to do pull-ups or crush a beer can on my head.

The girls are excited and acting like they're hyped up on loads of sugar and caffeine as we make our way down the hall. They bounce, skip, and giggle all the way to the classroom. It won't be long before Kadin and London get the call from this school informing them that the girls are going to have to go somewhere else for their educations. I can't even imagine the disruptions they cause in the classroom.

Anastyn pulls open the door for their classroom, holding it open for her younger sister to bounce through. I grip the top of the door as she steps in herself.

"Girls," A woman says. "Take your assigned seats."

The girls calm immediately. What kind of witchcraft voodoo is this shit?

"Yes, ma'am," they both say in angelic voices.

I watch in awe as the two little spawns of Satan turn into completely different children.

I cut my eyes toward the sorceress, prepared to ask for her spell book and stop in my tracks. Piercing green eyes, surrounded by more dark hair than you'd see in an expensive shampoo commercial, look over at me as the door slams closed. I'm so enchanted by her attention toward me that I released my hold on the door. The sound rings through the quiet classroom and echoes off the walls, breaking the trance she's holding me under. I blink several times, unsure if I lost seconds or entire days.

She's nothing like I normally go for. Her thin, almost lanky frame, and from what I can tell, tiny breasts, are nothing similar to the thick thighs and double Ds of the headmistress I was hoping would be down for some fun this evening.

She gives me another quick smile and looks down. I'm certain my cheeks flush when I realize my dick must be straining against my jeans.

Chapter 2
Lexi

The first week of school is always complete chaos, even more so when you're teaching kindergarten. Granted, this is only my second first week of school, but if I recall, last year was pretty rough as well. I may have almost given myself alcohol poisoning with my wine consumption that first weekend.

No matter how much planning you do, you can never really prepare yourself for the ruckus that comes with fifteen tiny kids in their initial week of a structured educational environment. If they're not crying because they don't want to be separated from their parents, they're out of control and have absolutely no manners.

You'd think things would be different with the children of some of the richest parents in Washington; it's not. Tiny humans don't really understand money, responsibility, and image at such a young age. Lucky for me, I've always managed quite easily with children.

My secret? I don't really have one. What I have found that works best is to make sure they know how much fun they can have, and then whisper. That's right, whisper. Yelling over them doesn't work. It will become a competition. Forcing them to get quiet or miss out on the fun is accomplished by lowering my voice. I read it in a book once, and I thought it would never work, but to my surprise, it works like a charm. You have to get your bluff in early of course.

What frazzles me most is being late, which of course on the third day of school, is the situation I find myself in this morning. The house next door to mine is in the process of being torn down, and every morning this week I have found bits and pieces of that destruction in my own damn yard. After the storm that blew in last night, the debris in my yard was more than normal. Hence, the reason I'm running late. My grandmother took great pride in her yard and would roll over in her grave if she knew I just walked away and left it a mess.

I tuck my head to my chest and do my best to slide past the front office unnoticed. The clearing of a throat tells me I've failed. I stop in my tracks, knowing if I just keep going there will be more hell to pay than just standing there and taking whatever chastisement Headmistress Amelia DuPont deems fair for a four-minute tardy.

"Should I expect behavior like this to continue throughout the entire school year, Ms. Carter?" Her voice is like a highbrow Minnie

Mouse and grates on my nerves more than someone tapping the end of a pen in an otherwise silent room.

I roll my lips between my teeth and take a deep breath, reminding myself that I need this job, and I serve a purpose in the lives of the children entrusted to my daily care.

"Should I?" she prompts again.

"No ma'am," I respond.

I could tell her about my morning. Most people would understand. Honestly, most people wouldn't bat an eyelash at a four-minute tardy. I only had one last year because I witnessed an accident on the way to work and pulled over to render aid. Ms. DuPont, however, doesn't care.

She doesn't take into consideration that four minutes late is still twenty minutes before the children start to arrive. She's hated me since day one, this being my second year and her third. Granted, I'm the youngest teacher here, and the one closest to her in age, but she's had it out for me since the beginning. Luckily, I toe the line and never give her any reason to admonish me.

"The formal reprimand will be ready in the office this afternoon," she says with more joy in her voice than necessary at a time like this. "I'll expect you to come by before leaving for the day to sign it."

My right eye twitches uncontrollably. I take a calming breath and blow it out slowly; it's the only thing keeping me from scratching her eyes out. I'm not a violent person, but she brings out the worst in me. I nod and walk away.

Crazy thing about that little interaction? She held me in the hallway, asserting her power, longer than the four minutes I was initially late. Ironic, isn't it?

Deep breaths in and slow breaths out. That's my focus as I walk to my classroom. I refuse to let my bad start this morning reflect in my day. The kids in my classroom don't deserve any animosity that the headmistress forced into my soul.

Amelia DuPont is a prime example of how a rich daddy's money can buy you a position of power. I'm not even certain the woman has the educational background to run Edgewood Academy, yet here she is the tyrannical leader of the entire school. I'm not the only teacher who seems to have trouble with her. She tends to let her claws out with several of the teachers; female teachers, of course, never the males.

My pulse is almost back to normal as I use my teacher ID badge to unlock my door and step inside. I only have a few minutes to myself before my tiny wards start making their way into the classroom. I greet each child and parent by name.

Some parents still look apprehensive about dropping their pride and joy off at school, whereas others can't get out of the classroom fast enough. Those kids I keep a closer eye on. Those children are the ones who concrete my decision to become a teacher; the ones who even with the money their parents have are sometimes left without the comfort and love every child deserves.

"Thank you," I tell one parent as they hand over yet another huge bag of classroom supplies.

As they kiss their child goodbye for the day, I work to make room for the new bag amongst the overabundance of supplies other parents have left. Too much is always a good thing when it comes to supplies for the classroom, but parents at this school aren't supposed to bring supplies. Their pricey tuition is to pay for all things needed in the classroom.

The school's supply closet, however, has seen better days. That's a stretch of the truth. The closet is all but empty, and on only the fourth day of school, it's concerning. I'm not complaining about the supplies being brought by parents because Lord knows we need them, but finding a place for it all is posing a problem.

The classrooms are designed for minimal distractions. Even the kindergarten classes have very little storage space and shelving. I've piled everything as neatly as I can in a corner of the room, but I'm going to have to get creative to get it under control.

I would love to say most people are bringing the supplies out of the goodness of their hearts, but unfortunately, that's not the case. Some parents do, don't get me wrong, but many of the others see one parent bring supplies, and they have to compete with them by bringing even more than the first did.

I smile when I turn back around and see two of my favorite students walk through the door. Anastyn and Lennox Cole are the sunshine in my day. I know teachers aren't supposed to have favorites, but hey, I'm only human.

"Girls, take your assigned seats," I tell them.

They each chime back with a very respectful, "Yes, ma'am," and do as they're instructed.

My attention is then turned to the incredibly handsome man who escorted them in, definitely not their father, who is also extremely handsome in his own right.

He seems entranced when he looks at me, and I know my cheeks pink from the piercing blue gaze he's burning me with.

I smile and look down at his hands which are holding several bags of supplies.

"That for me?" I ask. My voice is huskier than it normally is. I clear my throat hoping he didn't notice

"What! No!" he says quickly taking a step back. I watch slightly confused as he shifts the purple bags in front of his body.

I cock my head to the side indicating my confusion. "The bags of Kleenex and Ziploc bags aren't for the classroom?"

He looks down at his hands as if he's forgotten he was even holding the bags. Odd duck this one. "Oh! Yeah, sorry," he says holding the bags out to me.

I take the bags from his hands and can't hide the gasp that escapes my lips when my hand touches his.

Cliché right?

Should I be thinking this man is my long lost soul mate? Fat chance. One, because I don't believe in that mess. Two, this man has a glint in his eye that informs me he's nothing but a playboy. Three, any sort of relationship with family members of the children, no matter how much I'd entertain the idea of a fling with this man, is absolutely against the rules.

I smile politely as his eyes wander from my sandaled feet to the pulse point in my neck that is working overtime just at his proximity.

"How do you do it?" he asks with a voice deeper than I would've imagined.

"I'm sorry. What?" I ask forcing my eyes away from his beard and perfectly pouty lips.

"How do you get them to behave?" He tilts his head and indicates Anastyn and Lennox.

I smile when I look over at the girls. "Those two angels?"

He huffs rudely. "Angels my ass," he mutters.

"They're two of my best students," I say somewhat offended. "They have better manners than many adults I've met." *Present company included.*

He shakes his head in disbelief. "They are total monkeys around me."

"And you are?" I let the question hang.

I could say I'm asking because I want to know all of the parents and guardians who are picking up and dropping off the kids, but honestly,

I really want to know his name. He looks quite similar to their father, Kadin Cole, but younger. The family resemblance is remarkable, but this man less refined. He doesn't have the tired eyes of a father.

It's uncanny how I'm attracted to this man, yet not his brother. Don't get me wrong Kadin Cole is extremely handsome, but knowing he's married, happily if the way he looks at his wife is any indication, puts him on the no-fly list and practically shuts down any attraction I have. It's the same with all the fathers, even the unmarried ones. These men are off-limits. I just wish my body was listening right now.

"Kegan," he says offering his hand. "Kegan Cole."

I take his hand in mine for a quick shake. "I'm their uncle; Kadin's younger, more handsome brother," he says bringing my hand to his lips.

I jerk it back before his undoubtedly soft lips can brush against my knuckles.

"Lexi Carter," I say, the huskiness returning to my voice.

"See you around, Lexi," he says with a wink and walks out of the classroom.

I blow out a long breath I didn't even realize I was holding. It isn't until the door opens again and I'm hoping Kegan Cole is walking back in, that I snap out of my daze.

It's the beard, I think as I smile at the next group of students who enter the classroom. Minutes later, fifteen children demand all of my attention, and I forget about Kegan Cole.

Chapter 3

Kegan

Green eyes. Dark brown hair.

Two things I couldn't pull my mind from as I left Lexi Carter's classroom. Two things I pictured when Amelia stopped me just before I left Edgewood Academy. She was keen for whatever I might have had on my mind as I entered the school.

She made sure her breasts were all but on display when she approached me. Usually, they would've distracted me, but for some reason, all I could think as I looked at her was how inappropriate her attire was for school. What kind of woman wears such a low-cut top and stiletto heels to work in a school?

The question in my head was rhetorical because I knew just what kind of woman she was. Difference is, that kind of woman holds no interest for me today, not after leaving the classroom of the most incredible woman I've ever had the pleasure of laying eyes on.

I shut Amelia down as politely as possible, regretting ever having touched her in the first place.

Regret. That's a new emotion for me, not on I'm very familiar with.

Amelia was a tigress in bed. I should've realized that her aggression between the sheets couldn't help but spill over into everyday encounters. Hell, the woman grabbed my cock within the first fifteen minutes of meeting me a few months back. I didn't mind, and I thought it was awesome that she didn't seem to mind when I bent her over her desk thirty minutes after that and fucked her stupid.

I know what you're thinking. I'm disgusting for fucking the headmistress in a school, but it was summertime with not a student in sight. Even I have standards, as low as they may be. You'll think even less of me when you're informed that her pussy wasn't quite tight enough, even for my package, but she had no problem with a little anal action.

That wasn't the issue, though. Fucking a woman I just met is no big deal. Going back for more, less than a week later was the mistake.

Twice was enough. As exciting as she was at the moment, she wasn't anything I committed to memory. Hell, when Kadin mentioned her this morning, I couldn't even remember her face. Her tits and ass? That was a whole other story. She has some of the nicest tits I've ever seen, the best that money can buy.

I frown as I pull up to the Westover project. This is an older community, but we've been hired to demolish an old home and build one of our cabins in its place. Our log cabins are known all over the world. It's still going to look out of place in this neighborhood, but rich people get what rich people pay for.

The issue really isn't building in this neighborhood, not for me at least. The problem with these older neighborhoods is dealing with all of the complications that come with it. People don't seem to mind when a beautiful new house is in their neighborhood, but they don't like the process that it takes to put it there. Noise complaints and just general bitchiness about the chaos that surrounds building in an established neighborhood is something I have to deal with daily.

I turn my truck off and take a deep breath. My foreman is on his phone and the entire crew is taking a break under a tree. This is the kind of shit that frustrates the hell out of me. It's way too damn early in the morning for no one to be working.

I walk up to Tony, my foreman on this project and a man I've considered a close friend for many years.

I raise my eyebrows to him in a 'what the fuck' expression.

"This house should be halfway, if not completely, torn down by now. What gives?" I ask with a frown looking over at the ten guys shooting the shit under a tree to the left of the property. I checked on this place yesterday. It was all but gutted when I stopped by on the way home from the other job site.

Tony shakes his head quickly, and I already know what the fucking problem is.

"Asbestos," he mutters as my mind says the same thing.

"How did we miss that?" Our inspector comes out to every demo job and is supposed to go through it with a fine-tooth comb so we can plan the best course of action.

"It's only a little bit, and it was tucked away in that weird room in the attic. I'd say since it's such a small amount we could just ignore it," Tony says.

I narrow my eyes at him. He knows we don't operate like that. We follow the letter of the law at all times on our job sites. It's one of the reasons we've managed to stay on top in the industry.

He holds his hands up in mock surrender. "Don't look at me like that. I've already called our guy in to come take care of it. I know you and Kadin would have my ass and my job if I didn't."

I nod at him. He may have an opinion about alternative ways to handle situations, but he'd never actually do it.

"Might as well get these other guys over to the project on Lamar Street. No sense in them sitting around all day."

I stand quietly as Tony rounds up his guys and directs them to the other project we have going on locally. I enjoy seeing their smiles. They'd rather be working than sitting idle all day. Not that they wouldn't enjoy a break, but time drags ass just sitting around.

Asbestos removal will set the project back a full day, so I know what I'll be doing on Saturday and it won't be sleeping late and watching the college football game like I'd planned.

I'm waiting around for the asbestos contractor to arrive when my cell phone rings.

Kadin.

"You must have heard about the asbestos," I say in place of a hello.

"What?" he says, confusion marking his voice.

"Tony's crew found asbestos in the attic of the demo house on Westover."

"You handling it?" he asks.

"Of course."

"Listen," he begins.

I sigh. Every time my brother is going to say something he knows I'm not going to like he begins with that word.

"I need you to pick the girls up from school at three," he continues. "London didn't like the answer the pediatrician gave her, so we're sitting in the emergency room at Sacred Hearts Children's Hospital."

"What the hell is going on with that kid?"

It has to be something because London isn't one to get overly concerned when the kids get sick. She was at first with Anastyn, but she's calmed down drastically over the years.

"We don't know, but he's only gotten worse. I'll let you know as soon as we find something out. We could be here for hours."

"Hours. You want me to take care of them for hours?" I can't hide the fear in my voice. They could murder me and dump the body in a couple hours.

He chuckles into the phone. I'd punch his shoulder if he was standing beside me. This is no joking matter.

"Mom will be by your house around six to get them."

Three hours. I can handle three hours, I think.

"Okay," I agree. What else can I do? I'd never tell him no, no matter how fearful I am.

"You have to feed them," Kadin says.

"I have salmon and asparagus planned for dinner. There's enough for them too."

"You know damn good and well that's not going to work. You need to think simpler than that. I'd go with fish sticks and macaroni and cheese," he offers in suggestion.

"I don't have shit like that at my house." He knows this.

"Well, take them to McDonald's or something. You'll have a fight on your hands if you try salmon and asparagus. Lennox wouldn't eat anything green even if she was promised a pony." From the sound of his voice, I'd bet my condo that he's tried something like that before.

"That shit is going to stunt their growth," I chastise.

"Don't give me that shit. They don't eat crap like that often. London has gotten very skilled with hiding vegetables and healthy shit in their food, but unless you have time to puree carrots and bake a damn meatloaf, I suggest you give it a rest this one time."

He's right; I'm not a parent and have no idea of the daily struggles they go through with such tiny, picky eaters. I know you can't force a kid to eat. I also know that I still gag when I smell cooked spinach. I blame my mother for that.

I resist giving him advice on a subject I know nothing about and smile when I realize I'm heading back to Edgewood Academy this afternoon. I may be picking up two tiny tornadoes, but I'm also going to see Lexi Carter again. Getting another glimpse of her is almost worth the violent death I'm sure to suffer before my mom can get the girls.

"Same routine as this morning?' I ask.

"No. You don't even have to get out of the truck. You just pull up, and they send them out to the vehicle. Just follow the line of cars."

My face falls knowing there's a chance I won't get a glimpse of Ms. Carter.

"Listen, I've got to go; they just called us back," Kadin says in a rushed tone before hanging up.

I work as long as I can, but I have to cut my day short in order to get the girls. I'm not too concerned with leaving early since the asbestos has caused an impromptu work day for Saturday.

I creep along in the long line of cars, waiting my turn to grab the girls. Much to my despair, Ms. Carter is nowhere to be found as the girls climb inside and buckle themselves up. I don't even try to hide the disappointment on my face.

"Where's mom?" Lennox asks from the back seat.

I have no clue how much they know about Easton and their parents' plans for the day, so I go with distraction.

"Who's hungry?"

They both scream like they haven't been fed in days.

"Can we go to McDonalds?" Anastyn asks excitedly.

"Fat chance," I say looking at her in the rearview mirror.

Her pretty little face drops and she crosses her arms over her chest. Just by the look in her eye, I can tell there will be hell to pay later.

Chapter 4
Lexi

I'm spitting mad as I get in my car in the teacher's parking lot. I have to try to calm myself down before I leave the school. Fifteen minutes late, that's what the formal reprimand I was all but forced to sign this afternoon said. Amelia had even printed out the time stamp from my badge swiping to unlock my door this morning. I know damn good and well that I would have only been four minutes, five minutes tops, late this morning had she not felt the need to assert her power over me in the hallway.

I could fight it. I could demand the video be pulled from the hallway, but I've learned to pick my battles, especially since making such a stink over something the board would consider trivial could compromise my contract from being renewed in the spring.

So I stayed quiet. I even stuck around to listen to her driveling on about punctuality and how important it is to our students for the teachers to be held to a high standard. She told me I needed to be more professional and that included arriving on time and not leaving early. All of this from a woman with more than half of her breasts pouring from her top.

I contemplate what I want for dinner and decide that an all-out carb-fest is going to be best.

I crank the car and wait for my phone to sync up with the hands-free.

"What's up, babe?" I smile when my best friend Jillian's voice sounds through the speakers.

"Shit day," I reply.

"Already? It's only like the second day."

"Third," I correct. I rest my head against the steering wheel and let the cool air from the A/C blow on my face.

"What did those tiny little bastards do to you now?" she asks playfully. Jillian knows full well I don't see my students that way.

"I was a few minutes late this morning."

"And they destroyed your classroom. How is it that the richest kids seem to be worse than those that go to public school?"

Jillian was all for me teaching at a private school. She knows why I chose such an elite place to teach. She also took me out of town and to a club to celebrate. Her wild ass ways are also what helped lead to my very first one night stand.

I've known Jillian since I was a teenager. She's a few years older, but the age difference hasn't really been an issue since she doesn't seem to go by society's standards of what a woman close to thirty should act like.

"Not the kids," I say. "Amelia DuPont."

I don't need to explain myself any further. She knows how much trouble Amelia gave me last year.

"What did she do this time?"

"Formal reprimand for being late. I tell you, she's a total bitch, but if it weren't for that damn construction going on next door I would've been on time."

"I know," she says in agreement. "You're the most punctual person I know. It's beyond annoying most days."

"One time," I say with a laugh. "One time I show up early to your apartment, and here I am judged for eternity."

"An hour, means an hour, Lexi." Here we go with the same argument we've had for at least a year.

"I know that now! Believe me, seeing you tied up to the coffee table being screwed in your no-go hole once was enough for me!" I can laugh about it now. Back then, I thought I needed bleach for my damn eyes.

She sighs. "Man, those were the good days."

I huff a laugh.

"You want to meet up for a bottle of wine?"

I know better than to say yes to her, especially on a school night. It's never just one bottle of wine. Most evenings with her end in at least three and a massive hangover the next day.

"Not tonight. How about tomorrow night?" I ask.

"No can do, friend. I have a hot date tomorrow."

"No, you don't." Jillian doesn't date. She gets laid, but there's only one man on her radar she'd deem acceptable to spend any length of time with, and as far as I know, her boss Hawthorn Pratt isn't interested in her that way.

"Well, I have a work thing. I'm bringing a date," she explains.

"To make Hawke jealous." She doesn't even have to answer. I know her well enough to know what she's doing.

Her silence is telling. I want to tell her to leave it alone. I want to encourage her to just date casually or actually give all of her focus to anyone other than Hawke, but I know she won't. She's been pining over him for years. I know they hooked up a few years back, but then nothing came of it. She's been lost to him ever since.

I can hear another phone ring in the background, telling me she's still at work.

"I have to go. I'll talk to you later. Raincheck on that bottle of wine?"

"Of course," I answer.

We say our goodbyes, and my mood has improved enough to drive safely.

I head straight for the place I know is going to make me feel better.

I love being a teacher for many reasons, but getting off work slightly ahead of most others is one of the best perks. Thirty minutes makes all the difference when it comes to speedy service at dinner time.

I pull open the heavy glass door, already digging in my purse for my frequent diner's card. I more than love this sandwich shop. The thick bread they slather with mayonnaise on their turkey clubs is exactly what I need after a day like today. Correction, only the morning and afternoon dealing with Amelia were bad. The middle with my students was actually pretty fantastic.

It's only a miraculous five-minute wait at the counter before my sandwich and chips are handed to me. I head across the restaurant toward the drink dispensers to fill my cup.

A squeal and a giggle draw my attention. Turning my head, I spot the head of a little girl I recognize in an all too familiar school uniform.

Calm, quiet, always respectful Anastyn Cole is running around one of the tables like a crazed maniac. No other than Kegan 'Sexy as Hell but Completely Off Limits' Cole is sitting at the table she's circling with his head in his hands. Lennox is messily trying to get the last little bit of yogurt from the long plastic tube. She seems to be wearing more than she's managed to get into her mouth.

I fill my cup with soda and begin to make my way out of the restaurant. All hopes of sneaking out unseen dissolve when on her next rotation, Anastyn spots me. Her eyes go wide, and she stops on a dime. I raise my eyebrow at her. Without losing eye contact with me, she backs up to her seat and sits down beside her uncle.

With the absence of noise, he raises his head and looks at Anastyn. The distraught look on his face is almost comical, and I have to wonder what kind of bet he lost to be put in this position. Following her line of sight, he turns his head and looks in my direction.

His face goes immediately from beat-down servant to dangerous tomcat. If I take a step closer, I'm certain I'd be able to hear the purr in his throat. Unable to leave without saying hello, I make my way to their table.

"You seem to have your hands full," I tell him.

"I'm being punished," he says. "I did something in another life, or hell even this life to be relegated to this."

I can't help but laugh. He sounds as if he's in a torture chamber, and by his inability to handle these two lovely girls, I'd say he doesn't have much experience with children.

I set my sandwich bag and drink on an empty spot on the table and grab a napkin from the dispenser.

"Eat your sandwich," I tell Anastyn as I lean over and wipe the light pink yogurt from the front of Lennox's shirt.

"Yes, ma'am," Anastyn responds and begins to eat her dinner.

"You're like the little girl whisperer," Kegan says with awe in his voice.

I shake my head in disagreement. "It's my job," I say dismissively. "Plus," I lower my voice to a whisper, "you can't show any fear. They sense it like a shark does when chum is poured in the ocean."

"I don't know if I can do that," he says, also lowering his voice conspiratorially. "They terrify me."

I laugh at his admission and reach down to grab my bag. He places a rough hand over mine. Chills shoot all the way up my arm and down my back at the contact.

"Stay," he begs. "They won't kill me in front of you."

My brain is urging me to decline, but the slight, sexy, upward curve of his lip decides for me. I pull out the chair across from him beside Lennox and pull my sandwich from the bag. I can feel his blue eyes burning into me as I empty the contents of my dinner onto the table.

Maybe he'll look at me differently after this. Maybe he won't be so flirty, testing my willpower. I've known men like him all my adult life. When I was younger, I sought out guys just like him. They're thrilling and great for an adventure, but never ready for anything more.

I know what his intentions are. I'm not conceded, but the sex appeal and attraction are rolling off of him in waves. He might as well be waving a bright flag that reads "I wanna jump your bones."

I snort at the idea, popping off the lid to the extra mayonnaise I always ask for when I come here. It's flavored with dill and lemon juice. I'm ready to argue that it's practically dip as I take a ruffled chip from its bag, scoop a chunk out and pop it in my mouth. I look up to find his eyes on my lips as I chew, not the grimace I was hoping for.

He licks his lips, never taking his eyes from my mouth.

Oh hell, that plan didn't go as I had anticipated.

"Look how calm they are," Kegan says after several long minutes of eating in silence.

I smile over at the two girls.

"Thank you for staying to eat with us Ms. Carter," Kegan says.

"Lexi," I correct.

"Lexi," he practically purrs.

I squeeze my thighs together. I know, that even though I turned down Jillian's offer of getting together with a bottle of wine, that there will in fact now be a bottle of wine in my future tonight.

Chapter 5
Kegan

I want to smirk at Lexi as I watch her shift in her seat, but I don't. I don't want to come off as cocky or arrogant any more than I already do. It's a character flaw, everyone has them, but let me explain. If every woman you've set your sights on since your junior year in college practically falls at your feet, it sets a precedent. Hell, it's almost a law after that much time.

My arrogance comes from knowing that I'll make arrangements with Ms. Carter for after my mom picks the girls up from my condo. Cockiness comes from the fact that I'm irresistible, and she knows it. My assuredness results from knowing without a shadow of a doubt that Ms. Lexi Carter will be coming on my dick in a matter of hours.

I smile wide when I think about asking her if she has a school uniform, but it then falters when I realize that's honestly creepy as fuck. The idea of that, while sitting beside my two nieces in school uniforms, makes my stomach roll. I wipe my mouth with my napkin and cover my food with it.

"Not feeling well?" she asks, her voice marked with concern.

"Tastes a little off," I lie. A quick change of topic is what I need. "You have plans this evening?" I give her the smile that has been dropping panties for over a decade. I usually don't pull out the big guns right off the bat, but she seems worth it.

She cocks an eyebrow at me, playing hard to get. This situation isn't the norm, but I've had it happen once or twice. Some women try to pretend they aren't interested, all the while their panties grow soggy, and their clit aches for my mouth.

"Plans, Lexi. I have a few ideas in mind for this evening. Every one of them involves you," I say after she remains silent.

She clears her throat and shifts her eyes over to the girls, who are oblivious to our conversation. I'm not concerned about them; they're too interested in the games on the back of the paper placemats.

"That's not appropriate," she finally says.

"What's not appropriate?"

"This conversation," she says leaning back in her chair and crossing her arms over her chest.

I smile wider. She thinks she's acting closed off, but all she's doing is drawing my eyes to her slender chest. My mouth waters to draw in her delicately small breasts.

"If you think this conversation is inappropriate, just wait until I have you alone." I wink and lean further across the table, closing in the distance she created when she leaned back.

I wait impatiently for her smile. It never comes, rather she frowns, and I'm man enough to admit she's just as beautiful with a scowl on her face.

I'm dumbfounded as I watch her wrap up her remaining sandwich and chips. She even takes the time to place the plastic lid back on the small container of mayo she was using as if it were chip dip. She's slow, methodical even.

She smiles at the girls and tells them she'll see them tomorrow in class, and she walks away. Anastyn reaches over and pushes my chin up, closing my gaping mouth.

"That's rough," she says with way too much intelligence for her age.

I have no clue where I went wrong. I laid it all out there. I whispered her name so she'd know what I'd sound like when I'm deep inside of her. The smile, the wink, the suggestion of what kind of dirty stuff I'm capable of between the sheets. All if it. The entire arsenal.

I put it all out there, and she walked away. *That* has never happened before.

The girls are happy enough with the ear damaging kid bop station on the way back to my condo. I watch them like a hawk when they bounce into my personal space. They don't come here often because it's not really suited for children.

My tastes are simple but expensive, and nothing in my condo is childproofed. I don't have children, so there's no real point.

Both girls pull off their light jackets and toss them to the floor. My house is always spotless, but I just don't have the energy to argue with them about where they should be hung up. As far as I'm concerned, they can stay on the floor until they pick them back up to leave.

Anastyn grabs the remote from the coffee table and pulls up Netflix on the TV like she's some technology guru savant or something. It took me quite a while and several Google searches before I had it down, and even now if I'm gone for long periods of time, I may have to refresh my memory with a quick online search.

I sigh in relief as they begin to watch some animated cartoon. It doesn't seem violent like the cartoons I watched as a kid. This show seems to be about animals living under the ocean and their fantastical adventures. There's no TNT or acts of violence with the polar bear and penguin on the screen. I have to say that their underwater suits are beyond fathomable.

I'd hoped they would've worn themselves out between school and acting all chaotic in the restaurant before Lexi arrived. I realize I'm one unlucky bastard when Anastyn holds up the remote, and the TV goes silent. There is no telling what's going to happen next. I dart my eyes across the room at the cleverly disguised fire extinguisher, wondering if I'm going to need it this evening.

"Are you going to tell us what's going on with Easton, or is everyone going to keep treating us like babies?" Anastyn asks.

Lennox's head nods up and down as she looks over at me. It's possible she's been thinking the same thing Anastyn has been. For all I know, they could've had a meeting about it. Normally I wouldn't believe they'd be capable of that level of organization, but I've seen some crazy things today. I remember how sneaky Kadin and I were when we were younger; all that plotting and conniving doesn't seem to have skipped a generation.

I shrug, trying to seem nonchalant when I actually feel like I'm being led blindfolded into a snake pit. "He doesn't feel well," I explain truthfully. "Your mom and dad took him to the doctor. I'm sure everything is fine."

"His doctor's appointment was this morning. Mom should've picked us up from school this afternoon." Anastyn is calling me out like I'm giving false evidence on a witness stand.

"My doctor appointments never last that long. Not even when I had step throat," Lennox says quickly.

"Strep throat," Anastyn corrects her, then looks back at me as if she's been waiting for an answer for hours rather than seconds.

"I don't know any more than what I've told you," I answer. I'm beginning to sweat under her six-year-old scrutiny.

I've heard horror stories about how parents do things that scar children for life, never having any intention of it. I've read posts on social media about how so many people are sitting back and attacking parents for how they raise their children, when they overeducate them or undereducate them about the goings on in the world. I'm between a rock and a hard place. Not only do I not have any information, but I'm also concerned with what I say because I don't want to start a ripple effect.

"Is it because Easton doesn't belong to daddy?" Lennox chimes in.

What the fuck?

I look back to Anastyn, who is shaking her head back and forth and slapping her hand on her forehead like a sixty-year-old who just watched a Wayans' Brother movie for the first time, embarrassment and frustration wrapped in one tiny little package. The slump of her shoulders even portrays her concern for the *younger* generation.

"I'm only going to explain this one more time," Anastyn says raising her eyes to her younger sister. "Just because Nikki's little brother went to live with his real dad doesn't mean that is what is happening to Easton."

Lennox looks like she's considering what Anastyn just told her, but she turns back to me for clarification. "So Mommy didn't have an affair? Nikki's mom did, and now her baby brother doesn't live there anymore. What's an affair?" Lennox asks with wide innocent eyes.

I shake my head, feeling as if the walls are closing in around me.

"I told you, Lennox. You've got to start listening to me. It's one of those things from the donut shop with chocolate on top. It's filled with cream. Mom always says she's being a good girl and never has one." Anastyn beams proudly after her explanation.

An éclair? Is that what the hell they are thinking?

A tear begins to form in the corner of Lennox's eye, just as her lip begins to quiver. "If mom eats one of those donuts, then Easton will go live with another daddy?"

Before I can break down their conversation into manageable parts, a light knock echoes at the front door. Without a backward glance, I jump up from my chair and pull the door open. Relief washes over me when my eyes land on my mom standing in the hallway.

"Thank God you're here!" I say with more enthusiasm than I should after three hours of parenting duty.

She reaches up and cups my cheek lovingly; then turns into a crazy woman when she slaps it twice, a little too hard to be mistaken for affection. She hates that I complain about the kids, and it's her only way to get me back.

I follow her into the living room. The girls have already begun arguing with each other.

Mom smiles. "Don't you just want a houseful of angels like them?"

"Hell no," I grumble softly. "This is a house of sin, not a playpen," I say with my arms swept wide for dramatics.

She huffs indignantly because she knows better. I've never come out and told my mother that I sleep around quite regularly. I've never mentioned that I don't bring women to my condo because it makes things incredibly messy. I've never told her these things, but she knows. She listens without listening. She's sneaky like that.

"Any news?" I ask on a whisper so the girls can't hear.

"Nothing yet. They're still running tests, but they have admitted him. I'm taking the girls to their house, but London and Kadin will be at the hospital all night."

"Do you need me to take them to school again in the morning?" My offer is hopeful, but Lexi Carter is the stuff dreams are made of, plus I want to help my brother out.

"I've got them. Did you girls have fun?" Mom says as she walks further into the room.

They agree they did as she helps them into their light jackets.

"Uncle Kegan got turned down when he tried to ask our teacher out on a date," Anastyn informs my mother.

My mother gives me a knowing smirk, fully reading into my offer to take the girls to school again. See? I told you she's sneaky.

I realize now why Lexi shifted her eyes to the girls during our conversation earlier. She's around children all day, so she knows just how much information they're not supposed to hear is actually retained.

I close my eyes briefly and try to go over our entire conversation in my head again, praying I didn't use some of my more vibrant words as we discussed my plans for us. I'm fairly certain I didn't, but if I did, Kadin will be sure to let me know if they start using their increased vocabulary around the house or at school.

I shuffle my mom and the girls out of the condo as quickly as I can. I've had a long ass day, and since my plans of spending some time inside a gorgeous kindergarten teacher have been thwarted, all I want to do is drink a beer and hit the bed.

Chapter 6

Lexi

I held out after I got home Thursday evening. I didn't drink the bottle of wine I was certain I'd chug the second I got home. The last thing I needed after having such a shitty day dealing with Amelia was waking up late because I didn't hear my alarm during my drunken blackout.

That, however, didn't keep me from putting away at least a bottle and a half last night, but Fridays were practically made for drinking. Since Jillian was busy, I had to drink alone, and I've never been one to police myself very well.

The pounding in my head matches the god-awful noise banging around my room. The beeping of machinery, crashes, and men yelling are not how I wanted to wake up this morning, especially not after barely making it up the stairs last night in my drunken stupor.

I hold a pillow over my head and lower my breathing. If I can just hold it there long enough to pass out from minor asphyxiation, then I'll get the much-needed rest I crave so dearly. It doesn't help one bit, other than to nearly make me vomit from my deathly rank breath. Plus, my bladder is near bursting.

As slowly as I can, I sit up on the edge of the bed. The urgency to urinate makes me want to move faster, but I won't give into it. I'd rather pee on myself than puke. I know most people wouldn't, but vomiting is the worst kind of sickness I could ever suffer with.

With a balanced equation of calm, for my head and stomach, as well as using the quickest movements not to upset the first one, I make my way to the restroom. My head swims as I take care of business. It's very possible that I'm still a little drunk.

I strip down and grab a shower. Feeling somewhat human again, I get dressed and head downstairs for some much-needed coffee.

The noise from next door is deafening. It's ten times louder down here than it was upstairs on the far side of the house.

I pull some pain reliever out of the cabinet and take it with a huge sip of water. Looking out the small window over the kitchen sink, I can see several men walking around. Each one is wearing a hard hat and bright yellow vest. My eyes land on the tiny clock on the window sill. The little hands tell me it's just after seven in the morning.

That can't be right.

I look over my shoulder, and the digital readout on the microwave verifies the ungodly hour. I only got just over five hours of sleep last night. Not close to being enough, especially after drinking so much.

I normally wouldn't complain. These men have a job to do, and I know it's only temporary. Eventually, the project will be done, the new family will move in, and I can be bitter about their dog shitting in my yard. For some reason this morning it's rubbing me the wrong way.

I pace in the living room as I wait for the coffee to finish brewing. Back and forth. Back and forth. With each step, I grow increasingly agitated. This would be different if I hadn't drank so much last night. I can't get in my car and park somewhere quiet because I'm not certain of my blood alcohol content, and drinking and driving is not something I'd ever do.

I go back to the small window in the kitchen. Watching a plastic bag roll into my yard like a tumbleweed on a western movie is the final straw. I don't care that I'm in a tank top with no bra and yoga pants. I couldn't care less that the only pair of shoes near the front door is my mismatched *Monsters, Inc.* house shoes. Jillian and I found these at the mall and couldn't decide which one we wanted, so we took one of each. It's like our version of friendship necklaces.

I hold my head high as I trudge across my perfectly manicured yard and into the demolition zone next door. I loved the man that used to live here. He was quiet and kept to himself. He never caused any problems or disturbances. I never even saw him outside very often. I'm well aware that he also kept to himself so much that he was deceased in his home for several days before anyone was the wiser, but this is a peaceful neighborhood, and it needs to stay that way.

Mike and Sully have never made me feel ridiculous before, but I'm regretting being too lazy to walk to the hall closet to grab a pair of flip flops. There's just something about the flash of lime green and electric blue on my feet that makes me not want to take myself seriously. If I'm feeling that way internally how do I get any of the men over here to take me seriously?

Catcalls and whistling begin the second I come into view of the guys working. "Animals," I mutter. Their unwanted attention fuels my anger as I look for someone who even seems like he may be in charge.

I cross in front of a large piece of equipment and stand with my hands on my hips. I make sure my resting bitch face is on full display. They may doubt me because of my shoes, but no one will question my intent from the look plastered on my face.

"Mister!" I yell at the man in the driver's seat of the machinery.

The machine silences quicker than I'd anticipated it would, leaving me yelling into the now quiet job site.

Familiarity tingles just below the surface, which is ridiculous. All men in hard hats and sunglasses look the same, and most of them have beards.

Did I seriously just stereotype construction workers?

"Don't ever walk in front of a bulldozer, unless you're looking to get plowed."

I gasp at the familiar voice, just as the man pulls his sunglasses off his face.

If there was any doubt in my mind that his comment is laced with sexual innuendo, it is washed away by the annoyingly handsome smirk on his face.

"You," I hiss.

"Ms. Carter," Kegan Cole says with more excitement in his voice than I'm comfortable with.

"It's not even eight o'clock in the morning," I complain looking down at my watchless arm. Great. Now, I look even more like an idiot, as if the fuzzy slippers didn't express it enough.

He's looking down at me from his high perch on the machine, but I can tell from the angle of his gaze that he's paying absolutely no attention to my feet. Nope. His eyes have zeroed in on my chest.

"For fuck's sake," I grumble, crossing my arms over my overly-enthused nipples. I should've grabbed a sweater before coming out into this cool fall air.

"You seem perky this morning," Kegan says finally raising his eyes to mine.

My scowl makes him laugh, which only infuriates me further.

I take a few steps back as he unbuckles and climbs down from the monstrous machine. Damn, the things this man does for a pair of jeans and a plain t-shirt.

I shake my head and snap my eyes back up to his, reminding myself that I'm out here to set things straight. The knowing glint in his eyes means I wasn't as covert in my appraisal of his body as I'd hoped I was.

Oh well, better luck next time.

"It's great to see you again," he says closing the distance between us and invading my personal space. "I knew you wouldn't be able to stay away."

"Mr. Cole," I say doing my best to keep the annoyance out of my voice. After all, his nieces are in my class, and I have to remain professional. "I wasn't aware you worked on the crew demolishing this home." I look away from his hauntingly beautiful eyes. "I would like to speak to the crew chief or whoever is in charge. I have a few issues I'd like to discuss with him."

I give him a polite, albeit fake, smile and take a step back.

"Foreman," he says stepping back into my space.

"I'm sorry?"

"The 'crew chief,'" he says with air quotes, "is called the foreman."

"Very well," I say standing my ground, refusing to take another step back. He registers my inflexibility to back down a second time, and the corner of his mouth pulls up. "I'd like to speak to the foreman then."

He grins wide showcasing a brilliant, perfect smile.

I look over my shoulder to see a group of the workers clustered together watching our interaction. They're too far away to hear what we're saying, but I can feel at least a half dozen pairs of eyes burning into my ass. I shift my weight uncomfortably. Sensing my discomfort, Kegan clutches my shoulders and switches our positions. His large frame blocks me from the other guys completely.

"This is my crew," he says.

Shit. Why would I mistake him for just any other worker? His brother is loaded beyond what anyone would consider normal; it only makes sense that Kegan would be wealthy as well. Kudos to him for getting out and getting his hands dirty, though.

Crap. I squeeze my eyes shut, trying to get the images out of my head about just how dirty his hands could get. I clear my throat weakly and look back up to him.

"Please feel free to express your grievances, Ms. Carter. We can discuss them out here or back at your place, say bent over the couch?"

"Not likely," I say with a hitch, my voice failing at my attempt to sound indignant at his suggestion.

"Your loss," he says with a quick shrug.

I'm sure.

I take a fortifying breath before I begin to complain about the issues that have been bugging me since they began working on this property. Suddenly, I feel as if I'm just being a whiney bitch. These men are only here to do a job.

I remember my assertiveness training and the things my therapist told me a few years ago.

You have to quit letting people run over you. If you don't express how you feel, they will never know. Internalizing it and not speaking your mind doesn't make it go away. Speak up.

He runs his hand over the scruff on his face. My eyes follow that hand down his chest, over his abs, until it settles in the front pocket of his jeans. And now I'm staring at his crotch.

When my eyes find his again, I realize what he's just done. I regain my fortitude and sneer in his direction.

"It's not even eight on a Saturday. The noise is out of control and more than a little disruptive. Every morning I have to pick up debris out of my yard," I complain. "The roads in front of this block are covered in clumps of mud from your equipment."

His smile never falters.

"And," I say taking a step closer and jabbing my finger into his rock solid chest. "I'm just hungover enough to smack that damn grin off of your face and not feel bad about it."

He catches my hand before I can pull it away and holds it flat against his chest.

"I know a few stress relieving techniques you'd benefit from," he says on a low purr.

Cue sexual innuendo and thigh clenching.

With a violent tug, I pull my hand from his grip. "You're incorrigible," I say and storm back to my house.

I don't know what's worse, the fact that he thinks he can talk to me that way, or that I actually want to take him up on his offer.

"Nice shoes!" he calls after me as I cross from utter destruction onto fresh green grass. I hang my head as I climb up my front porch steps. Why can't he just leave well enough alone?

Chapter 7
Kegan

I almost followed Lexi back to her house, but she seemed genuinely pissed. I avoid upset women like the damn plague, and even the beautiful Ms. Carter won't be an exception to that rule!

I remained distracted all day, my focus on her home rather than the job I was here to perform. Diverting my attention, especially while operating heavy machinery could prove fatal on a job site. I forced myself to pull my borderline obsessed attention from the house next door and refocus on the task at hand. I'm going to be working this job site for months to come; I'll have plenty of time to interact with Lexi Carter.

The day ends early since it's Saturday. I'd never force the crew to work a solid day on the weekend unless it was absolutely necessary. Since we're so early in this job, we'll have the ability to gain some ground later on.

I make sure the guys do a super good sweep of the job site, removing anything that could end up in her yard if there's a stiff breeze. I shoot over a text to the cleanup crew to have them come out as soon as they can to scrape the buildup of mud on the road just off the property.

What else did she complain about?

Oh yes, the noise.

Nothing I can really do about that, other than not work Saturdays. If everything goes as planned, Saturdays will be few and far between. I presume she leaves for work before the crew shows up during the week.

I tap out a text to Kadin to let him know our progress for the day; then I plan to head over to Lexi's and let her know that I've handled her grievances to the best of my abilities. In my wildest fantasies she repays my kindness with wild sex; in reality, more than likely, she'll claw my eyes out.

I'd be lying if I didn't admit that her clawing at me, especially my back, sounds like something I'd be interested in.

My phone rings before I can step over the property line. I wander back toward the half-demolished house.

"Hey," I answer. "This property will be clear by close of business on Monday."

"Listen," Kadin says into the phone. "They found out what's wrong with Easton."

"Good damn thing," I respond. "He's been in the hospital for two fucking days. What's wrong?"

"Spinal meningitis," Kadin says with an exhausted sigh.

"Fuck," I mutter. "That sounds extremely bad."

I slap myself on the forehead. I feel like a complete asshole for saying that. I have no damn filter. My mom's been complaining about it since I said my first words.

"Yeah," Kadin agrees, clearly familiar with my issue. "They've started him on an antibiotic therapy, but he'll be here for a while."

"How's London?" I ask.

"She's," he sighs again. "She won't leave his side. Fuck," he hisses. "I downplayed this, man. If she had caved and given in when I told her he was only teething, Easton would probably be dead. This is some serious shit he's dealing with right now."

"Hey, you can't think like that," I say trying to console him through the phone. "He's going to be okay, right?"

"Yeah," he answers. "The doctors think he'll make a full recovery. It's just going to be a while before he feels one hundred percent better."

"You have to focus on that, Kadin. Quit with the 'what ifs'. They don't help anyone."

He pulls the phone away and says something comforting to London.

"What can I do to help?" I ask.

I'd do whatever it takes to ease some of the stress they have resting on their shoulders.

"I need you to watch the girls."

Except that.

"Kegan? You there?" Kadin asks when all he gets is silence.

I had nightmares after the girls went home Thursday evening. How Kadin and London trust me with their children, I'll never understand.

"What's the game plan?" I ask reluctantly.

"After church tomorrow. You can grab them from mom and dad's house. They have a luncheon they can't get out of. You can drop them back off there at five or so," Kadin explains.

I do the math in my head. That's over four hours. I shudder at the things those two girls can accomplish in that length of time.

I look over at Lexi's house, and an idea pops into my head when a shadow crosses in front of the window facing the job site.

"Sure, man. No problem."

"Really?" Kadin asks, his voice marked with suspicion.

"Anything for you guys," I answer.

I hang up with Kadin as I walk toward Lexi's door. She loves kids; she'd never turn down an offer to help a desperate man in need.

I don't even try to hide the smile on my face when old school *Salt 'N Pepa* hits my ears. The front door is open, and the cool fall air is permeating the house through the front screen door.

I tilt and angle my head, trying to catch a glimpse of her before I knock. It's not really as creepy as it sounds, honestly.

Rather than seeing Lexi in the house, a loud crash echoes out of the door followed by her obscene curse.

"You stupid motherfucking cunt!"

My eyes widen at her foul language. She is a kindergarten teacher after all.

"Lexi," I say into the house, getting no response.

I say it louder, and it still goes unanswered.

Expecting the worst, I open the screen door and step into the house. Looking around, it's like I've traveled back in time thirty years.

"Lexi!" I yell.

"Back here!" comes her response from the right.

I follow the long hallway until I find her standing with her hands on her hips looking down at a mess of splattered paint and an overturned ladder.

"That's not good," I say without thinking. I chuckle when I look over at her. Her legs and almost indecently short cut-offs are covered in a thin layer of lime green paint; the same paint that is all over the hardwood floor and two of the walls.

"The ladder fell over," she says pointing as if I couldn't deduct that from the scene in front of me.

"Clearly," I say.

"Can I help you with something?" She uses her forearm to swipe at her forehead leaving behind a thin streak of green paint. My fingers tingle as I fight the urge to wipe it away as an excuse to touch her.

Maybe it's the lifelong construction worker in me, but seeing her in a tank top covered in splattered paint has my cock straining against the zipper of my jeans. This is the kind of dirty I've always fantasized about but never had the privilege of enjoying.

The women I go after are always dressed to the nines, enjoying a night out on the town. Interrupting a beautiful woman while she does home improvement tasks has never been offered to me before. Not that she's offering. Telling by the glare on her face right now, she's pissed I'm in the house.

"I heard the crash," I say pointing back to the front door. "I called your name, but you didn't answer. I was afraid you were hurt. Especially after your outburst."

I watch her cheeks flush. She's embarrassed I heard her use that type of language.

"I need to get cleaned up," she says dismissively as she kicks her sneakers off before leaving the room.

I follow her through the house because she technically hasn't asked me to leave yet.

"The lime green back there doesn't really go with the décor in here," I observe out loud.

"What are you some interior design specialist?"

"No," I huff. "That's a woman's…"

Her eyes shoot up to mine, halting my declaration.

Note to self. *Keep the sexist shit quiet.*

"I just mean lime green doesn't coordinate with your corduroy, floral print couch." I offer. "The green seems like you. The outdated furniture, not so much."

Like a lost puppy trying to find a home, I continue to trail her into the kitchen where she wets some paper towels and begins to wipe away the paint on her legs. I bite my tongue to keep from offering to help her clean up. Hell, I'd lick her clean and risk being poisoned from the paint if she'd let me.

"I inherited this house from my grandparents. I'm refurnishing one room at a time. I haven't made it to the living room yet," she explains never raising her eyes from her task.

"That makes sense," I say entranced at her hands wetting her long, tan legs.

"I started upstairs with my bedroom since that's where I spend my most time."

"I'd love to see it." I lick my lips at the idea of entering her bedroom, of entering *her*.

"Fat chance, Romeo." She tosses the now green covered paper towel in the trash and stands to her full height.

She walks through the house again, this time stepping into the living room. It's almost like a time capsule in here.

"I use the den mostly," she explains. "Well, that was until I splattered it with paint." She frowns as she looks around this room, which is clearly her grandparents' taste and not that of a vivacious twenty-something woman.

"Your grandmother and grandfather?" I ask pointing to a large picture over the mantel.

"Yes," she says sadly. "They've been gone for just over three years now."

"Together?"

She nods.

"That's horrible," I say without thinking.

She huffs a sad laugh. "Yeah. Car accident. Drunk driver." She offers nothing else.

I step closer to her, regretting opening my stupid fucking mouth since remembering her grandparents' death is bringing her distress. I cup her jaw in my hand and tilt her face up to mine. I lean in slowly to kiss her just as I realize how fucked up it would be to take advantage of this situation. Sad, broken Lexi Carter is not who she normally is. I'm an asshole most days, but today won't be one of them.

She blinks slowly as if accepting what I want to offer, but I take a step back instead. Her cheeks flush again as embarrassment hits her.

I really want to ask her details about the accident. My uncle's drunk driving accident was almost three years ago as well. The last name Carter isn't familiar to me, but just the thought that it could be the same crash makes my stomach turn.

I clear my throat, my mouth suddenly dry.

"What did you want?" she all but snaps in my direction.

There's the feisty woman I want to spend my time with.

"I'll have the girls again tomorrow afternoon," I begin. "I was hoping you'd tag along, so they don't murder me."

She laughs good-naturedly. Her change in mood relieves some of the tension in my shoulders. "Those girls don't have a devious bone in their bodies."

"Wolves in sheep's clothing," I mutter.

She frowns. "You don't have much experience with children do you?"

I shake my head. "No real desire to gain any either, but London and Kadin are in a pinch at the hospital and my parents have plans. That leaves Uncle Kegan. Believe me; I'm their last resort."

She gasps and holds her hand to her throat. "Easton?" I nod. "The girls have been scared for him."

"Spinal meningitis," I confide.

Her eyes sparkle with unshed tears at my news.

"I just need to keep them entertained for a few hours until my parents get back home. Want to help me out?" I smile wide and plead with my eyes. There also may have been a wink and smirk filled with innuendo thrown in for good measure.

"No," she responds without even giving it a second thought.

My brows knit together. Not the answer I was hoping for.

"Okay." I turn toward the door feeling thoroughly shot down. A woman immune to my charm? I guess unicorns are real.

"But," she says halting my feet in their tracks. "I will go to help them out. There's no telling what kind of trouble you'll get *them* into."

I wait until I'm out of her line of site and back at my truck before I fist pump the air.

Chapter 8
Lexi

What the hell am I thinking?

I don't mind helping with the girls when Kadin and London are in a pinch. I'm now Lennox and Anastyn's teacher, but I've known London for a while. I'd even consider her a friend. She and Jillian worked together for a while at the law firm Hawke and Justin own.

But, I know for a fact that help with the kids isn't all Kegan has on his mind. Still doesn't explain why he stepped back instead of kissing me. I could see the desire in his eyes. He wanted it, but something kept him from following through.

I cup my hand over my mouth and breathe into it. Nope, my breath is fine. Maybe the mood was wrong in my grandparents' mausoleum of a living room?

The bigger question is why am I even worried about it?

Did I want him to kiss me? I can admit that I had a weak moment and thought for a brief second that his lips on mine were the way to go, but I know I can't act on any type of 'extra-curricular' activities with Kegan Cole.

I shake my head, trying to get his blue eyes out of my head as I walk back to the kitchen and grab a container of Clorox wipes. I'm not looking forward to the mess in the den.

I try not to think about the disappointed look I know I'd see in my grandfather's eyes if he saw what I've done to his hardwood floor. After two hours of scrubbing every single dot of neon green paint off of the floor, I don't even have the energy to actually try to paint the walls. Besides, I'd have to run back to the hardware store to buy more.

So I do what I do every time I get bored, I call Jillian.

"What's up?" Jillian says as she answers the phone.

"Why are you breathing so hard? Oh God, did you answer the phone in the middle of sex again? Jillian, I told you to stop doing that!"

She laughs loudly. So loudly, in fact, I have to pull the phone from my ear until she calms down. "No. I'm at the gym. But there is a guy here who seems like he might be down for an afternoon romp."

"Romp? Seriously, Jillian?" I sigh and settle on my bed.

"Don't judge me," she says firmly, but I can hear the smile in her voice. "Just because you're all dried up doesn't mean I can't have a little fun."

"A little fun," I say with a laugh. "I've known hookers who are less promiscuous than you!"

"Hey!" she yells indignantly. "Enough with the slut shaming!"

"Okay, okay," I agree. This is another conversation we seem to have fairly often.

"Are you calling to try to make me feel bad about my healthy sexual appetite? Because you know that will never happen."

"I would never shame you," I say.

I'll never tell her that I'm actually jealous of her ability to go out and have a good time without feeling regret and reproach. Don't get me wrong, I do it on occasion, a girl has needs, but I don't live my life seeking the next man in my bed like Jillian does.

"Hey, handsome," Jillian coos at her next target.

"Jill," I sigh into the phone. "Did I tell you that I met Kegan Cole?"

"You didn't," she says returning her focus back to our phone call. "He's a fine specimen. I've seen him a few times in the office over the years. I think London told me her girls go to your school."

"Both of them are in my class this year," I confirm. "Kegan brought them earlier this week."

"Like what you saw, didn't you?"

"He just left my house a few hours ago," I say toying with her, knowing her mind is going straight to the gutter.

"You dirty bitch," she says in a hushed tone. "I'd climb that man like a stripper pole!"

A sick feeling hits my gut. "Have you? Did you and he hook up?"

"What? No! He's not really my type. You should know that," she argues.

I know what her type is, and I also know what type she pretends is her type.

"He's a construction worker, rugged, and hot as sin. That screams your type."

"He's a businessman and his family has more money than Croesus."

And there lies the problem. Her taste in men is very singular. Well, her ideal man is actually one man, Hawthorne Pratt, a lawyer, a businessman. So Jillian pretends her tastes go to the opposite of that, the antithesis of Hawke. She seeks out the tatted up bad boys, the men she'd never risk losing her heart to.

I remain silent because Hawke is a conversation we avoid at all cost, while we're sober at least.

"So no, I haven't touched Kegan Cole, but from the tone of your voice, you sound like you want to," she says.

"I'm helping him with the girls tomorrow. London's little boy is sick, and Kegan doesn't seem like he can handle the girls by himself," I explain.

"You have a date with him tomorrow?" she asks.

"Not a date," I answer.

"You've made plans to spend time with him. That's a date, babe."

"If anything it's a playdate."

"Uh huh," she says not believing a word I say. "Are you telling me he hasn't hit on you? Because if his reputation is true, he hits on anything with big tits... oh, sorry," she says with a chuckle.

"Ha ha," I say into the phone.

It's a fact; I have tiny little breasts. I don't have body image problems. I'm not one of those girls. I like to run, so my small breasts benefit me in that department. I've spent way too much time and money on therapy to have self-esteem problems.

For some reason, though, I feel the need to defend my sex appeal to Jillian.

"He's a relentless flirt." It's all I can really attest to, because when he had the opportunity earlier to kiss me, he backed off. So much for not having self-esteem problems.

Suddenly, I'm second guessing my call to Jillian to gossip about Kegan.

I know what her advice will be because it's always the same. *"Hit that."*

"You know what you need to do?" she says. "You know you gotta hit that."

I laugh at her predictability.

"Not gonna happen."

"No reason not to," she says.

"I can lose my job," I try to explain.

"Pish posh," she says dismissively. "Do you plan to marry him?"

"Don't be dumb," I tell her.

"Then what's the big deal. Hit it, get it out of your system, move on. Who would even know?"

She has a valid point, but still it's a huge risk to take.

Hold on.

Why am I even considering it?

"I'm really not that interested."

"If you weren't interested, we wouldn't be discussing it."

Good point.

"Hey, I've got to go. If I stay on the phone any longer, I may miss my chance. He's getting on a motorcycle!" she squeals before disconnecting the call.

Tomorrow is going to be… interesting.

"So what are you thinking?" I ask after telling the girls hello and clicking my seatbelt into place.

I almost embarrass myself trying to climb into this truck, but I have to admit, I feel pretty badass sitting up this high.

"I think a movie would be the plan," Kegan says as he lowers the volume on the radio, almost silencing a popular teen song.

I smile at him.

"Don't," he begs.

"I didn't really see you as a Belieber," I say referencing Justin Bieber fans. "But taking a longer look at you, I can totally see it."

He frowns. "This is what the girls like. So long as this station is playing, they don't try to kill each other in the back seat."

I look over my shoulder and see both of them with their hands folded delicately in their laps as they look at the window. They can feign indifference to the situation, but I'm well aware that they, along with every other child their age, are nothing but tiny little sponges that soak up information every second of their waking day.

"The girls, of course." I nod in agreement. "So the movies?"

"Yep," he says backing out of my driveway.

"They just got finished with church?"

"Yep," he repeats.

"No movie," I say. "Not yet at least."

"No?" he says confused.

"They've been sitting in a pew for over an hour. If you expect them to behave during a movie, they need to run off some energy."

"God, I'm glad you're here," he says turning right at the end of my driveway.

Fifteen minutes later, we're pulling into a small community park. The girls squeal in excitement as they bound out of the backseat of the truck and run toward the slide and swings.

"See," I tell him pointing at the girls. "They never would've kept that under control in a dark theater."

He points to a bench and guides me toward it with a hand on my lower back. I discovered something new today. Walking and clenching my thighs are almost impossible to do at the same time.

"Why are you fighting this?" he asks with his eyes still on the frolicking girls.

"Fighting what?" I ask even though I kind of know what he's talking about.

"Us," he says softly.

"Oh, I didn't realize there was an *us*." I pull my hand to my throat and bat my eyelashes like a damsel in distress, sarcastically of course.

His eyes widen when he realizes he just sounded like he wanted some sort of relationship. "You know what I mean. There's chemistry. Things between us would be explosive."

I have no doubt about that, but coming together in fiery passion and my heart exploding when he leaves really isn't something I'm interested in.

Kegan Cole satisfies an incredibly long list of traits I find damn near irresistible in men.

He's funny, insanely sexy, just the right amount of cocky, and has some of the biggest hands I've ever seen. I know what you're thinking, and the size of his hands doesn't have anything to do with me wondering about the size of his... you know. It does, however, have everything to do with how I love nothing more than huge hands spreading the expanse of my back, my stomach, thick fingers in my... damn is the sun suddenly closer to the earth?

I pull my t-shirt away from my chest and fluff it in and out to cool my warm skin.

His lip twitches up. Apparently, he's an expert on social cues as well.

"I imagine things between us would be explosive," I say quietly.

His grin widens as if he's already sealed the deal.

"I'm sure when my job found out I hooked up with a relative of one of my students, my life would be blown to smithereens." His smile falters. "Explosive," I say with hand motions of my life imploding.

"It's just sex," he says.

"*Just sex* isn't worth the risk," I mumble getting up from my seat to go push Lennox on the swing.

Chapter 9
Kegan

"Such a beautiful family," an elder lady says as she pats my back and continues on her way.

I cringe and look over at Lexi. Thankfully, she didn't hear what that obviously senile woman said. A wife and kids? Fuck that. Not even like 'consider it down the road.' Not gonna happen. Kadin is the family man, always has been. Me? I'm the one who is repulsed by women sleeping over after the kinky shit is done.

I watch Lexi's ass as she walks with the girls toward the soda machine at the movie theater. Tight blue jeans decorated with tons of studs and rhinestones on the pockets makes me imagine it like a present, and God do I want to unwrap that gift.

I pay the clerk at the counter after he finally pulls my attention away from the miracle that is Lexi Carter.

"Nice ass," he says brazenly when my attention is pulled back to her immediately after handing my credit card over.

I snap my eyes back to find him staring in the same direction.

"Boy, you couldn't handle an ass like that," I sneer with a lowered voice.

He chuckles softly. "From the way you're staring, it seems you can't handle it either."

Cocky motherfucker. I find myself almost resorting to high school and college age with this teenager. He's pretty much challenged me, and I never turn down a challenge.

I snap my jaw shut. I don't have a damn thing to prove to this punk, who, if I'm being honest, reminds me of myself at that age.

I slide my card back into my wallet and snatch the bucket of popcorn off the counter so fast it leaves a pile behind on the counter. Maybe while he's cleaning up the damn mess, he'll think about running his mouth.

Each of the girls carries their own snack pack containing a drink, popcorn, and a package of candy, while Lexi has both her drink and mine. Her drink, of course, is a large water.

"Water?" I asked when she placed her order. I seriously would've pegged her for a cherry Icee type of girl.

She just shrugged. "Saving calories for the wine I'll drink later."

My kind of girl. Sacrificing in some areas so she can splurge later.

I have the tickets and a huge tub of popcorn. With the tickets sticking out between the fingers of the same hand carrying the popcorn, I use my free hand and place it on the small of Lexi's back. The contact, although seemingly innocuous, is actually a pretty sexual gesture.

I almost groan when the tips of my fingers find the bare skin between her jeans and tank top. Feeling like this, aroused to the point of nearing an erection, is insanely inappropriate as I walk amongst a huge group of children.

Lexi must sense the electricity between us because she does exactly what I expect her to after the conversation in the park; she twists her body until my hand falls away.

Predictable. Most women are, and predictable women fall easily into my bed.

I smile wickedly. She may have gotten away from me now, but we will be spending the next hour and a half in a dark movie theater, surrounded by little kids enthralled with what's on the big screen. I let my mind run through seduction techniques that would be considered rated G, and I can't think of a damn one other than a light stroke of my fingers on her arm. It's not even a fraction of one percent of what I want to do to her, but considering our present company, it's the best I can do.

Crazy thing about it? I seriously can't wait for even that tiny touch.

I may have jumped the gun marking her as predictable only seconds ago.

I predicted that even though she pulled away from me in the hallway, she would most definitely give in and sit beside me in the theater.

Didn't happen. As I settled into my seat, she sandwiched both girls between us and turned her face toward the screen, ignoring me completely. What do I do in a situation like this? First, I remind her that she won't be able to reach the popcorn and motion for her to sit beside me.

She declines, waving her hand in front of her. "No thanks," her velvety voice says before she opens Anastyn's candy for her and begins watching the previews.

After my subtle attempt to get her beside me fails, I do what every man in this position would do. I question whether or not she's batting for the other team. I mean come on; I'm Kegan Cole, a hell of a catch. Well, a hell of a lay since I won't allow a woman to *catch* me.

If I'm being honest, the parts I watched were actually pretty decent for an animated kid flick. I do, however, feel like I need to go watch a Bruce Willis movie to continue feeling like a true man; especially after this movie made me laugh more than once.

I spent most of the movie watching the smile on Lexi's face, and I felt her gaze on mine when Anastyn climbed out of her seat and settled on my lap. I thought she was in a super loving mood and just wanted to snuggle with me. She made sure I knew that she was only there for my popcorn, since her tiny scoop was gone. She may want others to think that, but she kissed me on the cheek once. She can't deny she loves her Uncle Kegan anymore than I can deny I love my nieces when they're acting sweet like this.

The switch flipped by the time we made it to my parents' house. They were bouncing in the booster seats before I could even turn off the truck's engine. Seconds later, they were barreling out and heading to the front door.

I look over at Lexi with wide eyes.

Her giggle at my reaction to them makes me smile as well.

"Imagine if we didn't take them to the park first. The movie would've been a disaster."

I nod in agreement, grateful I asked her to come along.

Without thinking, I tell her, "Come on in. You can meet my mom and dad."

She climbs out of the truck and meets me around the front. I keep my distance this time. It isn't until my mother comes out on the porch holding Lennox's hand that I've realized my mistake.

I watch as a smile spreads clear across her face before she hides it with her hands. I'll never hear the end of this. I've just given my mother enough ammunition for a year's worth of family dinners.

"Oh, Kegan," my mother gasps as Lexi and I walk up the front stairs of the porch. "She's beautiful. You haven't brought a girl home since..."

"Mom!" I chastise cutting her off.

I feel like a teenager again, bringing home my first girlfriend to meet my parents. Granted, Lexi is the only girl besides the one in high school that has trekked up these stairs. Now, just like then, I want to crawl under the porch in embarrassment.

More because Summer is the last person I want to think about than my mom getting excited at Lexi being here. We dated for a few months my senior year in high school, went to different colleges, and mutually called things off. To hear my mother tell it, I broke her heart and any chances she'd have at having grandchildren.

Kadin was already married by then, and Savannah was very vocal about her desire never to have children.

"Honey!" my mother screams over her shoulder through the screen door. "Come out here and meet Kegan's girlfriend!"

My father makes his way out of the den faster than any man in his sixties should be able to move. A smile is on his face the second he crosses the threshold. He nods softly in approval at the sight of Lexi.

"Lexi Carter," I say in introduction to my parents.

"Friend," Lexi corrects holding her hand out to shake theirs. "Not girlfriend."

Friend. I can work with *friend*. At least she didn't identify herself as only the girls' school teacher.

My mom wraps her arms around Lexi in a huge hug, disregarding her proffered hand. If this is awkward for me, I can't imagine how uncomfortable she is.

My dad winks at me, a true lady's man in his own day. Lexi catches it and scoffs at our interaction.

My mom finally releases her and takes a step back. "Would you like to come in for a drink and a snack?" she offers.

"No, thank you," Lexi says quickly, and I can finally take a relaxing breath.

Any other woman in this situation would jump at the offer, and I'm grateful she declined. If Lexi stepped foot in that house, my mother would begin planning the wedding. She'd have the china pattern picked out before her homemade cookies hit the table.

Both girls make their way out onto the porch carrying a pack of fruit snacks, as if they didn't just eat their weight in candy and popcorn at the movies.

Lennox tugs on my dad's shirt until he leans down so she can whisper into his ear. "That's my teacher," she informs her grandfather loud enough for everyone to hear.

"The one who shot Uncle Kegan down when he asked her out last week," Anastyn adds even louder.

My mother's cheeks turn red, not in embarrassment for me, but rather because she's trying to bite back her laugh.

My dad doesn't even bother as he tilts his face up and laughs.

If it weren't for the slight smile tilting Lexi's perfect lips up, I'd wish this interaction never happened, but seeing her amused at my expense brings a certain peace to me.

"Must not happen often," Lexi says cutting her eyes to the side at me, but she's talking to my parents.

My dad sobers almost immediately. "Never, honey. He's a Cole." Nothing but seriousness marks his face.

Damn straight, dad. Cole men don't get turned down. That part goes unsaid of course.

My cheeks flame as my dad slaps my mom on the ass and makes her giggle. The girls follow suit, laughing at their grandfather's ridiculousness. They see it all the time between their own parents and mine. I was brought up in a very loving home, with parents who weren't afraid to show their affection. Kadin and London are the same way.

I'm in the fucking Twilight Zone.

It's Lexi's turn to roll her lips inward to keep from laughing. I'm glad she finds this shit amusing because after today and how my parents are acting, they can sure as hell guarantee I'll never let another woman step foot on this property again. Today was a slip of the mind.

"We should go," I tell Lexi.

"It was nice to meet you," she says politely to my parents.

I, on the other hand, sneer at them, letting them know I'm not happy about any of this.

"Come back soon," my mom says with slight disappointment in her voice as we turn back to the truck to leave.

It isn't until we're pulling away that I realize I didn't actually introduce her to my parents. My mom had me so flustered, formal introductions were never made.

Chapter 10
Lexi

The laid back flirtatious man I've spent most of the afternoon with is not the same man that just left his parents' house. Something has shifted his mood dramatically. I thought his mom and dad were endearing and funny. Clearly, he doesn't feel the same way.

I can't help but stare at his sandy-blond hair and strong jawline as we ride back to my house in silence. Seeing his father is like staring at exactly what he will look like in thirty years. Kegan, his brother, and his father all have the same handsome features. They definitely have great genes.

I'm not certain, but I think he was very uncomfortable with me meeting his family, which is seriously wrong because he's the one who told me to get out and meet them.

Judging by his mother's response to me, he doesn't make a habit of showing up at their house with women, a true testament to his playboy ways. At least he's respectful, hopefully keeping his extracurricular activities to himself and not flaunting his manwhore ways in front of his mother.

His dad? Totally different story. I caught that little wink Mr. Cole threw at his son. I bet he was a heartbreaker back in his day.

I sigh and pull my eyes reluctantly from Kegan. If I were in college, I probably would've already found myself climbing out of his bed. I'm wickedly attracted to him. The way he carries himself tells me he'd be a beast in the sack, but he's grown on me enough to know that he'd break my damn heart before I even realized I'd handed it over to him.

"Thank you for helping with the girls," Kegan says as we begin to cross from the cityscape to a more residential area of town.

I almost say 'anytime' like my manners and the etiquette classes my grandmother made me take say I'm supposed to, but I don't. I wouldn't mean it, and I pride myself on telling the truth.

Most of the time I tell the truth, but if Kegan asked me what I thought of him, or if I wanted to run the tips of my fingers down the light scruff on his chin, I would tell him no. That would be a lie. Getting my hands on him even though I know he'll crush me is *all* I can think about.

"No problem," I say quietly. "They're great girls," I say, continuing the conversation since he was the one to break the silence.

"When you're around," he says with a grin.

He can deny it all he wants, but I saw the way his face lit up when Anastyn climbed into his lap. He loves those girls. If he didn't, he wouldn't drop everything in the world to help with them when Kadin and London needed it, even though he's terrified of them.

"Your parents seem nice," I say.

He groans. "I'm sorry you had to see that. They usually leave the grab-ass out of the eyes of nonfamily members."

I can't help but laugh at his discomfort.

"It's nice to see an older couple clearly in love. You're very blessed to have parents that love you enough to get weird when you show up with a girl." I turn my head back to the window, even though there's really nothing to see.

"They're great," he agrees reluctantly. "What about your parents?"

I never should've even mentioned his family.

"They're dead," I say without an inflection of emotion.

"Damn, Lexi. I'm so sorry," he begins.

I hold my hand up to stop him from speaking. "I've been without parents a long time."

"Sorry," he says again.

Out of the corner of my eye, I can see him reach his hand across looking for mine to offer comfort, but I keep my hands wrapped around one another in my lap. He eventually pulls his hand back.

"Me too," I whisper.

The last thing I want to think about, ever, is the family I've lost and the one I never really had.

The rest of the drive is much like the first half, silent.

I climb out of his truck quickly when he pulls up in front of my house. He's crunching up the gravel driveway behind me, so I pause on the front porch. There's no way I'll be able to resist him if he manages to get me inside the house. I hold my keys in my hand, but don't move to insert them into the lock.

"Lexi," he says, his breath rushing over my shoulder. "I didn't mean to upset you."

I shake my head, trying to let him know it wasn't him.

He turns me to face him, and I watch as his eyes dart back and forth between mine.

"You didn't. Promise," I tell him.

I know what he's planning to do when his tongue reaches out and wets his lips. Hell, I knew what was going to happen the second I stepped out of the truck, and he followed.

So what do I do? I do what any warm-blooded woman would do standing in front of Kegan Cole as he leans in closer to their mouth; I close my eyes and wait for his lips to meet mine. I wait for the forcefulness that I've pictured more than once to strike my mouth, but it never comes.

First, I feel his warm, comforting hand cup my cheek. Next, his warm breath is ghosting across my lips, sending waves of goosebumps and a foreign tingle down my spine. Then I feel his firm, yet incredibly soft, lips brush against mine.

Soft and gentle. That is not Kegan Cole. He's abrasive and forward on his best day. This is pity. This is him feeling sorry that I didn't have parents, and he had two great ones. The last thing I need from Kegan Cole is fucking pity.

I push at his shoulders, breaking his delicate contact with my lips.

I try to step back, but he has one hand on my lower back and one gripping my ass. I was so engrossed with how his mouth was going to feel on mine, I was oblivious to where his hands were roaming. Now that they are there, I feel the same burn in his touch that I felt at the movie theater when his fingers brushed the skin on my back.

"Don't," I say with less force than I was aiming for. I want to be angry. I want him to know I'm mad, pissed that he's feeling sorry for me. I hate when people treat me like that. "I don't need your pity."

His hooded eyes open wider. "Pity? Lexi, there is nothing pitiful about you."

He flexes his arms and crushes me against his body. His mouth hits mine once again, but this time, he kisses me like I'd expect him to.

Giving me no time to stand my ground, his tongue is inside my mouth a second later.

Jesus, what a glorious muscle.

The same hands that were used to push him away are now clutching at him, trying to draw him closer. Heavy breathing and my own whimpers are the only sounds surrounding us as I feel his fingers flex and dig deeper into my ass.

I'm no angel by any stretch of the imagination; my college days were pretty crazy, but I've never been kissed like this. I was going about it all wrong, picking men the same age as me. There has to be at least a five-year age difference between us. Even though many wouldn't consider a thirty-year-old man an actual 'older man,' especially compared to me at twenty-five, but I'll be damned if that age gap doesn't make up for the difference.

There isn't any fumbling and bumbling. I'm not being pawed at and groped. The only other man who's had skilled, sure arms around me was Hunter. The thought sobers me immediately.

I push at his chest until he breaks free from my mouth.

"We can't do this," I say trying to catch my breath.

"Of course we can," Kegan says grinding his hips against mine. There's no way to ignore exactly where his mind is right now.

"We can't. I told you in the park. I'll lose my job. Plus, I'm not available," I lie.

I take a step back from him and wrap my arms around myself protectively.

I watch his tongue as it snakes out and licks my taste from his lips.

His eyes narrow momentarily at my admission; then they spark back to life. "We can keep it a secret," he offers.

Whatever fire he has been stoking the last week or so has just been completely drenched, and that is not a reference to my damp panties. I mean doused with water, no spark left. His mouth just ruined the moment we were having; the one I was fighting against.

"I'm nobody's secret," I tell him with my head held high.

"That's not..."

I cut him off. "The last guy that wanted me to be a secret ruined me."

He frowns at me, but I'm not sure which part is causing him the most concern: my admission of being hurt before or the fact that his dick is hard, and he's finally realizing I'm not going to be the one to take care of it for him.

"Please leave," I say sliding my key into the lock.

"Lexi," he says quietly as I push open my front door.

"Goodbye, Kegan," I say with resolve and close the door behind me.

His steps don't even falter as he walks off my porch. There was no hesitation when he quickly made his way to his truck, cranked it, and backed out of my driveway. Even though that was exactly how I expected him to act, I'd hoped he'd say something, knock on the door and try to explain that he isn't that type of guy. He'd be lying of course, but it would be nice to hear.

I flip the deadbolt in place and make my way up to my room without turning on a light in the house. It's still fairly early in the evening, but I don't feel like going through my usual routine for a Sunday night. I set my alarm on my phone for an hour earlier than usual, kick off my shoes, and fall into my bed.

I try to clear my mind as I close my eyes, but I can still feel his lips on mine. After a wasted hour, I convince myself I'll be able to deal with everything better tomorrow, and I fall into a restless sleep.

Chapter 11
Kegan

Just sex isn't worth the risk.

I'm nobody's secret.

I'm not available.

What the fuck am I doing?

I suggest, even after she tells me she's with someone that we still hook up in secret? I've lost my damn mind apparently. Married, or taken women for that matter, are a strict, hard limit for me.

I slam the heel of my hand against the steering wheel. That makes three times now that she's set off alarm bells in my brain. She's not a quick fuck, good time type of girl, yet I can't manage to stay away from her. She has relationship written all over her, which I guess is true since she just admitted to being in one.

Who am I kidding? No, she doesn't. She practically screams: I'm single and have no plans to change it, so leave me the hell alone; a contradiction to what she just told me.

I didn't imagine things; she kissed me back when my lips landed on hers. She's as into me as I am her, but something is holding her back.

I'm clearly struggling with the answer no. As the youngest in my family, I didn't hear it much growing up. I don't hear it much now. At work I'm the boss; in my personal life, I have too many women fighting over me. So what is it about Lexi Carter that makes me want to pursue a woman for the first time in as long as I can remember?

I don't even want to think about her any longer. No woman is worth the type of fight and energy required it is taking to bed Lexi, especially if she has something going on with someone else.

I pull into the first parking lot I come across.

My guard is down, that's all it is. It's been what, two days since I got laid?

I rest my head against the headrest and do the math.

The last time...

Kadin called me the next day because he needed help with the girls. That's the day I met Lexi at her school. Thursday. So that little blonde chick was Wednesday night. Today makes day number four. Well, that just isn't going to work.

I lift my hips and pull my cell phone from my pocket. I hate nothing more than being forced to call up one of the women in my phone, but this is practically an emergency, and I don't feel like going fishing at the bar.

I scroll through my contacts, and absolutely no one seems like a good idea. For a split second, I actually contemplate just going home and not worrying about it, but the slow throb and deep ache in my balls won't let it go. I've been stiff in my jeans off and on for hours today around Lexi, and that kind of torture is enough to drive any man insane.

I make it to the bottom of my contacts and scroll in reverse order. If anyone saw my contact list, they'd know for a fact that I'm a complete asshole. Most of the contacts don't even have legit names but rather nicknames. How do I keep them straight? I make sure I have a picture of them with their contact info, so when I 'search' I'm looking at their faces rather than their names, because I'd never be able to keep that shit straight.

Unfortunately, any of the women with long brown hair are automatically excluded from tonight's search, since it will only remind me of the woman who just slammed her door in my face, and I don't need that shit in my head ruining my evening.

'Ginger' will do just fine. I press call on my phone and listen to it ring through the sound system in my truck.

"Kegan," she breathes into the phone.

"Hey, doll," I say using a lower, sexier register of my voice. "You have plans this evening?"

I hear the beginning of a squeal before she fully covers up the mouthpiece on the phone. I smile and nod. That's how a woman is supposed to act when I offer to spend some time with them. Lexi should take notes from this extremely excited woman.

A long moment later there's an audible shuffle and then her breathing back on the line. "I had some stuff going on, but I can rearrange. You want to come over?"

"Nice of you to ask, doll. Text your address to me," I tell her.

"You've been here twice, Kegan. You still can't remember?" she complains softly into the phone.

I want to tell her that I don't even remember her actual name, but that won't lead to the conclusion I need for the evening.

"I get turned around, doll." It's a damn lie of course. I was an Eagle Scout, but that doesn't get me any closer to remembering where this chick lives.

"Don't worry, baby. I'll text it to you," she coos into the phone.

"Thanks, doll. See you soon."

We hang up, and I wait until the text comes in.

Fuck. It's all the way across town. I should start saving these women in my phone by geographical location; it sure would make things a lot easier.

Half an hour later I'm pulling into the subterranean parking garage of "Ginger's" building. I don't know what the girl does for a living, but she definitely has some money to live in a place like this.

I finger comb my disheveled hair in the mirrored wall of the elevator on my way to the tenth floor. I haven't even made my way to her door yet, and I'm already bored with the idea of how the next hour or so will go.

I step off the elevator, and just as I'm about to climb back on it and go home, her door opens. She must've been watching through the peephole waiting for me. Whatever boredom was seeping into my veins dissipates when my eyes find her standing in her doorway in the skimpiest negligee I can ever remember seeing. She might as well be naked with how little the silk and lace covers.

"Hey there," she says seductively.

My dick listens and pulses in my jeans.

"Hey," I say walking directly into her.

A second later her legs are wrapped around me, and her mouth is against my neck. I kick the door closed with my foot and carry her to the couch. I know I've been to her place before because it looks vaguely familiar, but I couldn't tell you where her room is. It's not a problem since I don't need a bed for what I plan to do to her.

As I inch her closer to the couch, she slides down my body. Her hands immediately find my zipper; she's on her knees a second later, and less than a breath after that, I'm halfway down her throat.

This is the kind of attention I deserve. Chasing after women is not something I do, so why do I still close my eyes and see waves of dark brown hair and bright green eyes staring back up at me?

"Thanks, doll," I say slapping this woman on her ass as she tries to stand from where I have her bent over the arm of her leather sofa. I quickly dispose of the condom and tuck myself back into my pants.

She moans like a whore after my hand makes contact. Now I remember why she's stayed in my contact list. Even though she just came on my dick, twice, she's ready for anything I'll give her.

"You want me to make you something to eat?" she asks twirling her fiery red hair around her finger. "I have another hour before my next client gets here."

"Client?" I say walking toward the door. "Are you a hair stylist or something?" It's late on a Sunday evening. Who does hair that late?

She giggles even though I didn't say anything funny.

"I don't do hair," she says quickly. "I fuck."

I stop in my tracks and turn back to look at her. "Excuse me?"

"I'm an escort," she replies.

I'm the one laughing now because there's no way I heard her correctly.

"Like dates and social functions?"

She shrugs. "Sometimes, but mostly I just fuck."

"For money?" I'm not one to judge but I've never paid for sex, and I'm not fixing to start now.

"Don't worry," she coos sliding up against my body. "I'll always fuck you for free."

I shake my head to clear it. I remember thinking she sucked dick like a professional, but it was a fleeting thought.

"Wow," I say. I mean, what else do you say in a moment like this?

As I make my way out of her apartment, with a noncommittal agreement to see her again soon, I step back on the elevator. I don't even know what to think in a moment like this. My brain tells me to stay far away; the last thing I need to be linked to is a paid call girl, but my dick loves how experienced and experimental she is.

I side with my brain, which doesn't happen often and delete her from my contact list and block her number for good measure. Kadin is going to get a kick out of this shit. On better thought, I won't even tell him. It's too much ammunition for him to bring up in later conversations, and it's not like he doesn't already have enough.

I head home to shower. I've slept with some pretty questionable women, but, for some reason, walking back to my truck with the new information I've just been given makes me feel dirtier than I've ever felt before.

I get the appeal of a paid companion, don't get me wrong. Quick, easy, a sure thing. In most cases, I'm sure it's a very discrete way to conduct sexual business, but it's not for me. I guess I know now how she affords to live in such a nice place.

Chapter 12
Lexi

Most people struggle with getting it together for Monday morning, but I know for me Friday is the most exhausting day of the week. Most Fridays I have to force myself to stay active when all I want to do is put on my pajamas and fall asleep in front of the TV.

This week has been even more exhausting since I'm leaving earlier in the morning and staying away until well after dark to ensure that I don't run into Kegan. I've been successful all week and avoided any form of contact with Kegan Cole. I wish I could say I felt good about the week with no sightings, but some evenings I feel like I miss him. Those evenings are the ones where an extra glass of wine helps.

I don't get to stay away from home today, however. Jillian, Justin, Hawke, and I get together once a month to hang out and share a meal. I'm hosting this evening, so as much as I want just to fall into bed, I can't.

I also don't have time to cook, so the local deli will be catering our meal this evening, and by catering I mean I called in an order of a ridiculous amount of food and picked it up on my way home from school.

I groan when I pull into my driveway and see that Kegan's truck is at the worksite next door. I pray he stays away for my sanity.

The food and my belongings require three trips to and from my car to get it all in the house. This is one of those times a man would be helpful. Sexist? Of course, but carrying bulky, heavy things is pretty much a requirement if you're a man. I do my best not to look distressed in case Kegan is watching me. The last thing I need is him trying to be helpful and following me into the house.

Thirty minutes later the doorbell rings for the first time this evening. I try to make out the person by the shape of their body through the silkscreened glass, but can't really tell who it is. I'm expecting three people this evening, but I know there's a big chance that Kegan will somehow make his way over before leaving his work site for the evening.

Thankfully, I find Justin standing on my front porch. I smile from ear to ear, but that still doesn't stop the tear from rolling down my cheek. I step into him before he can make his way into the house.

Did I mention that today is also the third anniversary of losing my grandparents? I lost so much more that day, but this is a grief that Justin and I share. He lost his grandparents that day as well. Justin had his own parents growing up, but Clive and Mona Carter raised me. They were practically the only parents I ever knew.

"I know," he says wrapping his arms all the way around me. "Shhh," he whispers in my ear and rubs consoling circles on my back.

He holds me for a few long minutes. He allows me to sob into his shirt and doesn't pull away until my shoulders stop shaking.

I finally let go of him and walk back into the house. No sooner do I get the bottle of wine he brought into the fridge and the doorbell is ringing again. It has to be Hawke because Jillian just walks right in like she owns the place.

Hawke's boisterous laugh, which I've grown fond of over the years, echoes off the walls. His exuberance is commonplace, but it's the soft tinkle of a feminine laugh that's out of place in my home. I round the corner and run into Hawke's chest as he makes his way into the kitchen carrying a bottle of wine.

I grab his arms to steady myself and look over his shoulder. A tiny pixie-like woman is standing in my living room with Justin.

"Who is that?" I ask a little too loud drawing both her and Justin's attention in my direction.

"That's Phoebe. My date."

He shoulders past me to the fridge.

"What about Jillian?" I'm in best friend tiger mode right now, and today is not the day for him to be bringing bullshit into my house.

"Jillian and I aren't together," he says dismissively.

"Does she know that?" Where did that even come from? I know Jillian and Hawke have a weird ass dynamic. They've been dancing around each other for years, and it seems they're the only ones who don't realize how perfect they'd be together.

"You're purposely goading her, Hawke. Our monthly dinners are only for us four, and you know it." I have no idea how Jillian is going to respond, but she's not one to bite her tongue and just let something like this slide.

"Tell her that," he says angling his head toward the living room where Jillian just walked in wrapped from head to toe around a man I've never seen, even though he looks remarkably like David Beckham.

This evening is going to be one for the books; I can already tell.

Any other monthly get together someone would give me a hard time for not cooking, but everyone who's important to me knows what today is; it's one of the reasons we decided to do this today rather than the second Friday of the month like we usually do.

The other two, Phoebe and Mark, don't know any different. They're here today, and we'll probably never see them again. Neither Hawke nor Jillian is one to have any sort of long-term relationship. Hawke is the definition of a playboy, and Jillian has trouble committing to one brand of shampoo. Relationships to them are the equivalent of mythical beings and unicorns.

I'd love nothing more than to rip into both Hawke and Jillian for breaking the sanctity of our dinner, but I don't have the energy even to concern myself with them. They're too busy trying to one-up each other even to notice my mood, and that hurts my feelings more than I should let it.

The whole evening has been one hell of a show. They are both purposely baiting each other, acting as if their date is the declared love of their life. Phoebe looks like she's in heaven as she bats her fake eyelashes at Hawke's attention. Poor Mark looks like he may have food poisoning at Jillian's fawning. If he gets sick at her lovey-dovey act, she will be cleaning up the mess.

Normally, we would play *Cards Against Humanity* or some other game, but it wasn't even suggested this evening. I had hoped that tonight would be a distraction from the anniversary, and it has been, just not the type of distraction I'd hoped for.

I cut my eyes to Justin as Phoebe nuzzles her nose against Hawke's jaw. He huffs a laugh when Jillian mimics her behavior and does the same to Mark.

"How's work?" I ask Justin pulling my attention away from the couples who are acting more like they're in a club than my house in the suburbs.

"Steady," he responds. "We're considering bringing in another attorney to help with the workload."

"That's a great problem to have. Any front runners?"

"We've had a few resumes sent in, but we haven't decided on anyone yet. How's life in the education industry?"

"Chaotic," I tell him. "The first part of the school year is always crazy, but my kiddos are settling in pretty well."

A low moan grabs my attention, and I look over at Phoebe and Hawke. I narrow my eyes when the pillow on Phoebe's lap moves over Hawke's hand.

"Okay!" I say slapping my hands on my lap and standing from the sofa. "Well, I'm so glad everyone could come tonight, but I'm super tired and need to get some sleep."

If I let this go on any longer, I'm going to have to have my couch dry cleaned.

I make eye contact with Jillian, doing my best to communicate my disappointment. Her face sobers, and she has enough humility to stop her performance immediately. Hawke, on the other hand, is so engrossed in production that he doesn't cease his actions until Justin stands and clears his throat rudely.

Jillian looks despondent at his actions, but clearly doesn't take her own behavior into account. I love the woman to death, but accountability is not one of her strengths.

"I'll call you tomorrow," she says after a quick kiss on the cheek. She squeezes my hand in lieu of apologizing.

Hawke mutters a quick "thanks" and leaves with Phoebe.

Thankfully, Justin sticks around long enough to help me get things cleaned up before making his way to the door. I follow him out on the porch and wrap my arms around my waist.

"You going to be okay?" he asks stepping in for a hug.

"Of course," I tell him. It's the truth. I've accepted my grief; it's become a daily part of my life, but I don't let it control me.

"Liar," he says in my ear. "I'm here if you need me."

"I appreciate that," I whisper softly as he pulls away and kisses my cheek.

I watch as he makes his way to his truck. My eyes follow his taillights all the way down my driveway until they disappear into the night.

I'm home alone when all I really need right now is a distraction from life.

Chapter 13

Kegan

It's official; I'm a creeper, borderline stalker.

I've resisted any and all urges to cross over onto Lexi's property all week. I've worked shuffling other jobs so I can focus solely on this one. I haven't seen her in days; if I had to guess, she's been deliberately avoiding me. It wasn't until I saw people show up at her house that the urge became irresistible.

Two couples and a man I know not only from work, but also because of London, showed up. Deductive reasoning tells me Justin Bland is there for Lexi. He is the man who had his eyes set on London after she disappeared for months while pregnant with Anastyn. I have a working relationship with Justin, but it's strained because of his previous interest in my sister-in-law.

I'm not available.

Those three words, spoken last week, echo in my head as I sit in my truck and stare at her house like some detective on a stakeout. Her words are clear as day. She has no interest in me. It's the hiccup in her body's response to me that's making me take pause and ignore our conversations. Her mouth says not interested, but her body is screaming for me to take charge. But, since I'm a firm believer in no-means-no, I've taken a step back.

I've left her alone all week, but watching Justin on the porch wrapping his arms around her, is my limit. His lips brush her cheek and my resolve snaps. She told me she was in a relationship, and I was willing to leave her alone, but she could do so much better than Justin Bland.

What are the chances that he's been the one separating both Kadin and me from the women we're focused on? More so Kadin because she was carrying his child when Justin tried to make his move. Okay, it was incredibly more complicated than that, but still.

Jealousy, a feeling I don't experience often, is creeping into my bones. As much as the infrequent emotion makes me nervous, it's still not enough to keep me from getting out of my truck and walking over to her door.

I knock with determination and stand, waiting for her to answer.

The door is pulled open. "Did you forget your...?"

Her question stops when she realizes it's not Justin coming back after realizing a peck on the cheek wasn't good enough on a Friday night.

"Kegan," she says in a tone that hints at more relief than annoyance.

See? Mixed signals all over the place.

"You've been avoiding me."

"I have not," she says standing a little straighter.

Her cheeks flush a light shade of pink betraying her lie.

"Week before last you were home every day before five. This week we're gone before you get home."

"Are you stalking me now?"

Busted.

"No," I backpedal. "It's just an observation."

She smirks at me, not believing a word I say, which she shouldn't, since I'm full of shit.

"What brings you over tonight?"

The smile is still on her face, but there's also an air of sadness surrounding her. Any other time when a woman presents with emotional drama, I'd do my best to remove myself from the situation. For some reason, though, I'm finding myself actually wanting to know why the light I'm used to seeing in her eyes is dull.

"I saw your company leave."

She cocks an eyebrow up. "It's been dark for hours. Were you just driving by and noticed them leaving or have you been sitting next door waiting for them to leave?"

Busted again.

I ignore her question and busy myself swatting away the bugs that are swarming around her porch light.

She watches me and glances back over her shoulder to the screen door.

"Damn it," she mumbles. "Come inside." She's the one offering, but at the same time, she's acting like I'm forcing her invitation.

I'm not going to turn it down, but I take note of her annoyance at the suggestion.

I follow her through the house to the den; the very room she told me previously she spends a lot of her time in. I can't help but glance at the living room in all its outdated glory. Nothing seems out of the ordinary. I don't even know what I'm looking for, dishevelment maybe? Justin wasn't here very long after the others left. I'm not discounting the notion that he may be a quick in-and-out kind of guy, but Lexi doesn't look like she's been thoroughly fucked.

I smile at the thought. It means I'll be even more appealing to her.

It's apparent she's invaded my senses and is doing something to my integrity, because before Lexi came along I'd never even consider poaching another man's girl. Add that to the fact that it's Justin Bland, and I'm all for stepping on toes to get what I want.

"Your reason for visiting?" Lexi asks again as she settles on a comfortable looking couch.

I look around the room and nod in appreciation. I honestly didn't know how the lime green was going to look since it's such an off the wall color, but somehow she's made it work.

"Justin Bland?" I say. "You turn me down for Justin Bland?"

"What are you talking about?" She honestly looks confused.

"I saw him leave. Nice little PDA on the front porch."

She narrows her eyes, and I know I need to tone it down a bit.

Even though my brain tells me to back off, my mouth just keeps digging the hole. "You told me you weren't available. I get that, but Justin Bland? You could do so much better than him."

"Seriously?" she says with more than a little aggravation in her voice.

"I guarantee spending time with me would be much more enjoyable than him. Time is precious," I add. "You shouldn't be wasting it on him."

"That a fact?"

"Yep," I nod in agreement and sit in an armchair across from her.

"Who do you think you are?" I don't respond, assuming the question is rhetorical. "You don't get to dictate who I spend time with."

She has a point, but I'm nowhere near giving up on the idea of getting her naked.

I watch as she brings her hand to her face. Her fingers pinch the bridge of her nose, and my smile falls. I'm upsetting her, seriously upsetting her. This isn't one of our back and forth banter conversations like we had last week. I suddenly remember the sadness in her eyes on the front porch, and I want to kick my own ass for being such a shithead.

"I'm not dating Justin," she says quietly.

Thank fuck.

"So he's not competition?"

She looks up at me. "Competition for what?"

"You," I simply say.

"I'm not a conquest, Kegan."

"Of course you are." Hello, asshole. "I only ask about Justin because I need to know what's standing in my way."

"I'm not a fucking toy. You wanting to fight over me for whatever end you think is there is ridiculous." Her anger is growing exponentially, as it should with the stupid shit that just came out of my mouth.

I have nothing left in my arsenal since my panty-dropping smile doesn't seem to work on her.

We spend the next couple of minutes just looking at each other. The longer I catalog her face and that soft spot on her neck right below her ear, the more determined I am to get her in bed. Who am I kidding? Bent over the couch, up against the wall, or on the floor would suit me just fine

"Justin Bland is my cousin," she says finally breaking the silence. "Our mothers were sisters."

I want to smile at her admission, but even I have the sense to know now is not the right time.

I sit back further in my chair and spread my legs wide. When I rest my hands in my lap, I notice her eyes following them, resting a few inches lower than my hands.

My lip twitches as I remain silent while her eyes pause on my crotch. I clear my throat abruptly. If she keeps gawking at my jeans, she's going to get more than an eyeful since my cock is already thickening at her attention.

Her eyes snap to mine, and she has the decency to blush at being caught.

I grin at her.

"You're incorrigible," she snaps.

"Don't put this off on me, Lexi. You're the one staring at my dick, not the other way around."

She cuts her eyes to the other side of the room, and once again I can't read her mood.

The urge to ask her if she's bipolar skates across my mind, but somehow I'm able to keep the question off my lips. With the way her emotions seem to be all over the place tonight, I run a real risk of her killing me and burying my body next door at the job site.

"Why are you here, Kegan?"

I grin from ear to ear. She's asking a question she already knows the answer to.

Chapter 14

Lexi

The glint in his eyes and the huge grin on his face explains exactly what his intentions are. I should expect nothing less from Kegan Cole. The man emanates sex appeal without even trying. I can see why women probably throw themselves at him. It's probably the reason he's struggling so much with my numerous rejections.

My own lips tingle, an automatic response to his domineering personality.

Wasn't I just thinking a distraction would be the best thing for me right now?

The only problem is using Kegan as a distraction has disastrous consequences of epic proportions. A decision like the one he's expecting me to make right now, shouldn't be done when I'm in this mind frame.

The anniversary of the car wreck is clouding my judgment and forcing my emotions all over the place.

"What's it gonna be, beautiful?"

The tone of his voice and the way he's already concluded I'm a sure thing grates on my nerves, but it doesn't stop me from wondering exactly how much he could change my mood. I watch his fingers stretch out and curl back up on his solid thighs.

Am I actually considering this? Would letting him take my mind off the shit bouncing around in my head be worth the repercussions if anyone found out? Would that type of fallout be worth the hour or so of distraction he may be able to provide?

I could easily say my brain is fighting my baser urges, but honestly half of my brain is on Team Get It Over With.

I'm fighting a losing battle here.

What does it matter if I sleep with him today or two weeks from now when he finds another reason to show up at my house and tempt my resolve with his quirky smile and gorgeous blue eyes? That's the fact, plain and simple. I will eventually cave to him. I know it as sure as I know that no matter how much grief is controlling my emotions right now, that the sun will rise again tomorrow.

"What do you mean?" I ask trying to stall until I can think of something else to say.

He remains silent with nothing but a grin on his face.

"Why are you here, Kegan?" This is the third time I've asked the question. The first two times have gone unanswered. I know the answer; I'm not an idiot, but I need him to verbalize his intention.

I stiffen when he leans in, placing his elbows on his knees. The action causes the sleeves of his t-shirt to strain around his thick biceps.

"You know why I'm here, Lexi."

Still not really an answer.

"You want to get laid." I swallow roughly and place my focus on one of the loose strings hanging on to a tear in the knee of my jeans.

"I want to fuck *you*," he clarifies. "Look at me, Lexi," he demands.

My eyes shoot up to his.

"Don't deny yourself, beautiful."

"A quick fuck is what you're looking for?"

He chuckles softly. "Quick? No babe, I got all night."

The sensual promise makes me want to clench my thighs together, but the stupid pet name infuriate me.

I stand suddenly from the couch, my decision instantly made.

"You want to fuck?" I ask grabbing the hem of my t-shirt. "Let's fuck."

His smile falters as I pull my shirt over my head and toss it on the table in front of me. I can sense his uneasiness at my angry aggression, but it doesn't stop him from staring at my breasts encased in a lacy bra that covers absolutely nothing.

I use the toe of one shoe to begin kicking off the other. Once they're cast to the side, I begin to unbutton my pants.

"No expectations right?"

"None," he confirms watching my hand work my zipper down.

"Let's do it then. I've lost everything else. Why not throw my damn dignity into the pile so it can burn right along with the rest."

Tears of anger and grief flood my eyes and fall down my face.

"Lexi," Kegan says trying to get my attention. I don't look up at him. If I meet his gaze, I'll lose my determination.

I continue to undress, shoving my jeans down past my knees and kicking them off.

I sense movement from across the room and look up, even though it's the last thing I should do.

Kegan darts up from his chair and makes his way toward me.

"Lexi!" he shouts when I unsnap my bra and add it to the pile of discarded clothing. "Stop."

I don't listen to him. I hook my fingers into the lace of my panties at each hip and start to shove them down as well.

He grabs my hands roughly to keep me from getting entirely naked. I close my eyes as violent sobs threaten to make their way up the back of my throat.

"Not like this," he says with more kindness than I ever would've thought he is capable of.

He shifts his weight, and the soft fabric of the throw blanket from the back of my couch is wrapped around my shoulders.

"Not like this," he says again as he pulls me against his chest. "When I finally get inside of you, the only tears you'll be crying will be tears of pleasure."

He moves us, leaning back to sit on the couch gently urging me to follow him. What would all of his conquests think if they saw him now? I can't imagine anything more out of character than Kegan Cole comforting a crying woman.

He holds me to his side and whispers soothing comforts in my ear. My head is lowered and tucked against his shirt. Even in my despair, I can appreciate just how good he smells. Pure masculinity, sweat, and the slightest hint of cologne or body wash infiltrate my senses. He's been working outside on a job site all day, and he smells amazing.

I inhale deeper and hope it's convincing enough to pass as only trying to calm my sobs.

"Did you just sniff me?" Geez, this man has no filter.

"No," I say pulling my head off of his chest. I wipe at my eyes removing tears from my cheeks. They continue to fall even with my effort and determination to halt them.

"Hey," he says quietly. "No more crying."

I'm pretty sure I'm making him uncomfortable. It's been a very long time since I've had an outburst like this. I could blame it on stress, but I know it's the anniversary and Jillian's ridiculous behavior. Combine that with him being here with his cocksure attitude, and all of it is just too much all at the same time.

"You should go," I say trying to get some distance from him.

"You sure?" He says pulling me against him.

I give him a weak smile and nod.

"I don't mind staying." He doesn't release his hold on me. "Now that I'm sitting here with you, knowing you're practically naked under this blanket, I'm reconsidering turning down your offer."

I pull away from him and stand from the couch, making sure the blanket remains wrapped tightly around my body.

"Last chance," he says that cocky grin returning to his mouth. "I can make you come on my mouth in a minute flat."

I tilt my head to the side at his words.

"Maybe some other time," I offer before thinking. There goes that damn finishing school training again.

He licks his lips as he stands from the couch, taking my words to heart. The next time he comes over and I refuse him, he's going to label me as a tease. At this point, I don't even care, so long as he leaves before I give into him.

He closes the few feet of distance between us and wraps his arms around me again. His lips find mine with a searing kiss. His tongue strokes along mine, and I allow it. Before long my body is responding to his, my tongue countering his movements.

Just as I'm about to drop the blanket from my shoulders, he breaks the kiss, leaning in one last time to kiss my forehead.

Before pulling away he leans his mouth near my ear and whispers, "You have an amazing fucking body, Lexi. I can't wait to taste every inch of it. I'm looking forward to the day I'm buried so deep inside of you that you see stars."

I'm a split second away from begging him for it now, but he releases his hold on me, runs his hand down my cheek, and takes two steps back.

"Get some sleep, Lexi. I'll see myself out," he says before quickly disappearing toward the front door.

I jump slightly when my heavy front door opens and shuts a few seconds later.

I should go to bed and put an end to this horrible day, start fresh tomorrow, but I can't find the energy to do that just yet.

Instead, I walk over to the small bookcase in the corner and pull a well-worn photo album from the top shelf. Carrying it back over to the couch, I settle in for the final loop in my rollercoaster of a day.

My fingers gently stroke over the black and white pictures my grandmother was so proud of. As I flip through the pages, my grandparents' entire lives play out. First, their marriage, where my grandmother is standing in her simple wedding dress beside my grandfather in his best Sunday suit.

I flip faster, almost without looking, as the next couple of pages show up in the sequence. My grandmother spent most of her time on these pages, the ones with my mother in them, but they're the ones I won't let myself dwell on. The final page is where I nearly break down again.

My finger traces the black and white paper-printed picture, circling around the image of the little girl I'd placed so many hopes and dreams in not so long ago. The tears begin to fall again, only this time I do nothing to stop them. She deserves every one; just as I deserve the guilt I've felt every day when I realized I was the only survivor of that car accident.

Chapter 15
Kegan

"Hey," I whisper into the dark hospital room.

Kadin shifts his weight on the horribly uncomfortable looking recliner, sitting it up. It's super early in the morning, but he sent me a text yesterday and wanted me to stop by before work.

In the dim light of the room, I can make out London's form. She's sleeping in a similar recliner next to the one Kadin is standing from. Her arm is outstretched, and her hand is between the slats of the small medical grade crib that Easton is sleeping in. She's not quite holding his hand, but the tips of her fingers are at his side.

Kadin catches me watching them, and the look on my face must convey my worry.

"She won't leave his side," he says with a loving look on his face.

I just nod and wait for him to wash his face in the small sink on the far wall. We walk out together and catch the elevator to the cafeteria.

"Are you really going to wear that thing in here?" He points to the hard hat on my head I didn't even realize I had put on. Old habits and all that.

I pull it off my head and run my fingers through my hair.

"You really should wear one without all of those stickers." I look down at the yellow hard hat and chuckle. "Seriously though. You're a Cole. You should probably be more professional."

"Really? This is your old hard hat, Kadin."

I hold it for him to see. It's littered with inappropriate things that are very common around a construction site. (Vagitarian,) (I'm not a gynecologist, but I'll take a look,) and my personal favorite and the way I live my life, (Please don't ask to borrow my tools, and I won't ask to borrow your girlfriend.)

After buying a couple of cups of coffee, we find an unoccupied table in the corner. I sit my "inappropriate hard hat" in the chair beside me. Honestly, I forgot I even put it on this morning. I'd never wear a hat that says 'I Love Sushi' with a picture of a guy going downtown in a children's hospital.

"How's he doing?" Easton has been in the hospital for quite a while, and the longer he stays here, the more concerned I am for him.

"Much better," Kadin says scrubbing his face.

He's exhausted; his eyes are sunken, and his beard hasn't had a trim in a while. My brother, who has been so put together since meeting

London, now looks like he did the year and a half he was alone after Savannah died. Only this time, it's the stress of a sick child and lack of sleep rather than bottle after bottle of whiskey.

"I can't stop thinking about what would've happened if London wouldn't have stood so firm about something being wrong," he mutters with a distant look in his eyes.

"You can't think like that, Kadin."

"I failed him. I'm his father. I'm the man of the house, and I let him down." He hangs his head, resting it on hands that are propped up by his elbows on the table.

"You didn't fail him. Being a parent is about sharing and two people shouldering the load. It was London's turn is all."

I have no idea where this little nugget of support is coming from, but it breaks my heart to see my older brother like this. My heart clenches for his pain even though I have no idea what he's going through on a personal level.

"Any idea when he'll get to go home?"

He shakes his head. "The doctors don't want us to get false hope. They are telling us he should make a full recovery, though, so that's a positive. We just have to wait it out and see how his body responds to this last dose of antibiotics." He takes a long sip of coffee and looks past my shoulder. He's too much in his own head to focus on much of anything right now.

"That's great news," I tell him before raising my own cup of coffee to my lips.

Kadin turns his gaze to mine as if remembering something suddenly.

"Tell me about this woman you brought home to meet Mom and Dad." His stupid grin tells me he knows exactly who she is.

"She helped me with the girls that Sunday. She was in the truck with me. I didn't bring her to meet them. She just happened to be there as well. I'm not such a dick that I would've left her sitting in the truck."

"Yes, you are," he says with a light chuckle.

It's true. I've pulled up with a chick in the car more than once when I had to run into my parents' house for something.

"Tony tells me you pulled him off the Westover project just so you can work every day next door to her house." He raises an eyebrow at me, daring me to lie to him when he has the inside scoop.

"Tony gossips like a fucking woman," I say attempting to divert his attention.

"Fucking the girls' teacher and not wanting to talk about it? That's a first for you." He pauses, waiting for me to answer. He's baiting me, and I won't fall for it.

He's a genius because after several long moments under his scrutiny I cave. He's always been like this, knowing exactly which buttons to push and what to say to get me to spill my guts.

"I haven't fucked her," I admit. The declaration makes my mind wander back to her stripping down in her den last week. I shift uncomfortably in my chair at the image in my head of her lean, perfect body.

"You like her," he says on a mild gasp.

"I want to fuck her," I correct.

"But you haven't?"

"Nope."

"Why not?" He's asking an honest question. Even Kadin knows that most women can't resist me, and if by chance I find one who's not interested, I divert my attention somewhere else, immediately.

I stare at him as if he's an idiot. "I'm not a sexual predator, Kadin."

His laugh is loud and emanates from his gut. It's also out of place in a hospital cafeteria at six in the morning. All eyes in the sparsely populated room shoot in our direction.

As if by osmosis, Kadin's laugh makes other people smile and chuckle in response, even though they have no idea what he's laughing about. I narrow my eyes at him. It's great that he's laughing rather than looking as beat down as he did a few minutes ago, but now I feel like the entire room is laughing at me.

"Seriously?" I ask quietly trying to get him to calm down.

He swipes at tears that have begun to form in the corners of his eyes. Without saying a word, he pulls his cell phone from his pocket and snaps a quick picture of me.

I frown when he turns it around so I can see the unimpressed look on my face.

"What are you doing?" I ask with annoyance in my voice.

"I'm going to call it the *Kegan got shot down, and he's bitter about it* picture. It's going in the photo album. Hand to God, this is epic." Eventually, his chuckles calm, and we can carry on a conversation that I'm beginning to wish wasn't even happening.

"She didn't really turn me down," I say with exasperation.

With any other woman I encountered, I wouldn't have an issue with laying out the details about how she stripped down naked and begged me to fuck her. I mean, I might avoid the part about comforting her, if only to keep myself from looking like a pussy. I know that's not the reason I remain quiet about that part. I'm not disclosing that type of information to Kadin, the man who knows every dark and dirty sexual act I've ever accomplished because I value Lexi on some level. As much as I'd like to deny it, she's different from the other women.

"The timing just wasn't right," I say in explanation giving him nothing more.

"Like I said, Kegan. You like her. There's nothing wrong with that. I don't know her very well, but she seems like a great woman. You could do worse at picking the first woman to fall in love with than Lexi Carter."

"What the fuck?" I hiss at him. "Love? I'm not falling in love with her. I want to fuck her, and for some reason, she's worth the actual chase she's forcing me into, but this isn't nor will it ever be love. I don't do love. Ever. Plain and simple."

He rolls his lips between his teeth before responding. "You sure are arguing really hard against it," he says. "My experience is, the harder you fight it, the harder you fall."

I know what you're thinking. You think I'm falling for her, and I just don't realize it myself, but let me tell you, you're wrong. So way off base that you're standing alone in the desert. This is in no way love or even infatuation. I want to fuck Lexi Carter.

Is she smoking hot? Yes. Do I fantasize about sinking balls deep into her? Fuck, yeah I do. Would I even consider her anything more than an acquaintance who I fucked once? Not in a million years.

I'm going to respond to Kadin's entirely misguided observation of what's going on between Lexi and me, but my phone rings in my pocket.

I answer the phone as I watch him sit back in his chair, arms crossed over his chest and a smug, satisfied look on his face.

"Hello," I bark into the phone, unable to mask my annoyance.

"We've got a problem boss." This could mean absolutely anything, but I pray it's nothing major. My day has already turned to shit thanks to my meddling brother.

"How big of a problem, Julian?" The call is coming from the job site I should already be on my way to.

"Broken window," he says.

"The house isn't even up, Julian. Are you at the Westover site? How is a window broken?"

"Yes, sir. A rock broke one of the window's next door." Lexi's house.

"Is Ms. Carter home?"

"No. I went over and knocked even though her car isn't in the driveway. No one answered the door."

"Alright, thanks for calling. I'll take care of it."

I hang up the phone and look over at Kadin.

"Work crew already causing problems this morning?"

I grin from ear to ear. "This isn't trouble, brother. This is an opportunity."

I grab my hard hat, leave Kadin sitting in the cafeteria, and head out to the job site. He was in a much better mood than when I first pulled him out of Easton's hospital room this morning.

Repairing a broken window isn't what I had on my agenda today, but I'll never turn down an opportunity to run into Lexi. The day is starting to look up for me.

Chapter 16
Lexi

My weekend was spent being depressed with loads of tissues and even more wine, but as the week has progressed my mood has gotten much better. It's hard to stay upset and antisocial when you're surrounded by a classroom full of jovial, excited children.

It's Thursday and, as great as my week has been, I've got my eyes set on the weekend. Jillian came over Tuesday night, and after hours of groveling and begging for forgiveness with the way she acted Friday night, I forgave her. She knew I would because I always do. We spent the night curled up on the couch watching chick flicks and eating more chocolate than should be legal. We also made plans to go out Saturday night, which I normally don't do, but I'm extremely excited about it for some reason.

My day has pretty much been perfect. The one kid in my class that causes the most problems was out today, and that reduces stress and tension in the classroom. I don't dislike the kid, but he's a handful. Today I'm grateful for the reprieve.

Well, it's perfect until I pull my cell phone out of my desk during my conference period and notice a text from an unfamiliar number.

One of my guys broke a window. Will have it repaired ASAP

The text has to be from Kegan, and even though my window is broken and I've not seen him once this week, I can't help but smile. The way he comforted me Friday night was a blessing I didn't even realize I needed, until his warm, strong arms engulfed me.

I've thought about his touch more than a few times this week. I've let my mind wander to things I've got no business fantasizing about, but that doesn't stop the sexy thoughts from popping up.

I clear my throat and try to force all thoughts of Kegan Cole from my brain. I turn my focus to next week's lesson plans. Before too long, I'm back in the classroom for the final hour of the school day. I didn't text Kegan back, even though it took all the strength I had. I did, however, allow myself to save his contact in my phone.

It's just after four when I pull up to my house. I let my eyes wander to the job site in full swing next door, but I don't see the man my eyes are desperate to land on. With minor disappointment, I unlock my front door and put my bag on the small table just inside the door.

Small noises from inside the house scare me at first, until I force myself to remain calm. Instinctively I know it's Kegan, who's more than likely fixing the window he texted about earlier.

I follow the noises and stop cold when my eyes find him in my den in front of a pristine, new window. I'm not in awe over the window, rather the man standing in my house shirtless.

I swallow roughly and watch him as he gathers his tools. The bending and squatting make the impeccable muscles of his back bunch and knot. The fine specimen of a man doesn't realize I'm ogling him until I'm forced to grab the doorframe to steady myself.

He looks over his shoulder and grins salaciously.

"Hey," he says huskily. "Sorry about the window."

"Thank you for fixing it," I manage to say with a soft voice. "How did you get in? My front door was locked."

When he turns and faces me, my brain turns to mush. Corny, I know, but this man's body is beyond spectacular. My eyes rove over every delicious dip and valley on his sculpted chest and abdomen.

Deadly. He's positively deadly.

Kegan Cole has the body of an Olympic athlete. The light smattering of hair on his chest and stomach only accentuates the hard definition of each and every muscle. I make a mental note to scout out construction sites if this is what men who work with their hands all day look like.

He points. "I climbed through the window."

Ignoring his explanation, I lick my lips as my eyes follow the trickle of sweat from the base of his throat clear down to the waistband of his jeans. My tongue tingles at the prospect of tasting his sweaty skin. If I'd known this is what he's been hiding under his t-shirts, I never would've had the ability to resist him.

Taking in every inch of his exposed skin, wishing he was wearing even less, reminds me that my little battery operated friend in my bedside table has been less than satisfying these last couple of weeks. It's almost as if my body knows what it's missing, and it exponentially increases my desire for satisfaction. From the looks of Kegan and his cocky attitude, there's not one ounce of doubt in my mind that he'd be able to give me what I need.

"You like what you see?" His voice makes my skin prickle with awareness.

I shift on my feet, resisting the urge to squeeze my thighs together and failing entirely.

I regretfully lift my eyes from the bare skin of his chest and finally make eye contact. The storm that is brewing in his baby blues makes me realize I couldn't have been more obvious in my perusal of him.

"Clenching those thighs together is giving you away," he says dropping a hand full of tools in a bucket and taking a few steps closer to me.

His movement draws my eyes back to the rippling muscles of his abdomen.

"You want me to fuck you."

It's not a question. He knows what I want. Hell, at the way my body is responding to his right now, he can probably *smell* what I want.

"How do you stay so fit?" Dumbest question in the world. Of all of the things I could say right now, and my brain allows my mouth to spit that mess out.

"I fuck a lot," is his response.

As much as that declaration should turn me off, it does the exact opposite.

His rough, hardworking hand makes its way into my line of sight, interrupting my view of his tan, sweat covered body. I follow his hand as it roams down his body and grips the straining erection in his jeans.

Sweet mother of all things holy.

I release a breath I didn't realize I was holding as I watch him stroke his jean-clad cock. I tangle my hands in the sides of my skirt to keep myself from reaching for him.

I feel a sense of disappointment when he releases himself, but immediately become aware of every sound and movement when he steps closer and circles my body like an animal on the hunt.

I close my eyes as he steps in against my back.

"I want to fuck you too, Lexi."

I shudder as his breath mixes with the light sheen of sweat covering my neck.

Warm, plush lips touch my neck, and I nearly crumple to the ground until a strong arm wraps around my stomach to steady me. I can feel the heat and dampness of his skin through my thin, silk shirt.

"Can I fuck you, Lexi?"

My brain scrambles, trying to find a reason to say no, but can't manage a single coherent thought with his body against mine. So, I do the only thing that feels right; I nod my permission with a jerky shake of my head.

"Right answer," he says with a cocky tone in my ear.

The arm banded around my waist flexes as he pulls me harder against his body. The two fabric layers of my clothes and his jeans do nothing to mask the stiffness in his jeans. I moan in anticipation.

I know I was looking forward to the weekend, but I think Thursday has just become my new favorite day of the week.

Both of his hands slide up my body and begin to work the delicate buttons of my blouse. I don't know if the back of his hand grazing my hardened nipple was intentional, but it sure got my attention.

My skin responds with racing goosebumps when the warm air of the room hits my flesh as he lowers my blouse down my arms.

Lips and the occasional lick of his wandering tongue set me on fire as his mouth teases my neck with the attention my body is demanding elsewhere.

"Please," I whisper as deft fingers toy with my nipples through the lace of the camisole.

"I've been wondering for weeks what your voice would sound like begging for more," he breathes in my ear. "I can't wait for the plea when I'm buried so deep in you that you never want me to leave."

"Quite sure of yourself," I mutter then groan as he pinches a puckered bud between his thumb and forefinger.

"Just wait and see," he counters playfully.

I don't want to wait, I want to tell him. I want to beg and plead for him to end the needy ache that's building up in my body, but now that he's called me out, challenged me, I refuse. I want him to take me, but I won't concede to his every whim.

He turns me around and holds me at arm's length as his eyes rake over my body from head to sandal covered toe.

I'm not very exposed, but from the look in his eyes, he's seeing more than a lace camisole and calf-length skirt.

Agile fingers slide the silk straps of my lingerie off my shoulders until my arms are free, and the fabric is bunched around my waist.

I'm reminded of Jillian's declaration that Kegan Cole is known for wanting women who have large breasts. I raise my arms to cover my small chest, but his large hands grip my wrists, preventing me.

"Don't," he says, licking his lips as he leans in to take my right nipple in his mouth.

The hot, wet attention of his tongue is divine. The swirling, stroking, and sucking of his mouth is pleasurable beyond measure, but it's the nip and the slight sting of pain that follows that has me on the edge.

"Fuck you're gorgeous," he says releasing my wrists and drawing both hands to my breasts.

I automatically reach for the button and zipper on his jeans as his lips find mine. He pushes my hands away before I can even get the top button undone. His tongue dips inside of my mouth, taking over, taking charge. Lush slides of his tongue and playful nips on my lips heighten my arousal.

I feel his hands begin to bunch my skirt up, and my body sighs in relief that this is finally heading in the direction I've wanted it to the second I saw his skin glistening in the sunshine in front of my newly repaired window.

"Hold this," he growls into my mouth.

My hands instinctively obey and reach for the gathered fabric. He continues to bite and lick my neck as his arms once again circle my waist. Lifting me off my feet, he carries me several feet further into the room.

I hiss when the coolness of the window meets the bare skin of my back. Before I can wrap my legs around his waist, he lowers my feet back to the ground and turns me, forcing me to face the window.

"Fuck," he groans gripping each cheek of my ass in his rough hands. He has an unobstructed view as he grips my hip and applies pressure with one hand to my back. I bend at the waist at his unspoken command.

A jolt of electricity torments my body when thick fingers rub my slit over the silk of my thong.

"So wet," he says appreciatively. "So tight," he commends slipping his fingers past the fabric and directly inside of me.

"Oh God," I sigh at the relief I immediately feel at his intrusion.

"So greedy," he declares as my core clutches at his fingers.

I whimper, disappointed when he pulls his hand from the apex of my thighs. A gentle but authoritative hand grips my neck and pulls me up against his chest.

"So sweet," he says pulling his fingers from his mouth with a smack.

My body trembles with need as he reapplies pressure on my back, urging me to bend over again.

"Grab the window frame," he instructs as he takes a step back.

My body teems with excitement at the rasp of his zipper and the crinkle of a condom wrapper.

I jerk in mild surprise when he grips one hip holding me in place. My unsure, trembling legs barely hold me up when I feel him slide my thong aside and rub the thick head of his cock against my slit. Every action since I walked into this room has been a layer to his seduction; each well-placed movement is a new tier on his enticement.

"Please," I plead as he teases my clit with the tip of his erection. I refuse to acknowledge that he was right about the begging, but no doubt he'll taunt me with it later.

"Your wish," he grunts as he slams inside of me. "My command."

The forceful action forces me onto my tiptoes as my body fights to adjust his size.

"Oh!" I scream as he pulls out of me to the tip and repeats the action.

Damn, he's going to kill me, and my body clings to him, begging him for more.

"So much better," he says more to himself than me.

I tilt my head and rest my cheek against the cool glass as my fingers white-knuckle the window sill. *I pray the glass is sturdy, and his thrusts don't force my face through the window*, is the last thought I have before I'm nothing but sensation, boneless.

My eyes fall closed as my orgasm builds to a crescendo faster than any one before it.

Expert fingers toy with my clit until my body convulses and grips him in pulsing squeezes.

My body goes lax, forcing him to wrap his free arm around my waist.

"More," he demands as his hips continue to thrust, not even slowing for my release.

"I can't," I whimper.

"You will," he counters leaning over my body. "Grip the window sill, Lexi."

Fingers, having gone lax from my previous surrender, regrip the wood at the bottom of the window. The arm around my waist relaxes and is pulled away as his chest rests against my back. His hand is now gripping the window frame near my head as he slams into me repeatedly, relentlessly.

The angle of his intrusion changes, and my body sparks with renewed hunger.

"Kegan," I pant, my breath fogging up the glass against my cheek.

"That's it, Lexi." His voice betrays his control as my core begins to quicken once again. "I need you to come."

His words, combined with the fact my body was already on the precipice, send me over the edge. Again.

"Fuck!" he growls before his teeth sink into the flesh of my shoulder. Seconds later, I can feel the pulsing of his orgasm through every cell in my body.

I feel his tongue lick at the indentions his teeth surely left in my skin before he stands up, keeping a steady arm around me.

I sense him straightening his clothes before I'm picked up and placed on the couch. I watch him with heavy eyelids as he removes the condom, ties it off, and tosses it in the trash at the end of the couch. His cock, I notice, has barely softened, but he shoves it into his jeans and zips up anyways. This man is beyond virile and potent.

He leans in and brushes his lips against mine. "Thanks, doll," are the only words spoken before he gathers his tools, winks at me, and walks out of my house.

Chapter 17
Kegan

I don't know how today is going to go, but I do know I set an early alarm on my cell phone and made it to the job site before the sun crested over the horizon, with the hopes that I can catch Lexi before she leaves for work.

I'm scanning through social media notifications on my phone. Okay, I'm actually scrolling through Tumblr, which has managed to become nothing more than porn clips.

I miss Lexi coming out of her front door but catch a brief glimpse of her as she rounds the front of her car and opens the driver's side door. I spring out of my truck and shout her name, trying to get her attention before she locks herself inside.

Her eyes lift to mine, and a smile spreads across her face as she leans in the opening of her car door.

She winks at me, and without another word, she climbs in her car and leaves me standing halfway between her house and the job site.

I chuckle to myself because the vixen just used one of my own moves against me, and damned if it doesn't make me rock hard in my pants.

I left her yesterday within minutes of pulling out of her deliciously sweet body. I had to. Everything in my body was telling me to stay, to carry her to her room and spend the rest of the night pleasing her. Honestly... it freaked me out more than I want to admit.

Don't get me wrong; she's not the first woman I've had the urge to stick around for another taste, but it was more than that. I didn't just want to get inside of her again. I saw myself waking up with her in my arms and getting up early to make the coffee. That shit has never happened before.

I'm not that guy. I'm not the guy who sneaks into the bathroom and joins her in the shower. I'm not the guy who wants to ask a woman what her plans are for the weekend and pray that I'm a part of it. Yet, all of those urges were there. The sense of calm in my blood that I seek after such a release never came. If anything, my desire for her was elevated.

So, I did what I always do. I thanked her the same way I do every woman I conquer, and I left. I told myself walking out of her house that I'd got what I came for, and my insistence on doing it again was over. I reminded myself repeatedly that I don't do emotion; I don't do complicated, and Lexi Carter has complicated written all over her.

It lasted through the night. A very restless, sleep-deprived night.

I woke up this morning with the fierce need to see her again, to touch her again.

It seems the tables have turned, if her little response this morning is any indication. That beautiful woman should come with a warning label cautioning men that once indulged, immediate addiction is a real risk.

The first part of my day is ruined when one of the guys broke a major plumbing pipe that was extending out of the recently poured concrete foundation. The guys are going to be the death of me; I just know it.

While waiting for the plumber to show up and fix the damage, I head over to Lexi's house and clear her gutters. Fall is fast approaching, and it looks like she didn't have them done last year.

Either she hasn't noticed the buildup or she's been single for over a year. Any man, who's been to this house, if he's a good man at least, would have noticed and taken care of this for her. I don't allow my brain to analyze exactly why I'm on a damn ladder clearing them out. I just turn up the music louder in my headphones and finish the job.

Kadin calls right after lunch, needing another favor. Lennox has a dental checkup. The good news is that the doctors think Easton will be able to go home tomorrow, but that doesn't help Kadin and London today.

Since the appointment time is so close to the end of the day, he advises me to grab both girls from school. Normally, I would be slightly frustrated, but heading to Edgewood Academy to pick up the tiny little devils has just become the highlight of my day. Not only do I get to see Lexi again, but the girls' dental hygienist, Sadie is hot too. Two lovely ladies in one day... perfect.

I step into the school, head to the front office for my visitor's pass, and pray the headmistress is gone or at least out of the office. Thankfully, the front office manager is the only one inside, and I'm on my way to the classroom a few minutes later.

Unfortunately, the classroom is empty, and I have no idea where to even look for the girls and their incredibly sexy teacher. I wander down the hall looking for someone to help me. My luck holds up when I peer in an open door and find the sexiest ass I've ever seen loading a shelf with colorful boxes of Kleenex.

"Finding Dory on a box of tissues is actually a thing?" I ask startling her.

Several boxes of tissues tumble to the ground, and I do the only chivalrous thing I can think of as she bends over to collect them. I grip a handful of her ass while she's vulnerable. I expect her to slap my hand, punch me in the nuts... something. I did just walk and leave her yesterday after she came on my dick... twice. But, all I get from her is a shy smile.

"Amanda, one of the parents, brought those for her son. Apparently, rich kids are very particular about where their snot goes," she explains.

"Ridiculous," I mutter shaking my head.

She shrugs, placing the boxes back on the shelf. "Not really. You have to keep in mind that these kids are still very young. They believe a Ninja Turtle Band-Aid will fix a severed finger. If Finding Dory tissues are what keeps them from wiping snot on their shirts, hey, I'm all for it."

"Good point," I concede stepping in closer to her. I pull the door to the small supply closet closed as I crowd her, forcing her back against the shelving.

"What are you doing?" she asks quietly glancing over my shoulder as if some random person is going to walk in on us during the five minutes we're here alone.

I flex my hips against her stomach. Her eyes widening means she feels my thickening erection in my jeans.

"Absolutely not," she chastises. "You're out of your mind."

"I'll be quick," I promise in her ear before licking down her neck.

She groans and shudders against me. Her hands roam up my back as I take a handful of her dark hair in my hands, using my grip to tug her head back.

She presses her palms to my chest and urges me away. "I can't," she says.

"You already have," I remind her.

"Yesterday didn't happen, Kegan," she says with an eerie sense of calm to her voice.

"I beg to differ, *Lexi*. If I recall, *both* of your orgasms were very real. You can't deny something I'll remember for the rest of my life. That's just not fair." I lean forward, resting her hands on my chest and nip at her earlobe.

"I'm not having sex in the supply closet of the school," she hisses.

That's what her mouth says, but it doesn't stop her from tilting her head to the side so I can suck gently on the pulse point in her neck.

I remove one of her hands from my chest and guide it down my body until she's gripping my cock. I roll my hips instinctively.

"We don't have to fuck," I tell her with a wicked smile on my face.

She shakes her head at my brazenness, but the smile never leaves her lips.

"I'm not sucking you off in the supply closet either," she counters.

"You owe me," I say with seriousness.

She huffs indignantly. "Owe you? How did you come to that conclusion?"

"That little wink and then taking off this morning," I explain. "You could've avoided this if you'd just talked to me."

She cocks an eyebrow at me. "Is that so?"

I nod.

She grips my cock harder and leans in closer. I nearly lose my shit when I feel her hot breath on my neck. "You want a blowjob," she taunts.

"No teeth," I add.

She takes a step back. I'm coming to terms with the fact that she's not the type of woman that's going to hit her knees in a supply closet at her job, when I feel her nimble fingers open the top button on my jeans.

She reaches inside the loosened fabric and wraps her hand around my straining erection.

"That's all you want?" I follow her line of sight as she lowers her eyes to my dick.

"For now," I breathe when her fingernail scrapes gently over the head.

"I bet. And what do I—"

The door opens before she can finish her thought.

Scrambling, she pulls her hands from me, but there's no denying what we're doing in here. Our profiles are facing the open door, and well, my dick is out.

"What in the world is going on in here?"

I turn my eyes to the intruder. The headmistress.

I tuck myself back into my jeans and zip up. I don't rush because there's really no point.

A sniffle comes from Lexi, and when I look over at her, I notice a tear roll down her face. My gut clenches. I put her in this situation, and there's no clear way to make things better for her.

Amelia crosses her arms over her chest and taps her foot.

"We have a clear no fraternization policy, Ms. Carter. Not to mention the fact that you're also engaging in sexually deviant behaviors in the supply closet, during school hours." The look she's giving Lexi hints at more hatred than just getting caught with her hands on my cock, and for some reason, it rubs me the wrong way.

"Sexually deviant behavior? On school property?" I say turning my full attention to the spiked-heel bitch that's berating Lexi.

"Yes," Amelia spits. "This school has higher standards than teachers who are involved in such things."

"Really?" I hiss at her doing my best to keep my voice down because we are in an elementary school. "Where were your complaints about school property and sexual deviance when I was fucking you in the ass on your desk a couple months back?"

Amelia's indignant attitude falters, but it's the gasp coming from my right that demands my attention.

My fucking mouth.

I watch as full realization dawns in Lexi's reddened eyes. Her face switches back and forth, looking at me then Amelia.

The slap in the face that comes a second later is much less than I deserve. I close my eyes, unwilling to watch Lexi as she walks away.

"A little too much attitude for a fuck toy, don't you think?"

My blood boils at Amelia's words. "Don't ever talk about her like that."

She disregards my anger and sidles closer, attempting to run her long fingernail down my chest. I step out of her reach.

"Don't be angry, Mr. Cole. I can satisfy you more than she ever could. Since when do you go after the homely kind?"

I dump every ounce of my gentleman nature at my feet and close the distance between us. Her seductive smirk tells me she's not reading the situation right.

"Since fucking whores like you left me unsatisfied."

I turn my back on her and reach for the door handle.

"She'll lose her job for this," she spits.

A single calming breath is all I allow before I turn back to her. "If she loses her job for touching my dick in a closet, imagine what will happen when they find out you got fucked in the ass while an apple paperweight was shoved in your dirty cunt."

She finally takes a hint and backs away from me. My fists clench, but I know even as enraged as I am, I'd never hit a woman. I walk away from her as calmly as I can to get the girls and get the hell out of here.

Chapter 18

Lexi

I went back to my classroom yesterday to finish my day and waited for my pink slip that was sure to arrive before the final bell rang. It never did. I even went by the office after school was out, ready to face my dismissal. Amelia was nowhere to be found. Sharon, the front office manager, said she had left before last period started.

The same time Kegan would've been leaving.

I was told by my recess paraprofessional that he came and picked the girls up early, so I know the chances are slim she went with him, but the idea still niggles.

I can't stop the racing thoughts in my head. My brain has been running scenarios since I laid down last night. I roll over again, not really wanting to get up, but knowing I can't stay in bed any longer.

I grab my cell phone and look at the time. Almost ten. I stayed in bed later than I thought.

I head to the kitchen to make coffee and revel in the silence around the house. No machinery is making noise; no loud instructions are being yelled by workmen. Just silence.

Kegan didn't call or text to explain. I don't know why I expected him to, but it doesn't ease the sting of not being worth an explanation. I know I told him that Thursday night didn't happen; he knows why I turned him down the half dozen times he wanted to hook up before, but that didn't keep shit from blowing up in my face.

I sit on the back porch and enjoy the serenity I'm sure won't last. Selecting Jillian's contact in my phone, I press send and wait for her to answer.

"Nope," is her greeting.

"Nope what?"

"You're not calling to cancel our plans tonight. I don't care how much you want to. You need to go out more than anyone I know."

"I'm calling," I begin, "because I want to know what you're wearing. The last time we went out we practically wore the same thing. I want to look different, noticeable beside you, not like your cross-dressing brother."

I don't really look like a boy, but beside Jillian and her plump ass and way more than a handful breasts, anyone without curves looks a little masculine.

"What were you thinking?" she asks as if she didn't just preemptively bite my head off.

"That half maxi dress. You know the one with the turquoise bottom and shimmery, black, flowy top."

"The one that's super snug and short?" I can hear the thrill in her question.

"Yes, that one."

"Perfect," she praises. "I think I'll go with the coral mini skirt and a new white sequined top I got last week."

"Sounds great. Pick me up at eight?"

"Seven," she clarifies. "We're heading out of town tonight. We've exhausted the waters in town. Tonight calls for a fresh hunting ground."

"I'm not hunting, Jillian. I just want to have a few drinks and dance."

"Well, I'm hunting. So just deal with it."

"You're always hunting," I mumble under my breath.

"What's that?" she asks.

"I'll see you at seven," I tell her before hanging up.

Jillian may be older, but sometimes I wonder who the twenty-five-year-old is in this friendship.

True to Jillian form, she was twenty minutes late whereas I was ready half an hour beforehand. One of these days she'll be on time, but today isn't her day. A plus is that she hired a driver tonight since we're going out of town and planning on copious amounts of alcohol.

I can feel the sidewalk vibrate under my feet as we walk up to *SWEAT*. I don't know why they'd name a club that, but the name is not keeping people away. After twenty minutes in line, a guy walking up and down the sidewalk picking people at random selected Jillian, and I got to tag along. When I say random, I honestly mean he's looking for the best-looking people to head inside ahead of everyone else. It happens at almost every club we go to, and Jillian almost always gets picked. If she doesn't... well, we never go back to that club again.

She'd mentioned wearing a mini skirt, but I should've known that her idea of a mini is actually a micro-mini. The lower section of her butt cheeks were visible, but hey, it got us off the sidewalk and into the club, so I'm not complaining.

The pulse of the music seems to change the rhythm of my heart as we step up to the bar and order shots. We decided on the ride over that tonight was going to be wild, so fruity cocktails had no place in our evening.

We start with two shots each, but that turns into three when a guy down the bar buys us each a shot with a wink. We raise our shots to him in thanks but turn our attention back to the dance floor that's vibrating and moving with dozens of people.

Jillian has a rule about guys that send shots without approaching first. She feels like if they don't have the balls to come over and offer to buy a drink in person, they're not worth the time. Me? I just like free booze. So it's pretty much win-win.

"Want to dance?" she yells over the music.

I nod and smile. I want to get lost in the rhythm. I want to forget the fact that come Monday morning I may not have a job. I want to get Kegan Cole out of my head. He's taken up too much space over the last couple of weeks, and it's time to replace him with something else.

I contemplate taking up yoga for the whole, free your body and mind techniques, but then I remember I'm a klutz and nearly killed myself trying the downward dog in my living room a few years back.

Jillian takes my hand and tugs me toward the dance floor. We're only several feet away when a hand snakes out and grabs mine.

I turn suddenly, gearing up to yank my arm from the stranger's grasp. "What the fu—"

My eyes meet those of my cousin.

"I thought you were going to attack me!" he hollers over the raging beat of a techno song.

I laugh at the wide-eyed look on his face. "I think I almost did!"

I can feel Jillian at my side, and my body registers the angry vibration of hers. I look past Justin's shoulder and see exactly what she's pissed about. Hawke is huddled in close to a woman wearing a lime green wig of all things. She's not the only one wearing fake hair in the club, but the fact that Hawke is even talking to someone who'd wear one is the oddity.

"Why the fuck are y'all here?" Jillian spits at Justin.

I place a calming hand on her shoulder, but she shrugs me off.

Justin just looks at her like she's asking a question she already knows the answer to.

"You know exactly why we're here." He gives her a frustrated look and takes a long pull on his beer.

I shake my head. It's clear Justin is as annoyed as I am about the bullshit Jillian and Hawke put each other through. I can tell we're an incident or two away from an intervention with them.

I tug Jillian's hand and pull her toward the dance floor. I didn't come out tonight to watch her and Hawke one-up each other, and if that's how the night is going to go, I'll leave right now. I've grown weary of Justin and I being dragged into their antics.

Five songs later and I'm covered in sweat, and the mild tingle of the liquor has settled into an incredible languor. I stopped paying attention to Jillian, who's done nothing but stare at Hawke sucking face with Wig Girl, and found my rhythm dancing with different people on the dance floor.

I motion to Jillian that I'm going to grab another drink and head to the restroom to towel off. She waves me off because I blocked her line of sight. The guy dancing behind her has one hand on her bare thigh and is cupping a breast in his hand, but it's almost as if she doesn't even realize he's there.

Pitiful. I remind myself to never get so wrapped up in a man that I refuse to tell him how I feel. I'd rather put it all out there than dance around each other for years. The mental affirmation automatically brings Kegan to mind. I shake my head as I walk toward the restroom.

I can't keep my mind off of him. I'm so focused on him that my mind formulates his scent as if he's standing right beside me. I close my eyes for two brief steps and inhale deeply.

Just like out on the dancefloor, my arm is grabbed again. I don't mess around. This isn't the bar area where I'm surrounded by other people; this is a more remote area of the club. I turn on my feet and send a closed fist punch through the air.

By the time I recognize the blue eyes looking back at me, it's too late to stop the momentum of my hand. Pain radiates up my arm as Kegan grabs his jaw with his free hand.

I cover my mouth in surprise at what I've just done.

"That's twice now you've hit me in the face," he says rubbing the injured flesh.

"And both times you've deserved it. You should know better than to grab women the way you just did."

I shrug out of his grip and cross my arms over my chest. To him, I hope it looks as if I'm closed off and unapproachable, when in fact, I'm doing it to keep my hands off of him. The sight of him in blue jeans and t-shirt, combined with the sexy man scent he seems to carry around with him, is almost too much for my senses.

"I was standing right over there," he says pointing to the other side of the narrow hallway. "I thought you saw me and were just being stubborn."

"What are you doing here?" I ask.

"Would you think I'm a freak if I told you I followed you?"

My eyes widen. My heart beats faster. We're nearly forty-five minutes away from my house. What does it mean that he's willing to go so far?

"Are you freaking stalking me now?"

He shakes his head no.

"I was about to pull into your driveway and saw the town car leaving. I made a hasty decision."

"Why would you do that?"

He shrugs. "After you didn't call or text yesterday, I felt like I needed to see you. I want to explain about Amelia."

I hold my hands up to stop him. "You don't owe me an explanation, Kegan. But, I'm not that girl. I'm not like Amelia. I lost my head for a minute in the closet, but I don't do that stuff. *Ever.*"

He takes a step closer. I take a step back. This happens several times until my back is against the wall. My body is thrumming with electricity at his proximity.

"I know you're nothing like Amelia," he says as his eyes land on my lips. I lick them instinctively. "Do you think I'd follow her just to explain something to her?"

"I have no idea, Kegan. I don't know a damn thing about you." I attempt to sound indifferent, but my words come out breathy and aroused.

"Yes you do," he says closing the remaining couple of inches between our bodies. "You know how I feel when I'm deep inside you." He licks up my neck to the sensitive spot below my ear. "You know how hard I get just being near you." He rolls his hips against mine; his blue jean clad erection comes tauntingly close to my clit.

I tilt my head to give him more access. "I bet half of Spokane knows all of those things about you."

I yelp when he takes a retaliatory nip at my earlobe.

"Are you wet for me?" he asks as his hand glides up my thigh. "Amazing," he breathes as his fingers slip past the lace of my panties.

"Mmm," I groan as they slide through the slickness that began to build the second I realized he was the one grabbing me.

"What are you doing?" I whimper when I feel his fingers hook into either side of my thong.

Without a word, he bends and glides the lace down my legs.

"Kegan," I gasp as he pulls them past my heels and nips my inner thigh.

"Tell me to stop," he says as he stands, dangling my lingerie between us.

"I can't," I confess with a harsh pant.

He makes quick work of his zipper, pulling a condom out of his back pocket.

I glance around, terrified someone is going to walk up, but not really caring.

His mouth takes mine in a feverish kiss, his tongue stroking over mine relentlessly. Mouths still tangled, he grips my ass and lifts me. My legs circle his waist as he lines himself up with my entrance.

"What does all of this mean? What does this make us?" My eyes plead with him to explain his intentions.

I expect him to say fuck buddies or some lame shit like that, but he doesn't.

"Just feel me," he says raising my panties up and shoving them in my mouth. "No more talking, Lexi."

I bend my head forward into the crook of his neck and hold on as he powers in and out of me. The cool feel of the air against my flesh is an amazing contradiction to the heat of his cock as it slams home over and over.

"Fuck, Lexi. I can't –goddamn it," he groans in my ear.

I hold on to him tighter, wanting to kiss him but can't.

He leans his head back and then places it against mine. "I need you to come," he says never slowing his grueling pace.

His scent, the thrill of being with him again, and the excitement of virtually having public sex had my body on edge the second he entered me. His words, however, are what send me over the edge.

I scream into the fabric of my panties, never taking my eyes off of his, as my body comes with a ferocity I didn't know I was capable of.

"Jesus, Lexi. Fuck," he hisses as my body grips him in wrenching pulses.

His eyes soften, and his eyelids grow heavier the second before he climaxes. There's almost a hint of vulnerability on his face. I was facing away from him last time, so I don't know if this is how he looks every time he comes, but it's a sight to behold.

He pulls my panties from my mouth, tucking then into the front pocket of his jeans and kisses me as if it's going to be the last time. My heart is soaring and breaking all at the same time.

Chapter 19

Kegan

My feelings and the way my body responds to her scares the life out of me, but it doesn't stop me from buying a bottle of liquor and dragging her out to my truck.

I wanted to fuck her again. The second I saw her in the tight little blue dress, my cock demanded I make entrance into her body. My intentions, when I followed her and her friend to this club weren't one hundred percent innocent, but I never planned on fucking her in the dark hallway.

I watch from the corner of my eye as she tilts the bottle of bourbon back and takes a long swig. I drive as quickly yet safely as I can back to her house. I haven't had a drop to drink, but that'll be remedied soon. My mouth waters for a taste; the burn of the alcohol and the contrasting sweetness of her pussy is all I can think about as we make our way up her driveway.

She's not completely smashed as we walk up to her front door, but she's beyond able to get her key in the door. I make quick work of the lock and have the door closed behind us and locked before she can drop her purse on the table just inside the door.

Without a word, I scoop her up and carry her up the stairs.

"That one," she instructs, pointing to the door at the end of the hall.

I cover the space between the door and the bed in a few long strides. I shift her from my arms until she's steady on her feet. Grabbing the bourbon from her hands, I twist the top off and can't seem to worry about the lid when it hits the floor and rolls away.

I tilt the bottle back and drink deeply.

Lexi's hands are unbuttoning my jeans before I even pull my lips from the bottle. Lowering the zipper, she drops to her knees, tugging my jeans and boxer briefs down as she goes.

"I want to suck you off," she slurs mildly, tonguing the wide crest.

Her mouth is hot and beyond impressive. My brain wants to shut down and just let her have her fun, but I know she's had a lot to drink, and the last thing I need is her to gag on my cock and puke. There's nothing less sexy than vomit.

I pull her up my body and lick her neck.

"Next time, Lexi," I promise.

Her grin is radiant. Even with slightly smeared makeup and disheveled hair, she's absolutely gorgeous. My hands find the hidden zipper on the back of her dress, and I have her naked in seconds. She's not wearing a bra, which I absolutely love. Her breasts are just a little more than a mouthful and fucking perfect. Her panties are still stuffed in the front pocket of my jeans, where they'll stay. I have deviant plans for those when I find myself alone and needing her.

I kick my shoes off and shake my legs until my jeans and boxers fall to the side. Her hands find my chest as I pull my t-shirt over my head; the touch sparking a lust that burns deep. I'm rock hard, but her fascination with following each curve and rise of my muscles makes me grow even thicker.

Her attentive touch falters when she leans in and licks the top of my abdomen.

"And here I thought you were going to be the one getting licked tonight," I manage to say through her mouth's attention that's now focused on my nipple.

I lift her with an arm around her waist and place her in the center of her bed. I kiss and lick down her body, paying little attention to anything until my nose nudges her swollen clit. This is where I need my focus for the night. I have no intention on relenting until one orgasm flows into the next.

I don't even question the urge for domestic tasks as I leave Lexi lying in her bed to make my way downstairs to make coffee. Even though my balls ache from overuse, my cock still stands at attention knowing that Lexi is in her room naked as the day she was born.

As soon as there's enough coffee in the pot, I pour two cups. I'm taking a sip of mine when the front doorbell echoes through the house. Making my way out of the kitchen, I find myself grateful I threw on my jeans before coming downstairs.

I know it's not my place to open her door, but that doesn't stop me after waiting a minute to see if she's going to come down to answer it. After the second chime of the bell, I tug open the door.

I stare in amusement at the tall, lean woman standing on the front porch. I'd guess she's about forty-five, but with the amount of makeup she has caked on her face I could be way off base. I wonder if she's lost because the tiny dress that is almost forcing her fake breasts out of the top of her dress is a little out of place for a Sunday morning.

"I'm Cinnamon," she coos holding her hand out to me.

I shift my coffee cup to my other hand and shake hers. She slides her hand up my forearm before I can pull it back. I suddenly feel naked as her eyes roam over my bare chest.

"Kegan," I say politely.

"You are one fine man, Kegan." She takes a step closer to me and trails a long poorly manicured acrylic nail down my chest.

I take a step back and contemplate slamming the door in her face.

A hiss draws my attention to the staircase. Lexi is walking down with my shirt and shoes in her hands. Her eyes are narrowed, and she looks angry, but her focus is on the woman standing on the porch, not me. For that, I'm grateful. I had no idea how she was going to react to waking up with me in her house. Things are different the morning after. The light of day and the haze of alcohol lifting can have anyone questioning what they did the night before.

"Who are you?" I finally manage to ask. I'm trying to evaluate the situation, and if I'm going by the look on Lexi's face, this is not a woman she wants in her house.

"Her mother," she says looking past me to Lexi.

Mother? I don't remember many conversations I have with women, but every word Lexi has ever said to me has been playing on a constant loop in my head. I distinctly remember her telling me both her grandparents and her parents were dead.

I turn my attention to Lexi. "I thought you said—"

"That I was dead? Yeah, she tells everyone that," Cinnamon says stepping past me and into the house. "My key didn't work," she says to her daughter.

"I changed the locks," Lexi says handing me my t-shirt and shoes. The look in her eyes is pleading with me to go and let her handle this situation.

I put my shoes on the floor and begin to tug my t-shirt over my head.

"Don't get dressed on my account honey," Lexi's clearly not dead mother says. "This one looks much better than that asshole that knocked you up in college."

My eyes widen as I look over at Lexi, and the same reaction is on her face. Ah, secrets and lies seem to be a theme with her. Like I said before, this woman has complicated written all over her, and as much as I love fucking her, this shit is getting too deep for me.

I make my way into the living room and sit on the couch to tug on my shoes. I can feel Lexi's eyes on me, but I don't raise my head until both shoes are on and tied up.

When I finally raise my eyes to hers, I can tell she trying to analyze my thoughts, trying to get a read on my reaction to her mother's words. My thoughts are so scrambled I know she can't get an accurate read. That would be an impossible task, seeing as I have no idea how I feel about all of it.

I could be pissed that she has so much in her past. I could be livid that she lied to me about her mother, for no other reason than she seems to have been doing it for years. Yet, if I judge her for her past and her way of coping with Lord knows what, then I become her, the same woman who slapped me in the face for coming face to face with a woman in my past.

Unfortunately, it's the lies in my past that make me call everything into question. The fact that she did it so easily as if it was second nature is the cause for concern. It's the reason the alarm bells going off in my head are louder than the ones informing me she's more of a relationship type girl than the quick fuck kind.

I make my way toward the door, having nothing left to say. I don't know why I stop walking when I feel Lexi's trembling hand on my forearm.

Chapter 20
Lexi

"Cindy," I groan in frustration.

"Cinnamon," she corrects.

I shake my head and look at Kegan, grateful he stopped when I reached out to him. I have no idea what to tell him, but my mother standing in the middle of the living room isn't helping the situation at all.

"That's your stripper name," I counter.

I know what you're thinking... how dare I speak to my mother that way? Yeah, you have no idea about this woman.

"You," she says aggressively taking a step toward me. "Are the reason I'm a fucking stripper."

I feel Kegan's body tighten. I take a step back, and he repositions his body as if to shield me from the angry woman.

"I wasn't going to be a stripper, Lexus." *God I hate my name.* "I was going to be a showgirl! I had dreams!" she screeches, growing angrier as each word comes from her mouth.

"Cindy," I say in a calming tone trying to stop this before things get out of hand.

"Cinnamon!" she yells. I watch as her face turns a brilliant shade of red that almost matches the color of her dyed hair. "If that piece of shit producer hadn't knocked me up, I'd be famous by now."

The famous part she's always thrown in my face. As long as I can remember she's blamed me for her shortcomings. I don't know why; it's not like she didn't drop me off with my grandparents the first chance she got. The newest addition, though, is her mention of the producer being my father.

My paternity changes to suit her mood. I've come to realize over the years that there's a very real chance Cynthia Carter has no idea who my father actually is, but her poor choices in choosing sexual partners are somehow all my fault.

I sigh at the realization. Like mother, like daughter.

Suddenly my desire for Kegan to stay, if only as a defense against my belligerent mother, evaporates completely. The longer he stays, the more he'll realize that I'm a complete mess.

"You've ruined my life!" she continues. "I was destined for fame, and what do I have now? Nothing. I have nothing to show for years of hard work other than being the lead at Marky's Muff Mansion in Portland."

I want to laugh at her declaration, but it catches in my throat as Kegan takes a step toward her.

"Sounds to me that you've got some pent-up frustrations," he says with an edge to his voice.

My mother nods, seeking his sympathy.

"Seems you're pretty upset, made some bad decisions in your life," he continues.

She nods. "Horrible decisions. I didn't know I was pregnant until it was too late for an abortion," she whimpers.

Kegan's back muscles tense up at her words. For me, it's just another day with my mother. I'm so thankful that these random visits are so few and far between.

"She ruined my life," my mother says.

"It's a damned shame you feel that way, *Cynthia*." I smile at his use of her name. "Lexi is the most amazing woman I've met, other than my own angelic mother."

He turns his back to her and looks me in the eye. "I need to go. Unless you want me to stay?"

I shake my head. He's seen enough. After this, I may never see him again.

He kisses my forehead but lingers a second longer than necessary. "We need to talk about the lying," he whispers in my ear before walking out the front door.

"He may be good looking, but he's sort of an asshole," she says picking up the half empty cup of coffee Kegan sat on the side table before putting on his shoes.

"I'm not talking to you about Kegan," I say walking out of the living room and heading in the direction of the coffee I smell in the kitchen.

"I just don't want you to make the same mistake I did," she says halfheartedly as she follows me.

This is my mother. She gets belligerent, puts on a performance around others, vying for sympathy, then calms down to just spiteful and backhanded comments.

"I did make the same mistake," I remind her.

Falling for a man who used me. Check.

Getting pregnant and then left by that man. Check, Check.

"You were lucky, though," she says

I close my eyes and take a deep breath. This may be another thing she's adamant about, but it's also the one thing that makes me want to throat punch her.

"I wouldn't call it luck," I mutter taking the full cup of coffee Kegan must have poured for me and heat it in the microwave.

"It is lucky," she pushes. "You weren't saddled with a kid your whole life."

I huff at her distorted memories.

"Why did you have to bring up the baby in front of Kegan?"

The laugh that follows my question reeks of malicious intent.

"What? You didn't tell your boyfriend that you trapped a guy in college?"

"I didn't—" I stop my words. There's no sense in arguing with her. I never get anywhere when I do. I pinch the bridge of my nose between my fingers. "He's not my boyfriend."

She laughs again. "Neither was the last one."

I shake my head and pull my cup of warmed coffee from the microwave. I could argue with her that I thought Hunter and I were together, exclusive even, but I seem to have a problem with reading cues from men.

"Why are you here, Cindy?"

I look over at her, arms crossed over her chest and a glare in her eyes.

"I need money," she all but demands.

"I don't have money to give you," I respond quickly.

"You spent all of your inheritance?"

"That money is mine. I'm not touching it, and neither are you."

Her body stiffens, and I wonder briefly if she's going to attack me. She's never resorted to violence before, yelling and degrading is more her thing, but I wouldn't put it past her. She grew angry quicker today than she has in the past.

"You owe me," she spits holding her clenched fists by her sides.

"I don't owe you a thing," I say as calmly as I can manage.

At what point does a parent get things so twisted in their head that they honestly believe that giving birth to a child guarantees them everything that child has?

I totally get taking care of a loving parent when they need it. Hell, I wish this was the case. Had my mother been around, had she nurtured me and loved me the way a parent should, I'd give her every penny I had if she needed the help. That is so far from the case I'm dealing with now; it's almost comical that she expects a penny from me.

"That money was supposed to be mine. That's my parents' money, not yours." She's seething, which isn't anything new.

She only shows up when she's down to her last dime, and she comes back each time because I give into her. She is my mother after all. My grandmother would help her out. It's what I saw growing up.

Cindy would show up, beg for money, and my grandmother would give in if only to get her out of the house. Things were always chaotic when she was here, and it didn't take long before she wanted things to go back to normal.

"They didn't leave it to you," I say pouring out the coffee. I look at the clock on the wall, wondering if it's too early to start drinking.

"You manipulated them," she counters.

"I did no such thing." I head to the fridge to grab the unopened bottle of wine. If she stays too long this time, I may be an alcoholic before she leaves.

I clutch the bottle to my chest, reach in the drawer for the corkscrew, and don't even bother to grab a glass.

"I need money," she says again as if I didn't hear her the first time.

"What do you need money for?" It's always some big excuse: car trouble, apartment got robbed. Last time she was here she needed money for another abortion. She's had several. I don't believe in abortions as birth control, but there's no way I'm okay with her bringing another child into the world.

"I have tickets," she says, but her eyes dart away from mine. You'd think after all these years of manipulating people that she'd get better at lying.

"Well," I say calling her bluff. "Write down the information for the court and I'll get online and pay them."

"You can just give me the money. I'm a grown-ass woman. I can take care of the paperwork myself."

I raise an eyebrow at her. "You want to pull that 'grown-ass woman' mess with me while you're standing in my kitchen begging for money?" I huff and make my way to the door.

She practically growls at me, and it brings a small smile to my lips. It's the little things.

"You'll have to make the bed upstairs if you plan to stay," I tell her as I walk out of the kitchen.

"Some fucking host you are," she says to my back.

I turn around and face her. "I'm not hosting you. That's for when people show up because they're expected, wanted. I'm not asking you to leave, but I'm sure as hell not going to cater to you."

"I'm your mother," she spits.

"Yeah," I say turning back around. "Just my shitty luck."

I leave her to do whatever it is she does while she's here. No doubt she'll spend a few hours rifling through the house, trying to find things to pawn or sell.

Chapter 21
Kegan

I couldn't tell you why I kissed her before I left, but even with the anger coursing through my veins, I knew I couldn't leave without doing it. Call it instinct, need, or ownership. I have no idea, but my nerves calmed a fraction when my lips met her skin.

Just a fraction, though, because I don't do lies. I don't do complicated, and after hearing what her mother said, this situation is nothing if not complicated.

She told me her parents were dead. She never mentioned having a baby. I struggle with faulting her with that omission. We don't have a relationship. We fucked. We had sex. Amazing, mind-blowing, incredible sex, but sex nonetheless.

There are things about me she doesn't know. Things no one knows. I know it's shitty of me to be angry about her past, but the lie about her parents... that's not okay on any level.

She tells everyone that.

Her mother's words ring in my ears. So she's what? Embarrassed. Hell, after meeting Cindy, I can see why. That woman is a train wreck and a half. I hated leaving Lexi there to fend for herself, but I'd say things I'd regret if I stayed.

I make it to my house in record time. The only thing I have on my mind right now is researching her grandparents to see if she lied about their deaths also. At this point, I don't know what's been the truth and what has been lies.

I fire up my computer a second after walking through the door. I carry the laptop to the kitchen for a bottle of water, then settle on the couch with it on my lap. I type her name and 'car accident' into the search engine. The results populate immediately.

My eyes land on a newspaper headline "College Graduate Sole Survivor in Fatal Drunk Driving Crash."

My hand shakes as it hovers over the link. I close my eyes and pray that this isn't the accident my uncle Scott was involved in. My anger at her lies suddenly dissipates when I realize that my drunken uncle, who killed three people while driving drunk three years ago, could be the one who murdered her family.

I swallow roughly and click on the link. I begin to read the article:

A drunk driver claimed the lives of two people this morning after a wrong-way collision on Interstate 90. Clive and Mona Carter were pronounced dead at the scene. Jake Bellows, of Orchard Prairie...

I breathe a sigh of relief. Everyone, me included, feels enough guilt over not doing something about Scott's drinking. I couldn't handle it if he was the one who ended her grandparents' lives. I continue reading.

...walked away from the scene with minor injuries and a blood alcohol content of 0.14, nearly twice the legal limit. An unidentified female, wearing a graduation gown, was pulled from the wreckage and transported to an area hospital. More updates to come.

I scrub my hand down my face and close the lid to my laptop. I can't read any more than what I've already seen. I lie back on the couch and close my eyes. From the date on the article, I know the accident happened three years ago. As a matter of fact, three years to the day of when she stripped naked in her den last week. I knew something was off for her that day.

Three years ago, and I still have the urge to rush back to her house and comfort her for her loss.

As much as I don't want to be around people right now, my mother would never let me live down missing a Sunday dinner. There is an unspoken rule, that if you are in town, you are at Mom and Dad's at six on Sunday evening.

The only one I've missed was last year. I only got the reprieve because I had the flu and was banished from the house since London was pregnant and the girls were so susceptible to germs.

I don't bother to knock as I enter my parents' house. Squealing and screaming greet me just like it does every week. I grin from ear to ear as I turn into the living room and see London walking around with Easton in her arms.

"Here," Kadin says stopping me with a hand on my arm. "You have to wear this."

I take the surgical mask from his hands and gladly put it on my face. Just the air surrounding him is lighter than the last time I saw him. I knew Easton had been released Friday, but this is the first time I've seen them all together since I picked the girls up and carried them to school several weeks ago.

"How's he doing?" I ask walking up to London and touching my nephew's foot with a gentle hand.

"Good," she answers. "He still gets tired easily, but he's much better than he has been."

She goes back to walking around with him, rocking him gently as he drinks a bottle.

"The masks?" I ask Kadin.

He shrugs. "She thinks we all need them. I'll never question her instincts again."

I nod, knowing exactly what he means. I have to wonder how long he's going to beat himself up for not trusting her when Easton first got sick.

"Oh," my mom says stopping short in the living room entrance. "You're alone?"

"Just like every week, Mom."

"But I thought you'd bring Lexi." She's practically whining, and the disappointed look on her face is almost comical.

"I told you. We're just friends."

"*She* said you were friends," she corrects. "I read between the lines, and I know there's more to it than that."

I watch with grateful eyes as London walks out of the room to lay the sleeping Easton down in the nursery my mom has here. The last thing I need is a bigger audience watching this mess.

"There were no lines to read between, Mom. *Friends.* That's it." Kadin chuckles beside me, and I want to pop in the back of the head. He's having too much fun right now and needs to be knocked down a peg or two.

She narrows her eyes at me. "*You* brought her *here.*"

"And?"

"You never bring girls here unless it is serious."

"Serious? I've never been serious about a girl," I lie. No one in my family but Kadin knows about Rhonda, and I'm not explaining that shit now.

"That girl in high school," my mom prods.

"Rachel?" I ask. "You insisted we come over for prom pictures. She was here under duress."

She huffs indignantly.

"Still, you brought Lexi over." She will not give up.

"She was in the truck, Mom. She was helping with the girls. Nothing else," I insist.

The words fall out of my mouth, and I mentally want to slap my own face.

My mom finally leaves it alone, for now. I know we'll revisit this conversation while we're all prisoners around the dinner table.

"Just friends? Really?" Kadin is getting a kick out of this apparently.

I sigh and walk to the liquor cabinet. Pouring three fingers of a dark scotch into a tumbler, I turn back to him. "Lexi Carter has more drama than a season of Game of Thrones," I tell him and take a seat on the couch.

"Every woman has drama, Kegan." Kadin sits on the cushion beside me. "You just have to decide if she's worth getting tangled up in the middle of it."

I laugh and toss back the remainder of my drink. "No woman is worth the drama."

He looks over at the doorway where London is walking back in with the girls. "You couldn't be more wrong," he says softly. "Some women are worth all of the drama."

I watch his eyes as they soften looking at his wife across the room.

Before I can respond to him, Dad sticks his head in the door. "Hey, son. Where's Lexi?"

I groan as my brother belts out a laugh beside me. This is going to be one long ass dinner.

An hour and four glasses of scotch later, my mother is still going on about Lexi. I can't really argue with her observations.

She's very pretty. Truth.

She's cordial. Another point well made, unless you've got her pinned against the wall in a dark club. There's nothing cordial about her then. *Your dad and I talked about her for an hour after you left the other day.*

She'll be an amazing wife and mother. Truth... hold on... what?

"That's not even on my radar, Mom." I toss back another glass and ignore the scowl my brother is giving me. "I'm never getting married." I look over at the girls who are using their mashed potatoes for lipstick. "Kids really aren't my thing."

London's chuckle draws my attention. "What?" I ask her.

"Nothing," she says with a shrug and a grin.

"I get it. You and Kadin are great parents and partners. That's not me. Kadin was born to be a dad. That's not everyone's goal in life."

Kadin leans in and whispers in her ear. The light giggle and the pink that flushes her cheeks make me wish for a fraction of a second that Lexi was here. I'd much rather be whispering salacious things in her ear than listening to my family drone on about settling down.

"You're thirty-four, Kegan. You don't want to start a family too late," my mom says cutting into my mental escape plans.

"No family, Mom. Those," I point to the girls, "and Easton are the only kids I need in my life."

I pour a large glass of wine and drink almost the full glass. My parents don't allow hard liquor on the table, but drinking a full bottle of wine is acceptable.

I should've thought about my little Sunday evening drinking binge. Now I'm going to be stuck at this house all night, which means I'll get to have the same conversation again over breakfast tomorrow.

Chapter 22
Lexi

I groan and roll over in bed. My head is pounding, and my mouth feels like it's stuffed with dirty gym socks. Drinking all day and half the night isn't as easy to recover from as it was in college. I know I sound like a broken record. I think the same damn thoughts every time I wake up from a night of overindulging.

Deciding just to sleep it off, I turn to my stomach and shove my hands under my pillow. My eyes widen when my arm hits something that's not supposed to be under there. I sit up as fast as my hungover body can maneuver and lift my pillow. I'm alone in the room, but it doesn't stop the heat from rushing to my cheeks.

I shoot a look at the door to make sure it's closed before turning my eyes back to my purple vibrator that I must have stashed under my pillow last night. Did I mention that a drunken Lexi is also a super horny Lexi? That's how I ended up pregnant in college. Hunter and I were both drunk. Going without protection seemed like a good idea in our inebriated state. It was the only time I made that mistake. Hunter is another story. He had two other girls pregnant before I graduated from college.

It's also why I didn't stop Kegan when he pulled my panties off at the club. As angry as I was with him, the thrill of getting it on with a super hot guy in such a public place was a total turn on. I need to reevaluate my life because the more I reflect on my actions, the more I realize I'm a freak.

I normally wouldn't feel shame about finding my plastic boyfriend under my pillow, but I know that I'm not the only one in the house. My mother is lurking around here somewhere. The idea of facing her again today makes me want to go downstairs and grab another bottle of wine from the fridge.

I put Big Ben back in the bedside table and head for the bathroom. Showering and possibly purging my stomach are the only two things that are going to make me feel even half-way decent today.

It's over an hour later when I muster enough strength to leave my room. A wide smile spreads across my face when I realize that the guest bedroom is empty. I pray my mother left, which means it will be another six to eight months before she comes back begging for money.

I close the door for now, even though I know I'll have to strip the bed and begin walking down the stairs. A noise from the back of the house makes me frown. The sight of my mother rifling through my grandparents' room makes me see red.

"What are you doing?" I ask from the doorway.

"What have you done with her jewelry, Lexi?" I watch as she drops the small drawer she pulled out of the vanity. Thankfully, the carpet keeps the antique from shattering.

"You mean the stuff you didn't steal the last time you were here?"

"She should've left all of this stuff to me," she says moving on to another drawer.

"But she didn't. You can stop destroying the room, Cindy. You won't find a damn thing in here worth money."

She slams the drawer closed and glares at me.

"What? You've already sold it all?"

I shake my head in disbelief. "No. I put all of their valuables in a safety deposit box at the bank. I knew you'd come back eventually, and I wasn't going to risk you selling them for a fraction of their value."

She sits on the bed, defeated by my news. "You've ruined my life," she mutters.

"Broken record, Cindy," I say turning out of the room. "Get over your bitterness."

Unfortunately, she follows me into the kitchen.

Other than her heavy, frustrated breathing, silence fills the room. There are no construction noises coming from next door. It's Labor Day which is the only reason I'm off on a Monday. It seems Kegan gives his crew the day off as well.

I begin making a pot of coffee, hoping that ignoring her will work, but I know better.

"I'm your mother," she spits.

I remain silent.

"You disrespect me every time I come here."

I can't help the snort that escapes my mouth.

"You can leave," I tell her deserting the coffee making. "This time," I say just before walking out of the kitchen, "stay away for good. Mother or not, you mean absolutely nothing to me. My parents died three years ago."

Jillian is my saving grace again today. I jumped at the idea of getting out of the house when she called and asked. Pig Out in the Park is the perfect distraction for me today, and the fried, greasy foods from the vendors are just what my hangover needs.

"I hate seeing you like this," Jillian says as we step away from the third food booth we've visited today.

"What?" I ask swiping at my face. "Is there mustard on my chin?"

She shakes her head no, so I take another bite of the foot-long sausage on a stick.

"I hate when Cindy comes to town. It's almost like she carries this dark cloud with her. You're different when she's here, sad and depressed."

"I hate when she's here as well. Then I feel guilty because the second she shows up, I wish she'd leave," I confess. "No one should feel like that about their mother."

"Don't do that," she chastises. "Don't you dare feel guilty about her. She's nothing more than an egg donor and incubator. That's the extent of her parenting."

"I know." We walk a little further in the park and find a small unoccupied spot on the grass as the band begins to warm up on the small stage.

"Enough about Cindy," Jillian says. "Let's talk about that hunk of a man you disappeared with on Saturday night."

I can't help the smile that graces my face.

"He slept with the headmistress at my school."

"Seriously? The one who always has her tits out and only got the job because she fucked some rich dude?"

"She's the daughter of a rich dude, but that doesn't mean she didn't sleep with a few to ensure her employment," I correct her.

She leans close to me. "You caught them together, and then went home with him? Lexi I taught you better than that."

"He said it was a few months back," I tell her.

She shrugs. "Everyone has a past, Lexi. You can't get pissed that he slept with someone else. He's ridiculously gorgeous. I wouldn't be surprised if he's slept with hundreds of women."

I frown at the thought, and my brows draw together. It's not as if it's something I haven't thought myself, but the realization still stings a bit.

"How is he?" I want to think she's asking about his health and general wellbeing, but when I look over at her with her lips wrapped around her sausage mimicking a blowjob with her eyebrows waving, I know that's not what she's asking.

"Adequate," I respond.

"You've got to be joking. Adequate? I want details, young lady."

"Other than Saturday night when we got to my house after the club, he's pretty much been an asshole." The look on her face tells me to proceed. "The first time we hooked up-"

"Hold on!" she says clasping my forearm. "The first time? You've hooked up more than once?

I nod. "The first time," I continue, "was in my den. He bent me over in front of the damn window. When he was done, he said 'thanks, doll' and left."

She chuckles. "I can totally see him doing something like that."

"The second time," I hold up two fingers. "Was in the hallway at the club. He stuffed my panties in my mouth and fucked me like he didn't have a care in the world."

"In the hallway?" I nod. "Stuffed your panties in your mouth?" I nod again. "That's crazy fucking hot."

"I nearly came the second he did it," I agree.

"And when you got home Saturday?" she prods.

"We were up until dawn going at each other. The man is a sex machine. I'm still sore."

"How did he act the next day?" she asks finally taking the last bite of her sausage.

I twirl the stick of mine in my hands, focusing on the rotation before answering. "Cindy showed up. We didn't get to talk much."

"That bitch ruins everything," Jillian says with disdain.

"She brought up the baby," I tell her.

"Fuck."

"Yeah, that and the fact I told him my parents were dead, may make him run for the hills." I begin to wrap my sausage in a paper towel.

"I'll eat it," Jillian says reaching for it. "Did he seem pissed?"

"Cindy was being a huge witch, and Kegan sort of stood up for me." I shrug. "He didn't seem mad, but he did tell me we needed to talk about my lying."

"Everything will be fine," Jillian says.

"You don't know that. I don't even know what I want from him."

"I do know that. If he was pissed and didn't want to see you again, he wouldn't have said that you need to talk later. He's a great catch. Handsome, beyond loaded. Seems to know his way around a clit. Top three priorities if you ask me."

I laugh at her shallowness. "That's not what I look for in a man, but Kegan has a lot of other stuff going for him. He's great with his nieces. His family is awesome."

"I thought you didn't want kids," Jillian says softly.

"I don't." I really don't. After such a loss it's difficult to have the urge to risk another one. "But knowing he's good with them is important. I like his mother. She's nothing like Cindy."

"Not many women in the world are like Cindy," she says.

"What do I do?" I look at her with a pleading somberness in my eyes.

She looks past me at the band on the stage. "I'm not the best one to ask relationship advice from, but I think you should wait for him to call you. If it goes longer than a week, shoot him a text or something."

I've got no better ideas so I might as well give her suggestions a shot.

Chapter 23
Kegan

"Damn it." I cover my dry eyes with my forearm as blinding light fills the room.

"You're not supposed to say bad words around me," comes from across the room. "My delicate ears shouldn't hear those things."

Anastyn.

I roll away from the noise and light, but the excruciating pain in my head doesn't subside.

"I'm almost certain you've been put on the earth for no other reason than to torture me," I grumble when I feel her climb up on the bed.

"Not true," she whines. "Momma says I'm here to bring everyone happiness and smiles."

I huff an incredulous laugh.

"Why are you here? Mimi and Granddad let you stay the night?"

"Something's wrong with your head," she says climbing on my back and knocking on the back of my skull.

"There's nothing wrong with my head other than the fact that you're banging on it and making it hurt."

"If there was nothing wrong with it, you wouldn't think you're at Mimi's house. You're in my house, Uncle Kegan."

That information has me rolling over and looking around the room. I grab Anastyn by the leg before she flies off the bed and smacks her head on the floor.

"Your house?" I crack my eyes open a tiny slit and look around. Sure enough, I'm in London and Kadin's guest bedroom.

"Daddy practically had to carry you in last night."

Awesome. My nieces got to see me in full-on drunken asshole mode. I'm winning awards over here people.

"Sorry about that," I tell her sincerely.

"No need to apologize to me, but I wish you'd get up so you can go buy my pony."

I laugh at her, but the look on her face doesn't leave any room for debate.

"Seriously?"

She nods. "Yep. I want a white one like Flynn Rider rode on Tangled!"

I release a long breath, trying to keep from puking as she stands up and begins to bounce on the bed.

"Anastyn." London's chastising voice from the doorway might as well be a holy song from an angel.

She stops bouncing immediately, leans down, and kisses me on the forehead. "A white one, Uncle Kegan."

A few seconds later her screaming echoes down the hallway.

"I promised her a horse?"

London nods. "You also promised Easton a speed boat, but I don't think he'll hold you to it."

I cringe. Clearly, I'm super fucking gifty when I'm drunk. "And Lennox?"

She laughs. "A new Barbie."

"Is that it?"

She nods. "Yep. It's Anastyn that has the expensive tastes. She reminds me a lot of you."

I ignore the jab because I never win when I fight with London. I've learned my lesson.

Kadin steps from the hallway and wraps his arms around his wife, resting his chin on her shoulder. "Hey. You're awake," he says way louder than necessary. He's doing it on purpose.

"Not like I can sleep when your devil spawn of a daughter came in and forced me awake."

His chuckle makes me realize she may have had some help in planning her attack.

"You ready to go pick out her horse?"

He has a smirk on his face, but I can't read whether or not he's actually serious. I narrow my eyes as if doing so will help me evaluate the situation. It doesn't

"She wants a white one," I say sitting up on the side of the bed.

"Like Maximus in *Tangled*," London adds.

"Right. I have no idea what that is. I also have no idea where to even go in Spokane to buy a damn horse." I scrub my face with my hands, but it does nothing to alleviate the pounding in my head.

"You should really reconsider getting drunk if you're just going to go all Favorite Uncle and make them promises you aren't going to keep," Kadin says with disappointment in his voice.

As his younger brother, there is absolutely nothing worse than that tone of voice.

"I'm not backing out old man. If I told the girl I was buying her a horse, then she's getting a damn horse." I give him a challenging look, daring him to think I'm bluffing. "But," I add, "Easton is going to have to wait on the speed boat."

London chuckles and looks over her shoulder at Kadin.

"You're actually going to do it?" he asks.

"Yep," I say standing from the bed and stretching my arms over my head. My back pops in several different locations reminding me I skipped my chiropractor's visit last month. Getting old sucks.

"Good," he says and kisses London on the temple. "I made the appointment last week. They're expecting us in two hours."

"Last week?" I ask his back as he walks away laughing.

I follow him out of the room and down the hallway to the kitchen.

"Last week?" I repeat.

London comes up behind me and gives my back a reassuring pat.

"Yep," Kadin says placing a steaming cup of coffee in front of me. "It's her birthday present."

"Yet somehow she asks me for it?"

Kadin shrugs. "Saves me some money. You know how I love a bargain."

"Asshole," I mutter blowing the top of my coffee.

"Want to talk about why you got plastered last night at the dinner table?" London says pulling out the chair beside me and sitting down. "You've never done that around the kids before."

"I just wanted to drink."

"Bullshit," Kadin says taking the chair across the table from me. "You're all tied up with that woman, and it's scaring the shit out of you."

"Lexi?" London asks with excitement in her voice. I look over at her, and her eyes have the same glint in them that my mother's had last night.

What is it with these damn women? Every one of them turns into fucking Cupid the minute I take a second look at a girl. This isn't London's first time to get excited over a girl. She did the same thing last year when she met my conquest for the night at a club we all went to together. Her mistake.

"I think she's great," London continues unprompted. Then she gasps and covers her mouth with her hand shooting a quick look at Kadin. "Please tell me you didn't one-night stand the girls' teacher?"

"I didn't!" I say defensively. Cutting my eyes back to Kadin was a huge mistake.

"I know that look," he says. "That look says you've slept with her more than once, but the real question is where does it go from here?"

"You're going to break her heart. She's going to hate me now. Do you know how bad it is if the teacher hates the parents?"

"I'm not going to break her heart." I have no idea why I made that promise. Who can predict the future? "I still don't know if I'll even think about taking things further."

Both of them just stare at me, blinking periodically.

"She lied to me," I inform them.

Kadin frowns, but it's his wife who speaks first. "What did she lie about?"

"She told me her parents were dead. Then her mother showed up at the house yesterday morning."

"You stayed the night with her?" Kadin asks with a grin.

"Leave it alone," I tell him.

"What's her mother like?" London angles her body at me as if I'm about to hand out some major gossip.

I cringe at the memories of Cindy. "She's horrible. Yelled at Lexi, said brutal things, blamed her for every wrong decision in her life. I was only there for like fifteen minutes after she showed up, but she managed to pack a whole lot of hatred in that short time. She claims it's Lexi's fault she's a stripper. She had all these grand plans for her life, and Lexi ruined them when she got pregnant."

London cocks an eyebrow at me.

"What?" I hate her scrutiny.

"Are you seriously telling me you're angry at her for lying about her mother after what you just said? Not everyone has parents like you guys do." She looks over at Kadin, including him in her appraisal. "A school teacher with a stripper mom? Can you blame her for lying?"

"She has to know I would've met them eventually," I mutter staring into my coffee cup.

Kadin laughs causing me to look up. "Does she, though? Have you given her any reason to think she'll be around for any period of time? Sounds to me like she figured you were just a passing fling and didn't want to get into anything personal with you."

London nods in agreement with her husband.

"Damn," I say softly. The idea that Lexi may be doing to me what I do with every other woman makes my gut turn.

"I'll be ready to head out in about thirty minutes," Kadin says getting up from the table and pushing his chair back up. London follows him out of the room, and I immediately hate the silence I'm left in.

Silence gives a voice to the thoughts in my head, and that's never a good thing.

I rub at my temples as Rhonda flashes in my mind.

Although I was a participating party in my relationship with her, I blame her for ruining me for all other women. Not in a good way either.

It was the little lies that she spewed that sent up the first red flags with Rhonda; those same red flags are rising with Lexi now too.

This isn't the same. Is it? I've been welcomed into Lexi's home, her bed. Lexi hasn't had issues with me showing up unannounced, and I completely understand now after taking a step back, the reason she lied about her mom. Cindy is beyond awful. Until meeting her, I didn't realize that people like that existed.

I have no idea how I feel about Lexi. I haven't really given myself the opportunity to think about her beyond any type of sexual relationship.

Liar, my brain tells me.

Looking back, I know I wasn't at her house Sunday morning because I got too drunk the night before. I wasn't there because it got so late I was too tired to leave. I was there because I wanted to be there. I stayed because having her in my arms felt right for some reason.

"You're looking for excuses," Kadin says coming back into the kitchen.

"She lied to me, Kadin. I can't get past that." Even though the words are coming out of my mouth, I don't honestly believe them myself.

"Of course you can. She isn't her, Kegan. This isn't the same thing," he assures me. "The question is, what are you going to do now?"

I shake my head slightly and rest my forehead in my palms. "I don't know."

"Take some time and figure it out. Lexi is a good woman. She doesn't deserve getting strung along." Kadin takes my coffee cup from the table, rinses it in the sink, and places it in the dishwasher. "But right now we need to go buy a horse."

"Where are you going to put a damn horse?" I ask getting up from the table and following him to the door.

"Out back," is his simple reply. "The barn and paddock were finished weeks ago."

He totally played me, and he used his not so angelic daughter to seal the deal.

Chapter 24
Lexi

"This is pitiful," I mumble setting out more plastic cups near the punch bowl.

"Tell me about it," I hear from beside me.

I cringe before looking over. A relieved sigh escapes my lips when I realize it's Renee, the second-grade teacher, beside me.

"Chex mix and punch? This is a private school. These parents pay tons of money for their kids' tuition, and we have open house night with cereal mix?" I shouldn't complain, out loud at least.

I just knew I would walk into work on Monday to my door code being changed and police waiting to arrest me for lewd behavior on a school campus, but it's blissfully silent. Amelia has kept her distance, and I can't help but wonder what Kegan told her, or promised her, to keep her from firing me.

Renee looks down at the pitiful refreshments on the table and frowns. "It wasn't always like this," she says in a whisper as if the walls have ears, and she'd be in trouble for what she's about to impart.

"Really? It was this horrible last year." This is my second year at Edgewood, but the lack of supplies and bells and whistles has always been an issue since I arrived.

"We used to have food catered in for every event we had. I'm talking real plates, cups, and silverware. None of this plastic junk," she says pointing at the tall stack of Solo cups.

"What's going on then? What's changed?"

"Two words for you, Amelia DuPont. She's cheap and doesn't feel like we should waste money on things like that." She grumbles something unintelligible under her breath. "Incoming," she groans softly and walks away.

I look over my shoulder and immediately jerk my head back toward the table. I busy myself tearing paper towels from the roll and folding them. No matter what nice way I try to fold them, they still look like cheap paper towels. I'm honestly embarrassed that this is what we're presenting to the parents of our children. Maybe some of the parents will be upset and cause a stink; hopefully, the next event will be back to the way Renee said it was a few years ago before—

"I'm keeping my eyes on you," Amelia says sliding up to the table. She purposefully hits it with her hips causing the tower of cups to fall over, several landing in the punch bowl. Thankfully the tablecloths are plastic, more than likely from the dollar store, and will wipe off easily.

I do my best to ignore her, but she's breathing down my neck. I try to calm myself with a few deep breaths before I turn to face her. True to her normal self, she's wearing a ridiculously low-cut top, and although her skirt is an appropriate length, her five or six-inch heels serve no purpose in an elementary school.

I can't help but notice her appraisal of me. She has a look on her face as if she's just taken a bite of spoiled meat. It bothers me the same way it did when the mean girls used to do it in high school. Of course, she would be one of those women.

"I have no clue what he even sees in you." I do my best not to let her snide remark rub me the wrong way, but it's almost impossible. "Kegan used to have class, but he seems to be slumming it these days."

I bite the inside of my cheek until metallic blood hits my tongue, but I manage to keep my mouth shut. Kegan left Sunday morning, and I haven't heard from him since. It's Thursday now, so I guess his silence is a clear indication of what he thinks of me. I don't have to justify myself to her, even though I want to. The last thing I'm going to do is risk my job justifying a man's decision, especially when he's not interested in me enough to call or even text.

I just smile at her and turn back to cleaning up the mess she just made.

"Ms. Carter!"

I turn to see Anastyn and Lennox Cole running toward me. Thankfully, Amelia steps out of the way as if she'll catch some kind of contagious disease if she gets too close to the children.

I reach down and hug them as each one wraps their little arms around my legs.

"We missed you," Lennox says softly.

"Missed me? That's silly," I tell her. "We were just in class a few hours ago. Did you show your mom and dad your caterpillars?"

They both shake their heads animatedly as if egg carton caterpillars are the best thing in the world.

"Good to see you again," London Cole says.

I lift my head to her, reaching out my hand to shake the one she's offering.

"Mr. Cole," I say to their father shaking his hand as well.

My heart flutters at the sight of him. He and Kegan look so much alike it's uncanny. Their father, although older, bears the same handsome features. I may be able to tell myself that Kegan Cole has no bearing on my life, but it still doesn't stop the thumping of my heart just being around his family.

"Where's Mr. Easton?" I knew the baby had been sick, but the girls told me he's out of the hospital and back home.

"At home with his Uncle Kegan," London says. My heart pounds harder.

My face must betray my reaction because she winks at me. Oh God. Do they know about Kegan and me?

"Momma doesn't want him to get sick again," Anastyn adds.

"Germs are bad!" Lennox chimes in.

"Yes, they are." I turn back to Kadin and London. "They're really excited to show you their work. They've been super busy girls since school started."

"I can't believe how much they've learned in a month," London says with a smile on her face.

Kadin remains quiet as we talk about the girls and how much progress they've made. It's almost as if he's evaluating me for some reason. I don't feel uncomfortable, but I just wish I knew what the silent interview was for.

Is he wondering if I'm good enough for his brother?

Maybe Kegan should tell him that ship has sailed. If telling me we need to talk and remaining silent for the next five days is his way of discussing things, then I've got no desire to explain myself to him or anyone else for that matter.

I make small talk with the Coles' for a few more minutes until another student's family comes up needing to discuss their child. We say our quick goodbyes, and I turn my attention back to the open house.

I'm exhausted by the time the school is cleaned up and back in order. Of course, Amelia didn't stick around to help, but I didn't expect her to.

A quick stop at the sandwich shop is the best I can do for dinner, and to save time getting into bed, I eat the whole thing on the way home.

Silence welcomes me when I open the front door. Cindy was here when I left this morning, but she doesn't seem to be around right now. Against better judgment, I leave the front door unlocked. We live in a nice quiet neighborhood, so it doesn't bother me. What would bother me, is locking it and having to get out of bed when she comes home drunk later tonight and bangs on it relentlessly, or worse yet, breaks a window to get in.

I smile at the thought of Kegan coming back over and fixing another window. I let myself imagine sitting on the sofa while he takes his shirt off like he did last time. I'd turn the heat up so he'd get all sweaty and delicious while I sit and drink ice cold lemonade.

I shut those thoughts down quickly. Fantasizing about Kegan before I actually slept with him was easy. Doing it after I know what he feels like in almost every position imaginable is dangerous. Those thoughts didn't lead to me grabbing my vibrator out of my drawer. Those thoughts led to me wanting to call him and invite him over, and that isn't as simple as it sounds

I kick off my heels in the front entry way and slide on my *Monsters, Inc.* slippers before heading upstairs and directly into bed.

Tomorrow will be better. Tomorrow I won't wonder about Kegan as much. Maybe tomorrow when I wake up I won't feel the fear I've felt all week that I'm going to lose my job. I don't, by a long shot, think Amelia is going to back down, but other than the insults tonight about Kegan's choice in women, she hasn't brought up the incident in the closet.

I don't know if I should be grateful or terrified.

Chapter 25

Kegan

I used to look forward to Fridays. The day only came second best to Saturday mornings when I didn't have to wake up early for work. Somehow, today doesn't carry the same thrill.

The week has been torturously long, especially when Kadin came to get Easton last night and made sure to tell me just how beautiful Lexi had been last night at the girls' open house. That little tidbit of information followed me into my dreams and haunted me all night.

I miss her. I'm man enough to admit that. I thought it was the sex and the way her tight body clings to me just before she comes that I was longing for, but as the week went on those carnal thoughts, although still there, turned into more than just a need for an orgasm.

I find myself wondering what she's doing, what she's wearing. I've wondered, more than once, if she is missing me the way I'm missing her.

I've been working with a different crew, starting another job across town and getting them settled. Today is the first day I've had the chance to even visit the Westover job. Her car's gone by the time I pull up at a quarter to eight. I knew it would be. What I don't know is if she's been leaving super early all week like she did that first week.

Is she avoiding me? I can't blame her for not reaching out and making contact; I haven't reached out to her either. I figured my body's need for her would dissipate over time, but it hasn't yet.

"A couple of us guys are going to hit the town tonight," Tony says meeting me at my truck. "You want to go?"

"Sure," I reply. Beers with the guys never sounded so good. "Where are we at with this project?" I ask walking up to the construction site.

Tony drones on about the foundation and supply list getting delivered on Monday, and I can't keep myself from looking over at Lexi's house. It isn't until my eyes land on the new window in her den that a genuine smile crosses my face.

I'm debating if this wasn't a horrible idea after all. Looking around the dimly lit bar, it doesn't have the same appeal as it used to.

Tony and the guys are chatting and laughing hard at a joke one of the other crewmen said. It would've been funny if it wasn't the same joke he tells every time he gets drunk.

I let my eyes wander as I sip on my beer. I got drunk twice last week, and I've got no plans to get that drunk again for a while. Eyes that would normally pause on the half-naked women in here, skate over them instead.

I blame Lexi for my tastes changing so quickly. It's the only explanation for not looking twice at the blonde near the bar. Big tits used to be my thing until I saw Lexi with her top off. I never knew small breasts would be so fantastic. I had always been a 'the bigger, the better' kind of guy. Now, all I want is a handful. Correction, all I want is Lexi.

Women with small breasts aren't my thing; Lexi is my thing.

I pull my phone out and check the time. We've been sitting here for hours, and it's already after eleven. If I call or show up at her house at this hour, she's only going to think I'm there to fuck her. It's the last idea I have in my head.

Tony nudges me with his elbow and indicates across the bar. My hopeful heart beats faster as I look over, expecting to see Lexi. I frown when my eyes land on the blonde I've been avoiding eye contact with.

I turn back to Tony and shake my head.

"Really?" he says unable to hide the surprise in his voice.

My skin crawls when I smell cheap perfume and feel the warmth of a woman's body slide up beside mine.

"Hey stranger," she purrs in my ear as she wraps her arm around my shoulder.

I have to angle my head back to keep from smacking my face on her implants. As gently as I can manage, I lift her arms from my shoulder. I keep ahold of her hand and place it in Tony's.

She pouts at my rejection but switches gears quickly when Tony raises her hand to his lips. Disaster averted.

I grin at Tony and the way he easily charms women. He thinks he's God's gift, but any woman who walks over with her sights set on one man and is so easily passed off to another, isn't a woman any man should get involved with. Unless he's looking for some quick fun, which for Tony is exactly what he's after. It's a match made in heaven.

I spend the rest of the evening passing easy women off to the other guys at the table. When they all decide to do a quick bar hop across town, I decline.

I climb in my truck and run through the contacts in my phone. My balls ache from my week long, self-imposed celibacy. My thumb hovers over Lexi's number. If I go over there now, we'll have the whole weekend together. If I go over there now, she may slam the door in my face.

I opt to drive over. I'll make the decision once I get to her house. If her mom's junky car is there, it will be a definite hell no.

Even though her mother's car wasn't in the driveway last night, I couldn't bring myself to knock on her door. All the lights were off and for the first time in my life, I didn't want a woman thinking I was showing up for a booty call.

Oh, how the mighty have fallen.

So I went home... alone.

Rather than run through my contacts to find another woman, I spent an hour deleting women from my phone. As I brought each one up, I spent a few minutes looking at their picture. Not one of them conjured feelings even close to what I felt when I came across Lexi's picture.

Like the asshole that I am, I took it last Sunday morning when she was sleeping. It was my way of getting things back under control after I willingly spent the night in her bed. I saved it under her contact information, just like I did every other girl I felt was decent enough for a repeat.

Looking back now, I feel like a total asshole, and she doesn't even know about it. Kadin has always told me when I find the right woman it'd feel like a punch in the gut. I'd meet her, and I wouldn't be able to think of any other woman.

I don't love Lexi, by any stretch of the imagination. After meeting her, I seriously wanted to get her naked, but it wasn't like an arch of light hit her, and I saw no one else. It's been more gradual than that, but the end is still the same.

I have to talk to her; I need to see where her head is at because this lack of communication and not knowing where we stand isn't something I'm going to deal with any longer. I need to know one way or the other, so I can make some decisions.

I get dressed with renewed determination. Today is the day I'm going to lay it all out. This will make the second time I've done this. The last time didn't work in my favor.

Chapter 26
Lexi

I hate yard work, maybe despise is a better word for it. If it weren't for the pride my grandmother had in this yard, I'd pave the whole damn thing so I wouldn't have to worry about weeds and curb appeal.

I tug the flat of fall flowers closer to me and begin planting flowers them; their frozen winter fate, already sealed. Waste of money if you ask me, but I somehow got it in my head that my grandmother is looking down on me, and this is what she expects. Too bad she's no longer here to massage my sore muscles away like she'd done every time before when we worked in the yard together.

I'd planned on doing the yard work as a way to avoid my mother, knowing she'd never offer to help. Apparently, nice hands on a stripper are a requirement. I guess reaching for dollar bills is much classier with a nice manicure. I don't have to worry about my mother though because I woke up yesterday to her absence and a note on the table reminding me how much of a disappointment I am.

The roar of a truck causes my pulse to pick up.

It could be anybody, I lie to myself. I'd recognize the sound of that truck anywhere. I wrinkle my nose in disgust when I realize I'm in ratty sweats and water boots. It's a far cry from the dress I was wearing last Saturday.

I don't turn toward the noise until the engine turns off and a door opens and closes.

My mouth immediately waters at the sight of Kegan in his tight t-shirt and form-clinging jeans. Damn, does this man have a set of thighs on him.

"Hey." I aim for nonchalance, but the high squeak in my voice ruins it. I am beyond ecstatic that he's here. Jillian told me he'd be the first one to reach out. I wasn't playing hard to get or anything, but the ball was left in his court when he left last week.

"Hey," he says walking closer. He shoves his hands down into his pockets. The closed-off behavior sobers my mood.

Silently, we just stare at each other, waiting for the other person to begin. Kegan gives in first.

"We need to talk."

I nod. I've been ready to talk since he left last week, but I'm terrified of the outcome. For weeks I've been trying to shove down feelings for him, not allowing my brain to actually acknowledge that I like him more than I have anyone else in a very long time.

I don't have a very good track record with men. I'd rather avoid them than get my heart broken again, but for some reason, I want to take that chance on him. My pulse pounds in my ears as I try to anticipate what he's going to say.

"I'm sorry I lied to you about my mom," I say. "If it's any consolation, it's what I tell everyone. The real story is not pretty, so I try to avoid it as much as I can."

He doesn't run like I thought he would, rather he sits down on the grass beside me.

"Yeah," he says. "Your mom... she's something else."

I huff a laugh. "That's one way to put it."

"I hate that you grew up with that kind of hatred." I can tell by the sadness in his eyes that he's sincere.

"That's the thing. I didn't grow up with that hatred. My grandparents raised me from a baby. I grew up in a loving home; it just wasn't traditional like the one you grew up in."

I hope I don't sound bitter because I'm not. It's a horrible thing to say, but my childhood was better without Cindy in it too often.

"Are you ashamed of her?"

I shrug. "Yes and no. She wasn't around much growing up to make any kind of impact, but when she did show up, we were miserable. My grandmother would cry when she'd leave again. Not because she was sad she was gone, but because she was happy when she left. She was ashamed that she didn't want her daughter around."

"I can see how she would feel that way." Kegan runs his hands over the trimmed grass but won't make eye contact with me. "I'm not upset that you tell everyone your mother is dead. I was upset that you lied to *me*."

"We weren't," I begin but pause. I don't even know what to say. "There was nothing between us but crazy chemistry when that easy lie fell from my lips, Kegan. I don't know what we are now, but if I had never spoken that lie and we were back in that situation now, after I've gotten to know you, I never would've said it."

"I don't do lies, Lexi." He's adamant.

"Most people don't," I agree.

"It's more than that." He looks out across the lawn avoiding eye contact. "I was in love once, in college. I met this gorgeous, older woman at the campus bookstore. We hit it off right from the start. Rhonda was everything I didn't even know I liked in a woman. She was funny, adventurous, secretive. That last part I loved until I discovered why she was so standoffish."

I busy my hands preparing the next flower to plant. I'll let him get his story out on his own time and pray he allows me the same thing when it's my turn.

"I fell hard for her. Even with the scheduled phone calls and not being allowed to go to her house, I just knew I'd spend the rest of my life with her." His face hardens, and his stare becomes focused on something nonexistent in the yard. "I bought her an engagement ring, planned out a special date. I was going to ask her to marry me. My brother thought I was crazy, but I was in love and couldn't be talked down. We met at a hotel like we always did, but she was different. I chalked it up to PMS or something, but the feeling wouldn't leave. I followed her home that night. My gut kept telling me she was cheating on me."

He runs a hand over his scruff so roughly I'm afraid he's going to hurt himself. "Was she cheating on you?"

He shakes his head no. "No, I was cheating *with* her."

"I don't understand."

"I'd always wondered why a woman as beautiful as her hadn't gotten married. Even in her early forties, she was gorgeous, a catch for any man with eyes. Even knowing that, I was gutted when her silver BMW turned into the driveway of her house, a family home. Turns out Rhonda, my sexy girlfriend was already someone else's wife."

"Shit," I mutter before I can catch myself. I take his chin in my dirty hand and force his eyes to mine. "I'm sorry I lied about my mom, but I won't ever lie to you again. It's not who I am. I have my own story to tell, and I will in due time, but I'm not a liar."

We sit in silence for a few long minutes. "I figured you were done with me," I confess. "All, *hit it and quit it* style."

Kegan laughs and shakes his head. "If you were any other woman, Lexi, I would've been."

"What makes me different?"

His eyes rake over every inch of my face. The softness in his eyes gives me hope.

"The first day I met you at the school, I was certain you were a sorceress. That's the only explanation I could come up with when the girls turned into compliant little children the second they stepped through the door of your classroom."

I shake my head in confusion. "What are you saying?"

"Clearly, Lexi Carter you've bewitched me, too."

"What are you going to do now that you've discovered my secret?"

His eyes focus on my mouth. "Kiss you?"

"Are you asking or telling?"

"Both." He grins. "I don't know what else you have in your black bag of juju."

He leans closer to me, and I pull back playfully. "I still have a few tricks up my sleeve, but only if you're a good boy."

He captures the back of my neck with a quick hand and tugs me closer to his mouth. "I've missed you this week."

"I've been right here," I say just before his lips brush mine.

He completely surprises me with his soft, tender kiss. I fully expected him to take my mouth like he has so many times before, aggressively and bordering on violence. The slow sweep of his tongue against mine sends a needy shiver down my spine. This man lights a fire in my blood that I can't even begin to explain.

With his free hand, he tugs on my hip until I'm straddling his lap. His slow licking into my mouth echoes at my core, reminding my body just how talented that tongue of his is.

He moans unabashedly when I suck it into my mouth and nip at the tip with my teeth. Both of his hands grip my hips and force them to rock back and forth against the hardness in his jeans.

I pull away from his mouth regretfully. "We should go inside," I whisper against his lips.

"You're safe out here." His grin is wicked. "If we go inside there's no telling what I'll do to you."

I kiss his neck and bite gently at his earlobe. "I'll take door number two, please."

He growls as he stands, lifting me up with ease. "I'll remind you tomorrow when you can't walk that you wanted this."

I squeal when he throws me over his shoulder and fireman carries me into the house.

Chapter 27
Kegan

When I drove to Lexi's this morning, I had no clue how the day would turn out. I sure as hell didn't have any intentions of telling her about Rhonda, but somehow she made telling that story much easier than I'd anticipated. The sting of pain I felt for months after I found out about her being married is no longer there. I'm not even angry at her, but I'm man enough to realize that my choices and all of my behaviors toward women since that day is a reflection of that betrayal. I'd hardened myself as a means to keep from having to feel that deep of a pain again.

As I carry Lexi into her house over my shoulder, I know that she's somehow slipped undetected under the fence I built around my heart. I haven't been miserable and unhappy since college, just the opposite in fact. I've had a hell of a time enjoying women, never wanting to settle down. Shit, I don't know if I want to settle down now, but thinking of that possibility with Lexi doesn't completely make me want to hightail it out of here.

Lexi stops mid-laugh when I slap her on the ass. I mean, it's right in my face. What else would I do with it? I contemplate biting it, but her sweats are covered in grass and dirt from gardening. The disappointing thud over the fabric of her clothes makes me want to strip her down and repeat the action.

"Put me down," she demands breathlessly.

I obey, but only because her mouth is nowhere near where I need it to be. Get your mind out of the gutter, *for now anyways.* Her lips on mine are the only thing I can concentrate on right now. I shift her weight and let her slide torturously slow down my body. My erection is still evident from our quick, outside make-out session. She tugs her bottom lip between her teeth as she feels it against her stomach.

"I'm filthy," she says holding her hands up so I can see the dirt and mud under her fingernails.

I'm all for dirty sex, but this kind is beyond anything I want to get involved with. I give her a quick peck on the lips and pull her behind me into the kitchen. A good hand washing is about all the time I have to dedicate to her clean up.

As she turns on the water and begins to use a small brush for her fingernails, I slide in behind her, grateful she has pulled her hair up to work outside in the yard.

I grin against her shoulder when my warm breath causes goosebumps to race down her arm. I don't miss the slight tilt of her head as she grants me access to her neck. She hums low in her throat when I gently scratch her exposed skin with the scruff on my jawline.

My hands find their way around her waist, and my thumbs immediately seek out the soft skin of her belly. Damn, this woman doesn't have to do a thing to get me riled up.

"I need to make you come," I whisper in her ear. The tremor my words cause can be felt from her knees to the racing pulse in her neck.

"Need?" she says playfully. "I mean, I'm not going to argue but..."

"Need," I growl and bite her earlobe.

With one hand splayed across her stomach, I let the other one dip past the drawstring of her sweats, brushing lightly over the apex of her thighs. It's a light, teasing touch and elicits the exact reaction I'm hoping for. Her knees bend and dip a few inches, but my hand on her stomach keeps her from melting to the floor.

"I love spending time with you," I confess into the delicate skin of her neck.

She chuckles softly. "Who wouldn't enjoy this?"

Her words force guilt into my chest. I don't know if she's being playful or if she honestly believes that all she is to me is a good time. In her defense, I haven't come out and said anything definitive about what we are or where we may be heading.

I struggle with indecision about what to say. Unsure if the words should leave my mouth because once they're out there, they can't be taken back. Once I admit that she's more to me than any woman has been for a long time, then hearts are involved, and that shit can get messy real quick.

"What's wrong?" she asks turning in my arms. The mood has shifted around us, and she can tell.

I look into her amazing green eyes, getting lost in the tiny flecks of gold. I can tell myself a lifetime of lies trying to convince anyone around me that I don't want to hurt her. I don't want her to invest in me too much because I may break her heart, but that's all it would be... lies.

It's my own fragile, yet guarded, heart I'm worried about. I'd rather be single for the rest of life than feel heartache again. And damn if that doesn't make me feel like a complete pussy.

"I need you," I admit, cupping her jaw in my hand. I can fight myself against her all I want. Hell, I've been doing it for weeks. I know how that ends. Just like it did today; with me pulling into her driveway and the urge to see her too strong to resist.

Her hands glide down my chest and grip the erection fighting to bust the zipper on my jeans. "I can feel that," she says with a quick wink.

"No," I say with a quick shake of my head.

Her eyes soften as I refuse to play along with her.

"Let the wall down, Lexi."

Her lip trembles as her eyes dart back and forth between mine. "You first."

"Oh, sweetheart. You knocked that fucker down weeks ago."

I pull her flush against my chest and take her mouth with every ounce of passion I have in my body. After lifting her up and making sure her legs are secured around my body, I make quick work of the stairs.

Last weekend we spent numerous hours wrapped around each other, but today is different. Not only does it feel different in my chest, but the atmosphere has changed. We're not hiding from each other with only the moonlight casting shadows over the room.

"Jesus," I murmur against her lips when her hands slide up my neck and grip handfuls of my hair. The tingle at my scalp makes my cock throb almost unbearably.

Slipping my hands past the waistband of her sweats, I grip her small ass and pull her against my body. I nearly lose my mind when she hikes her leg up on my thigh and grinds herself against me. Kissing Lexi has quickly become one of my favorite things to do, but my body is going to form a mutiny against me if I don't allow it more action than it's getting right now.

"Strip," I demand pulling my mouth away from hers and removing my hands from her body.

Nervous tension marks her brow when I take a step back. Her head gives a tiny shake.

"Close the curtains," she insists.

"Not gonna happen. Get naked." I take a step toward her aiming to remove the clothes myself if she doesn't do it.

"There's too much light," she argues.

"Wrong. There's not enough. I want to see every single inch of you," I say stepping against her body and brushing my lips against hers. "*Taste,* every inch of it."

"I don't look the same in the daylight," she complains but allows me to pull her t-shirt over her head anyway.

"You're stunning," I tell her as her shirt falls to the ground.

Another thing I have to add to my list about smaller breasts being perfect for me; no bra.

My mouth finds her nipple as my hands slide her sweats down her long slender legs. Crouching to slip them past her feet I let my mouth roam up her left leg, directly across her pussy and down the right side. Roughness hits my tongue causing me to pull my mouth away.

"Don't," she begs when my fingers reach up and tenderly touch the jagged scars near her right hip.

"Are these from the accident?"

Her eyes widen, and I realize my mistake. She never told me that she was in the accident; it was information I discovered on my own through internet research. She gives me a disapproving look and nods, but she doesn't say a word.

I delicately kiss the scars and turn my attention to other parts of her body.

She gasps when my tongue sweeps across the swollen bundle of nerves just above her slit, and I hope she won't be mad later about invading her privacy.

"Hold that thought," I say standing from my crouched position. I hastily pull off my shirt and throw it on the floor. My jeans and boxers are next. "Fuck," I hiss when I reach into my wallet only to realize that we used my last condom a week ago.

"What's wrong, handsome?" I look up to find her smirking at me.

"No condoms. You wouldn't happen to be on..."

She huffs incredulously. "No way, playboy. This isn't going to be one of those times where in the heat of the moment we talk about clean lab results and we both agree that you not wrapping up sounds like even a remotely good idea."

My face falls and my heart breaks a little bit. I was just about to ask that. I don't know if I'm more disappointed she can read me like a book, or that she completely shut down the idea.

"Don't give me that look, Kegan." Her eyes glint playfully. "You promised to make me come," she says turning back to her bedside table. "And if you do a good job," she says pulling out a long strip of condoms, "I'll see about making you come, too."

My eyes cloud with carnal desire as I stalk toward her, lifting her up and tossing her on the bed. She lands with a squeal, and I'm on her a second later.

"I thought you were going to make me go to the store," I say looking down at her.

"I was," she says circling her hips against my length. She leans up until we're nose to nose. "But I still would've made you eat my pussy first."

"I wouldn't have been able to walk away from you after even the slightest taste," I say against her stomach, relishing the way it jumps and quivers under my mouth.

I hiss when her hand tugs a handful of my hair, so I'm looking back into her eyes. "Do you want babies, Kegan?"

My eyes nearly bug out of my head at her question. "Fuck no!" I answer honestly.

"Well, neither do I. So you'll keep it wrapped, okay?" She gives my cheek two quick, playful slaps. "Proceed," she nods indicating where she wants my mouth.

"Yes, Ms. Carter." I love seeing this side of Lexi. Don't get me wrong, I love the snarky, bordering on pessimistic side also, but seeing her full personality at a moment like this is a breath of fresh air.

My eyes linger on the scar just above her neatly trimmed pussy. I kiss it softly and feel her body tense. Her mother's words fly back into my head, temporarily distracting me from my tasks.

"This one looks much better than that asshole that knocked you up in college."

"This one isn't from the accident," I whisper tracing the scar with the tip of my finger.

She shifts her weight up onto her elbows. "You promised to make me come," she reminds me ignoring my observations. She's trying to be playful still, but I can detect the pain in her eyes.

I wiggle my chin, which is pressing against her center. She hums her approval and goes to lie back down.

"Watch me." I swipe my tongue over her sensitive flesh just as she repositions herself on her elbows.

Chapter 28
Lexi

Kegan brings me to climax with expert precision. He tortured me for what seemed like forever, getting me close and forcing my body back down. Just as I thought he was going to taunt me again, he sucked vigorously on my clit while curving two fingers inside of me. I came harder than I ever thought imaginable.

"Your turn," I manage to say after what seems like half an hour of pulsing aftershocks.

I climb over him on languid limbs, straddling his legs. "Do your worst," he challenges with his hands behind his head. He's semi propped up on a pillow, and the mirth in his eyes urges me on.

Licking and nipping his thighs just as he did mine, I only give his cock light brushes. It jumps several times seeking the attention my mouth is denying it.

I look up and see Kegan has his eyes squeezed shut, his jaw flexes as he tenses it repeatedly. I watch his face as I snake my tongue out and lick the sensitive underside of his shaft. His mouth falls open, and his eyelids soften, a small moan slipping from his mouth.

I draw the thick head into my mouth and lose all focus on his face as I turn every ounce of my attention to his glorious cock. One hand cups his sack while the other scrapes fingernails down his taut stomach. I smile around his erection when his back arches off the bed. I suck vigorously, doing my best not to gag on his thickness, only failing a couple of times when his hips thrust up at the same moment I stroke down.

I can feel him tense under my body, hear the change in his breathing, and taste the difference in his precome. Knowing he's getting ready to come is a triumphant feeling. My elation on being able to get him to this point doesn't, however, stop me from torturing him just the way he did me.

I pull my hand from his heavy balls and remove my mouth from his cock with a loud pop. His eyes flash open expectantly, and I can't read the look on his face. His deviant smile either means he's anticipating my next move to be incredibly over the top, or he's about to pay me back in ways I could never imagine for doing to him exactly what he did to me.

My breath hitches in my throat when he flips me over onto my back.

"What's wrong?" I tease. "Was it not up to your standards?"

His wicked grin and the maniacal look in his eyes creates a light sheen of sweat to mist my skin. Anticipation of what he's going to do next tingles from top to bottom.

"You have a very talented mouth, Lexi. It's the provocative way you're trying to torment me that's the problem." He nips at my bottom lip when a smile crosses my face. "If we hadn't begun our day with such a serious conversation, I'd be tempted to tie you up to this bed and torture you for days."

"Mmm," I moan when his mouth sucks one of my nipples deep into his talented mouth. "What would that look like exactly?"

I watch as he leans back on his knees and quickly works the latex ring down his shaft. Leaning back into me, he rests his cock right on top of my throbbing clit. This seems like more torture than what he hinted at earlier. So close, yet way too far away.

"First," he says quietly as his fingers trail up my rib cage and down my arms. "I'd make sure you were as naked as you are now. I'd need to see every single inch of your amazing body." He slowly raises my hands over my head and secures them with one of his own. "I'd tie you down so you couldn't move. Force you to take everything I offer you."

His breath skates over the damp skin of my neck as his hips flex back. His length grazes over my sensitive nerves and down my silken seam. My arms flex against his grip, needing to reach out to him, urge him forward.

"I'd spank your ass until it turned as red as an apple." He slowly glides into my wet heat. "I'd pound in and out of you for hours. Fill you with my come until you beg me to stop." His hips flex outward again at a torturously slow pace.

His words are a contradiction to the movement of his hips, and I don't know if he's saying these things just to get a rise out me, or if he really wants to tie me up and fuck me silly. Either way, I'm pretty much down for whatever he has in mind. My body begins to quicken under his intrusion; my breaths escape in ragged pants at his words.

I whisper his name and pull my knees up high on his hips.

"Not yet," he chastises with a groan that says he's close too. He hisses loudly when I clench my muscles in an attempt to stave off the release I know will rock me to my core.

"I need to," I whimper. My eyelids flutter closed on a particularly expert stroke that causes the thick head of his cock to glide over the magical spot inside of me. "Please," I beg when he intentionally shortens his thrusts to avoid hitting it again.

"Look at me, Lexi." His voice is strained, betraying how close his own orgasm is. Those amazing blue eyes seem darker as he looks down at me. "No more lies," he insists.

"None," I promise. He rewards me with a long deep thrust of his hips.

"No more secrets," he adds.

"None," I repeat anticipating another deep thrust and moaning loudly when it's administered.

"Come with me, Lexi." He finally releases my arms and grips my hips in an almost painful hold.

My body comes alive under his command, seizing, clutching, pulsing down his length.

He hisses through clenched teeth a second before I feel his release throb inside of me.

"Fuck, you're amazing," he proclaims just as he pulls from me and crashes beside me on the bed. A second later, I'm tugged against his chest trying to catch my breath.

"Would you really tie me up?" I ask with a hint of shyness to my voice. People say tons of things in the heat of the moment, but I can't let it go. For some reason, the tantalizing thought of being controlled and relegated to doing whatever he insists on has kept my blood pumping wildly through my veins.

He chuckles and cocks his head so he can see me out of the corner of his eye. "Not tonight." He winks at me, and I have my answer. The thrilling aspect of it is that he not only wants to do something like that with me, but it's almost like he's making plans to be together again.

"Your mom called you Lexus," he says hesitantly from out of the blue.

"You caught that did you?" I feel a comforting hand wash over my back reassuring me that any judgment there is will be on my mother, not me. It's exactly what I need to open up. "Lexus Raine Carter is my full name. It's almost like my mother named me in retaliation for ruining her life."

"I think it's a beautiful name," he softly replies.

I tilt my head to look into his eyes. "I may have been near orgasm a few minutes ago, but I do recall you insisting on no lies."

He chuckles lightly. "Well, I think *Lexi* fits you perfectly." I rest my head back on his chest as his fingers dance across the sensitive skin on my lower back.

"Want to shower?" I hate to get up and put distance between us, but I was sweaty before coming upstairs from working in the yard and after the last hour, I'm in desperate need of soap and water.

"Sure," he says sitting up after I lift my tired body from his chest.

I turn on the shower and climb in as Kegan disposes of the condom. My face is under the spray of the shower when I feel him join me and wrap his arms around my waist. Stiffening when I feel his fingers trace over the scar on my lower belly, I pull my face back when my sharp gasp forces water down my throat. I compose myself quickly, but my reaction didn't make him pull his arms from my body.

I feel his chin rest on my shoulder. "Did you give the baby up for adoption?" he asks with sincere concern in his voice.

I turn in his arms as I shake my head viciously to the left and right. "I'd never do that. Even when Hunter suggested it, I wouldn't even let it be an option in my head."

Kegan sweeps damp hair from my cheek and kisses the tip of my nose. "What happened?"

"The car accident." I can't explain anything in detail. His eyes darken with empathy as his hand finds mine, giving it a light squeeze.

"You lost him."

"Her," I correct. "I was almost eight months along." I shake my head, unable to continue. It's too painful, even three years later I can feel the burn from my broken hip and the lack of movement in my stomach.

"I'm so sorry. Lex." He cups my cheek in one of his big hands and rests his forehead against mine. "You've lost so much."

His warmth and concern lands in my heart in the form of adoration I haven't allowed myself to feel in a very long time. I take a cleansing breath and pull my head back from his.

"Hunter," I say turning back into the spray. "Hunter treated me okay. He was my first serious boyfriend. My first well, everything. We stayed in my dorm room a lot. I didn't realize then, but he wasn't telling anyone we were together." I squirt body wash on my loofah and turn back to Kegan. I almost sigh at the sight of the white bubbles sliding down his tan skin.

"I fell hard for him."

"I'm sure he felt the same way," he says holding his arm out so I can wash it.

I shake my head. "No, he didn't. I was temporary fun for him, disposable. When I told him about Ella, he blamed me. I reminded him we were both drunk the night I got pregnant. He knew I wasn't on birth control and thought sex was still a good idea." I frown and look down at the pink bath sponge in my hands. "Don't get me wrong, I knew it was a bad idea, but I loved him so much I would've eloped and married him in a heartbeat. I knew pregnancy was a possibility, but at twenty-one, I wasn't thinking of it being a life-altering situation." I shrug. "Babies are cute. Who wouldn't want a baby with the man they love?"

Kegan takes the sponge from my hand and runs it over my shoulders and down my own arms.

"He wanted me to have an abortion, and when I refused, he pushed for giving her up for adoption. He told me from the beginning he didn't want anything to do with her. I accepted that and moved back in with my grandparents my last semester of school. Being on campus and seeing him move on so quickly with other women was more than I could handle."

"He's an idiot," Kegan says quietly.

"Funny thing is, he had two other girls pregnant by the time graduation rolled around. He stayed with the last one. Only five months after getting me pregnant, he was professing his love for another girl and telling anyone who would listen how happy he was about starting a family with her." I clear my throat to keep the tightness down. "For the longest time, I didn't feel like I was enough for him. He'd hidden me away while we were dating. I found out later on it was because he was dating tons of other girls." I look up into his eyes. "That's why I told you I couldn't be your secret."

Kegan looks down at me before kissing the very tip of my nose. "I'll scream it from the rooftop if you want me to, Lexi. I'm not ashamed of you."

I shake my head back and forth. "You can't do that. I don't even know how I managed to keep my job after Amelia busted us in the supply closet."

"Don't worry about Amelia. I took care of her ass."

I glare at him and his choice of words.

He throws his head back and laughs long and loud until his eyes meet mine, and he realizes I don't find a damn thing funny about what he just said.

"Sorry, sweetheart." He kisses my nose again. "Don't worry. If you don't want to tell anyone about us, that's fine." He leans in close until his lips are brushing my ear. "I'd love to be your dirty little secret."

He's seriously missing the whole point.

Chapter 29
Kegan

"Who are you and what have you done with my little brother?"

I roll my eyes at Kadin. He's been saying shit like that for the last hour. I look up into expectant eyes, and suddenly I want to force him to drop his pants just so I can verify he didn't grow a damn pussy since the last time I saw him.

"I'm just in a seriously good mood," I explain.

"I can see that. Where's cranky, pissed off Kegan? That's who left my house last week. You called me every name in the book when you had to reach into your pocket to pay for Anastyn's horse."

"I'm still pissed about that," I complain.

"Keep your mouth shut when you're drunk," he says tossing a fancy throw pillow at my head. "Or better yet, stop getting drunk."

I hold the pillow to my chest and set my beer down on a coaster on the table. "I was an asshole, Kadin. Sorry about that."

"I get it," he says. "You know all too well that I've been there, too."

"Getting stupid drunk because you're too afraid of your feelings to deal with shit?" I expand.

He laughs. "No, London had the opposite effect on me. One night with her and I sobered up really quick."

I nod and look into the fire across the room. Kadin has had it pretty bad, but I don't think he'd change the heartache he had all those years ago if it still meant he got to end up right where he's at now.

"So, where does this leave you and Ms. Carter?"

"I stayed the entire weekend with her. Been back to her place twice this week. I've had more sex in the last seven days than I've had in months." I grin in his direction.

"Damn it, Kegan. That's not what I meant, and you damn well know it." He frowns in my direction, and a sense of shame settles in my stomach. "Would you talk to the crew about her the way you just did me?"

"Fuck no," I say slightly offended.

"Then don't talk to anyone about her that way. She fucking deserves better," he lectures.

I pick up my beer and drain it. "Old habits die hard," I mutter setting the empty bottle back down.

"I didn't want to hear about your adventures before Lexi, and now that you have a woman you're falling in love with, I sure as shit don't need to hear it. That kind of stuff is private, man."

"I get it," I tell him. "Hold up... *falling in love?* That's not—"

He quirks an eyebrow at me, daring me to deny it. For the first time in my life, I shut my damn mouth without something idiotic coming out of it.

"You want her talking to her friends about how much of a stud and shit you are?"

I wiggle my eyebrows at him as a smile spreads across my face.

"Dumbass," he says with another pillow thrown at my head. I catch it with ease.

The mention of her friends reminds me of a conversation we had yesterday morning before I left to go back home and get ready for work.

"Did I ever tell you about Justin Bland?"

His eyes snap up to mine. His face remains impassive, but there's no hiding the small glint of jealousy in his eyes. Justin Bland made a move on London when she left Kadin after finding out she was pregnant. London worked for him at his law firm. Justin was in the process of pleading his case to her when Kadin finally tracked her down.

She was extremely pregnant with Kadin's baby, and Bland was trying to encroach on something that belonged to another man. I would've killed him, but I tend to lean more toward the violent side than Kadin ever has. He's always been one to internalize things and suffer in silence.

"I'm listening," he says flatly.

"Believe it or not, Justin Bland is Lexi's first cousin. Their mothers are sisters."

"No shit?" The tension in his shoulders relaxes a bit. I know his mind just went where mine did when I saw them standing, wrapped in a hug, on her front porch.

"Lexi and the people from Bland's office get together monthly for some dinner or shit. She asked me if I wanted to go with them."

"What did you tell her?"

I look at his face trying to decide which way he feels like I should answer.

"I told her I didn't think it was a very good idea."

"Why would you do that, Kegan? If the woman wants you to meet her friends, you should meet her friends." He makes me feel like shit, just like she did yesterday morning. She didn't call me out on it, but the disappointment in her eyes was like a flag waving in the desert.

"You already force me to sit in on meetings with that jackass, now you're telling me to spend some of my free time with him?"

"You hit on London within minutes of meeting her?" he reminds me.

I look at him with confusion. "What's your point?" Remembering how I acted around London the first time I found her in his condo years ago makes my stomach turn. I couldn't imagine her in any other way than the sister she is now, and I hate that I was attracted to her in the beginning; it feels creepy and borderline incestuous.

"She's gorgeous; I can't really blame Bland for wanting her either. He never even attempted to cross that line again after London and I got back together. You don't need to hate him on my account." He gives me a knowing look. "I think he and I would actually be friends if he hadn't, at one point in time, had his lips on my wife."

"Good point," I mumble, grateful that he's Lexi's cousin because I'd lose my shit if they weren't related and hanging out with each other.

"So you should go," Kadin prods.

"It doesn't feel right, man. It's almost like it's a violation of the code. He tried to take your girl; I'm your brother, and I'm obligated not to associate with him."

Kadin stands from the chair. "You, my little brother, are an idiot. You'd be hanging out with her family, not some guy trying to poach your girl. If this is going the direction I can see that it is, you need to care about the things she cares about."

"You have it so easy. London didn't come with family."

"Easy?" he asks giving me a hard look. "You don't know all of London's story, and it's not mine to tell, but I would rather her come with baggage than no family at all. Not having someone to rely on, no one to love is hard as fuck, Kegan. That shit can mess you up pretty bad. So quit complaining about having to endure a damn meal with Lexi's cousin."

He walks out of the room, leaving me sitting on the couch with my damn jaw hanging open. Just when I think I can't stack on any more disappointment in myself, he throws that little tidbit on top.

We didn't exactly make plans, but with the way last weekend went, I can't help but hope this weekend will be the same. My normal Friday night would include gathering up a few of the guys and hitting a bar or club. That's been gradually changing since I can't seem to get a sense of satisfaction with anyone but Lexi.

After leaving Kadin's house, feeling like a completely selfish asshole, I make a quick stop to grab a couple of bottles of Lexi's favorite wine and some beer for myself. We didn't leave the house once last weekend, and I know for a fact that we drained her stockpile.

I know she's not here the second I pull up and notice her car isn't in the driveway. It still doesn't keep me from hopping out of my truck and knocking on her door. Expected silence greets me even after pressing the doorbell numerous times.

Guilt washes over me at the realization that I should've at least texted her yesterday and today. I haven't spoken to her since she closed herself off at my refusal to her invitation at the dinner party. Kadin was right; I'm an idiot. I get the feeling that I'm going to end up ruining everything with Lexi before we can even get a decent start.

Taking a seat on the front steps, I pull out my cell phone and shoot off a quick text. After ten minutes with no response, I debate whether or not looking for an open window is a good idea. I decide against it after realizing just how psycho that seems.

I call her directly as I walk back to my truck, but the call goes straight to voicemail. I didn't even consider how important a stupid fucking dinner with her friends may have been to her, and now I can't reach her. I can't help but wonder if the two things are related.

Now I know what the girls feel like when they mess up and are forced into a timeout.

Chapter 30
Lexi

"You need to loosen up!" Jillian practically screams at me over the blaring music.

"I'm loose!" I debate.

"You are not!! That guy over there has been eye-fucking you all night, and you won't even give him a second look!" She points across the bar at the weird guy wearing a cowboy hat.

I don't correct her, but I have glanced his way several times, if only because I can feel his eyes boring into my damn back. I didn't give him a second look because I wanted to catch his already focused attention, I looked to make sure he's not sneaking up on me. Who in the hell wears a cowboy hat in a hip-hop bar?

"I'm not interested," I tell her before taking another one of the shots lined up in front of us.

"Oh come on," she groans elbowing me roughly in the side. I glare at her as I steady myself back on my stool. "You're no fun. He looks like he'd be fun!"

"Are you blind? He looks like a psycho. No matter how shitty as my week ended, I don't want to end my weekend cut up in a trash bag."

She looks past my shoulder and narrows her eyes at the man a mere twenty feet away. "You may be right," she agrees around the cherry stem hanging out of her mouth. "But I don't see any blood on his hands."

She's in serious contemplation over the possibility that the cowboy is an ax murder for much longer than necessary. I wish I could say it's because she's drunk, but it's not. She's thinking this over longer than she takes to decide if she's going to climb in bed with a man.

"So," I say breaking the criminal profiling she has going on. "Where's Hawke tonight?"

She scowls at me and tosses back another shot. "How the hell should I know? I quit my job this week."

To most people, this would be cause for concern. For Jillian? Just par for the course.

I throw back another shot and flag a waitress down for more. "How long did it last this time?"

She spins the lime wedge she just spat out on the table top. It's totally disgusting, but due to my buzz I'm actually mesmerized by her actions.

She shrugs, refusing to answer my question.

"When did you quit?"

"Tuesday. Right after lunch. He had some girl in his office. I couldn't do my damn job with all the giggling that was going on in there. So I snatched up my purse and left." She grins up at me. "I emailed him my resignation."

"Did you remember to change the date this time?"

She tosses the lime wedge at me, and I somehow avoid getting hit with it. "Yes." She looks up and to the left, and I can tell she's trying to recall if she did or not. "At least, I think I did."

"And when did you go back to the office?"

She turns her attention away from me and starts dancing on her stool. I grab her shoulder and spin her back around to face me. "When did you go back to work?"

"Wednesday morning." My brows knit together when I frown. "Don't look at me like that. He had a major meeting about an environmental dispute on some property. I wasn't going to let him do that on his own."

I shake my head. "Both of you are so fucking dependent on each other. Have you talked to him?"

"About what?"

I raise an eyebrow at her. We've been having this same damn conversation for years, and she knows exactly what I'm talking about.

"No, and I'm not going to. So just leave it alone. Let's talk about something else," she says with a slight quirk to her lip. "Tell me more about Mr. Rich Construction Man."

"There's not much to tell."

"Bullshit! You ignored every one of my calls and texts this past weekend." I mimic her actions when she picks up the salt shaker and licks her hand.

After a handful of shots, the tequila no longer burns on the way down. The hum of satisfaction rumbles in my chest. "I was busy."

"You were getting busy," she corrects. "Now spill."

The shake of my head causes dizziness. "Not gonna happen."

"Details!" she demands.

"My lips are sealed." Clumsy fingers lock my mouth and throw away the key.

"Holy shit," she hisses. "You like him *that* much?"

I can't keep the smile from gracing my face until I remember our last conversation. Reaching for another shot, I pray it washes away my disappointment in Kegan. This feeling, the one that's scratching at my heart, is why I have avoided men for anything other than quick fun. When the heart gets involved, it's no joke when disillusion rears its ugly head.

Holding my hand over my head, I flag down the waitress again. If I can still feel pain at his rejection to the dinner party invitation, I haven't had enough to drink.

Rolling over, I realize a second too late that I'm not in my bed. Air whooshes out of my lungs when my back hits the hardwood floor.

"Damn." Grumbling about being an alcoholic, I manage to get into a sitting position.

Noise in the kitchen makes my ears perk up. I don't know how, but even after the copious amounts of alcohol, I feel almost normal this morning. It never happens. Counting my blessings, I claw my way to standing by using the couch cushions.

Last night is hazy, but I'm hopeful that Kegan—

My face falls when Justin walks out of the kitchen with a cup of coffee in his hand.

"I rescue you, and you have the gall to look that displeased at my presence?" Shaking his head, he hands me the coffee. "You almost looked like you were hoping I was someone else."

"Nope." The lie falls easily from my lips. This is not a can of worms I'm opening so early in the morning.

A knock sounds at the door, and my eyes widen as Justin moves toward the foyer to answer the door. There are only three people who ever come over, one is standing in front of me, the other is probably face down in her own vomit, and the third—

"Kegan? What are you doing...?" Justin's head pivots on his shoulders and glances back at me.

I roll my lips between my teeth to stop the giddy reaction the look on his face is causing, confusion and amusement dance in his eyes. He's thinking about my reaction to him, and now all the pieces fall together.

"Justin," Kegan says offering his hand. They shake quickly with Kegan releasing his hand as soon as deemed acceptable.

"I'm going to head home." Justin leans in and kisses my cheek. "Great choice, but be careful."

His warning ricochets around my head as I watch him leave.

"Coffee?" I turn back toward the kitchen.

The echoing sound of his footfalls follow me out of the den.

"I stopped by last night." Leaning against the counter with his hip, his eyes burn into my back.

It makes me wonder if he's expecting an explanation, if he expects me to ask permission to hang out with my friends. Jealousy over my whereabouts is new for me. Hunter didn't give a shit where I was, so long as I was available to fuck when he wanted to. All of the signs were there from day one, and I still missed them.

I turn to face him, trying to read his expression. "Upset I wasn't here waiting with my legs spread for you?"

His head jerks back as if I'd slapped in the face. Guilt immediately washes over me.

"That's not what I came over for, Lexi." Turning back to pour him a cup of coffee, I resist the urge to apologize for my crassness. "What's going on?" His warm hands on my shoulders are comforting.

"Nothing," I mumble.

"Something," he counters.

"Want to go get something to eat? I haven't been shopping, so the fridge is pretty bare." I think a change of scenery would be best. I'm unable to think straight with my bed so close. Plus, I'm still upset with him, but struggling with not knowing if I even have a right to be upset.

I feel his warm lips against my neck. "I don't want to go anywhere," he breathes into the goose-pimpled flesh.

"You're treating me like your college cougar," I blurt.

He spins me in his arms. "Excuse me?"

"Didn't you tell me that she kept you hidden away? You never went out in public with her? She wouldn't come around when your friends were around?" My hand grazes over his chest, fingers flexing independently of my brains wishes. "You're *my* cougar. You won't go to Justin's for dinner. You don't want to leave the house, even for a late breakfast. I don't want to be your cougar, Kegan."

"Baby," he whispers as his lips brush softly over mine. "You aren't my cougar."

I smile up at him.

"You're younger than me."

Chapter 31

Kegan

She slaps my chest. "This isn't funny."

Her frown nearly breaks my damn heart. My large hands gently encompass hers as my face grows serious. "I'm not hiding you, Lexi. I've told you that."

"That's not what your actions say."

I reflect back. Other than the quick sex in the hall at the club and the interrupted almost closet encounter, we've been holed up in her house. I could argue that I don't 'date', so this is all new to me. It'd be true. Short of being seen picking up a girl, I'm not really the wine and dine type of guy. I mean, what's the point when they're a sure thing?

Surprisingly, I want that with Lexi. I want to be seen with her. I want men to look at me and know how much of a lucky fucker I am.

"I'm not intentionally hiding you away from anyone," I assure her. "Would I rather have you in my arms on the couch than sitting at a restaurant pretending I don't want to climb all over you? Hell yes."

I feel her body relax a small fraction.

"I'm not going to lie and tell you I don't want you alone all the time because I do. I don't want to have to explain to your friends or mine why I'm hiking your dress up over your head to satisfy a taste of that heaven between your legs. It would be...awkward, and I sure as fuck don't want to ignore the urge. That's just inhumane."

I pull her against my chest. "Really?"

I nod.

"You also told me that you don't want to be my secret, but if the school found out you could lose your job. I've told you before that I'd love to scream my affection for you from the rooftops. We can start with Edgewood Academy if you want." I remind her.

"I think that's all blown over. Amelia still has shitty comments and snide remarks, but she hasn't done anything."

"Let's hope she keeps it that way." Amelia is a snake in the grass, and I don't for a second think she's done.

Switching gears, I pull her hand and tug her toward the door. "Let's go get breakfast."

She resists me and shakes her head. "I don't want to leave."

The sight of her licking her bottom lip shoots straight to my cock. She saunters closer and runs her fingernail down my chest. Even through the fabric of my t-shirt, I can feel the tingle from her touch.

"You did fifteen minutes ago," I remind her.

"Things change," she pants against my neck.

Regretfully, I gently clasp her arms and take a step back. "We're not doing that."

Confusion is spread all over her face.

"Let's go to breakfast. I'm starved." She slips off her ridiculous house shoes near the door and makes her way up to her bedroom to change.

At the top of the stairs, she starts to strip naked, taunting me with her incredible body. "I'll wait in the truck," I croak and head outside.

"I'm not sure this is such a great idea," she complains as we pull up outside of an arcade. "There's a very good chance some of the parents from Edgewood are in there."

"They don't know who I am. It's not like I'm a member of the damn PTO or some shit."

I get out of the truck and tug her door open. She scoffs. "Everyone on this side of town knows who you are Kegan. The Cole men are very popular."

I clutch my hand to my chest. "You're embarrassed to be seen with me, aren't you?"

Her eyes tell me I'm an idiot, but the slight lift of her lips lets me know she also finds me adorable. "You're not the worst person to be seen with I guess."

I close the door, so she can't climb back in and press her against it. "Does this embarrass you?" I lick from her shoulder to her ear lobe and draw it into my mouth.

She squirms beneath me. "The shame is almost unbearable."

I rotate my growing cock against her. "The shame is going to be on me when I walk in there with an erection. I may get arrested."

She tilts her head to the side, allowing more room for my mouth. "You stand here completely unaffected. Doesn't seem fair."

"My panties are drenched," she confesses on a moan.

"Jesus Christ. This was a bad idea. Let's go..."

"You gonna fuck her in the parking lot or at least take her to a hotel room. I know you wouldn't care either way, but the lady should at least have a say."

I turn and glare at Tony as he and two other guys from the crew walk up.

"Tony," I snarl taking a side step to reveal Lexi. "I'd like you to meet my girlfriend, Lexi Carter."

He begins to laugh but sobers quickly, realizing I'm not trying to be comical.

"Really?" he asks in disbelief holding his hand out to her.

She smiles at him, unsure of what's going on. I didn't tell her we were meeting people, but I couldn't just ignore her complaints about not going out and being around other people. This is my olive branch so to speak.

"Back the fuck up." I shove Tony away from her as he tries to raise her hand to his mouth.

"You got it bad, huh?"

I look directly into her eyes and say, "You have no idea."

If melting into a puddle was physically possible, I'm certain just by the look in Lexi's eyes, she would've done it. Her eyes are expectant, loving, and full of hope. For the first time in my life, I find myself wanting to be everything a woman hopes I can be.

"What are you getting at, Cole?" Her glare burns a hole in the side of my face as I key in the security code to access the subterranean parking at my condo.

"All I'm saying is Piper would've greatly benefited from Crazy Eyes' protection. She could've avoided a lot of heartache with her as a wife." I'm not embarrassed one bit that we've been arguing over *Orange is the New Black* for the last twenty minutes.

"You're just as crazy as Suzanne," she mutters taking her eyes off me for the first time since leaving the arcade. "Where are we, Kegan?"

I turn off the truck and look over at her. "My place."

Her apprehension is palpable and remains intact until I open the door to my condo.

"Congratulations," I whisper in her ear as I kick the door closed with my foot. "You're the very first woman to make it past the front door." I chuckle. "I'd say past the front desk, but there was that one crazy chick."

She shakes her head, but there's still a smile on her face. I'm thankful my mention of other women didn't ruin our evening.

I waste no time getting her down the hall and into my room. If I were a gentleman, I'd offer her a glass of wine or a snack, but we've moved past that. She rubbed, bit, and teased me the whole time at the arcade. If there weren't so many teenagers around, she would've gotten fucked in the hallway again.

She tsks at me as I hastily kick off my shoes. "You have a lot to learn about women, Kegan."

"I shouldn't have said anything, Lexi. Seriously, I'm sorry."

She shakes her head. "Not what I'm talking about."

"Oh, baby. I know everything where that's concerned."

She continues with the back and forth of her head but crooks her finger urging me toward her. "Come here, handsome. I'm sure there are a few things I can still teach you."

I raise an eyebrow at her. "You're going to teach me like that? I think the lessons should start with you naked."

I pounce on her. Within seconds her shirt is off, and her bra is joining it on the floor. The rasp of her zipper is the wakeup call my cock needs. My mouth is on her the second the denim reveals her neatly trimmed snatch.

"Oh crap," she mumbles as her knees wobble.

"No, no, no," I chastise. "Don't go all gooey on me now. You're here to teach me a lesson, remember?"

"Mmm. Next time," she promises with a quick pat on my head. I lick her again. "Please don't stop."

"As you wish, Ms. Carter. I hope I get an A." I yelp in pain when she yanks on my hair before my tongue can slide back into her.

"Nope," she says with a scowl. "I teach kindergarteners. There's no appeal to me when you want to do the naughty teacher thing." I grin up at her. "I'm serious, Kegan. It grosses me out."

I pull my head back until her hand slips free, and then dive back in without another word. I lost count of her climaxes. All I know is somehow we ended up on the bed after the second one because her useless legs would no longer hold her up.

I'm naked, aching to be inside of her, and enjoying the sleepy, sated look in her eyes. With the tip of my cock, I tap her oversensitive clit. Sweeping it down, I bite my lip as it glides easily through her wetness. Heat engulfs my cock and bliss takes over every molecule in my body.

A hard hand slaps against my chest.

"What the hell are you doing?" she gasps backing away. "Get a damn condom."

I look at her like she's lost her mind. How could she just pull off of my cock like that? I was about to profess my love *of her pussy of course.*

"I don't have any condoms."

"You tried to pull that shit last week."

"I'm serious," I argue. "I don't bring women here, Lexi. There isn't a condom in this place. We used yours last weekend, remember?"

She sighs and points to her purse that was tossed carelessly by my bedroom door. "Hand me my purse."

Reluctantly, I climb off the bed and make my way to her purse as she mumbles some shit about being the only responsible one in this relationship.

I don't even bother handing it to her. I open it, pull the rubbers out, and have one sliding down my dick before I make it back to the bed.

"Better?" I snark.

She nods and reaches for my hips as I climb back on the bed and line myself up again.

"I should..."

I'm yelping again when her fingers twist my nipple. "Don't fuck angry," she says with a smirk.

"I'll get you back for that," I promise.

Her smile is radiant as she looks back up to me. "There's no place for retaliation in this bed."

I lean in and kiss her lips. "Our bed," I whisper sliding all the way back in.

Chapter 32
Lexi

Sunday mornings have always been my absolute favorite. In fact, they still are, but waking up with Kegan under my chin and my hand resting on his ridiculously defined stomach is like the whipped cream on a hot fudge sundae. I'd say the cherry on top, but gross; cherries are nasty.

He shifts slightly when my fingers tickle over the dips and crevices of his muscles.

"Morning." His voice is husky with sleep, and it makes me snuggle deeper into his side as if I wasn't already practically lying on top of him.

Warm lips brush across my forehead as his strong arm flexes around my back.

"I know it's cliché," I warn. "But I could get used to waking up like this."

I wait for him to tense up, backpedal from the words he spoke last night.

Our bed.

I'd assumed when he said the words he was in the sex fog right along with me, but his lack of reaction just now makes me wonder if he actually meant it. I seriously want to bring it up, but can't find the courage.

"You in my bed every morning? I can think of worse situations."

Not quite what I was looking for, but it works for now.

"How do you want to play this?"

I feel his head move, and I can't resist pulling mine back so I can look up at him.

"What do you mean?" His fingers reach up and swipe a clump of deviant hair from my face.

"You want me to get dressed and go? I don't know how you want to handle the whole morning after thing." My eyes dart away embarrassed that I asked the question. I'm fishing. I know that I am, but I've never been very good with subtleties, and I don't want to get this wrong

"Do you have plans or something today?"

"No, I just thought…"

"Stop," he insists. "If I had it my way, we'd stay in this bed for weeks."

"If we did that, I wouldn't be able to walk."

He shakes his head, mild frustration on his face before climbing over me and pinning my body beneath his. "You're not getting it, Lexi. I'm in this." His face hardens. "Wait, you are too, aren't you?"

I respond by cupping his face in my hands and kissing him senseless. He moans into my mouth, rotating his hips against me. The scorching heat of his erection is bliss against my swollen clit.

When he shifts his hips back and penetrates me with his thick cock, I almost let it happen, but the promise I made to myself years ago is stronger than the cloud of sexual need trying to obscure my brain.

"Damnit, Kegan. No!" I push back on him as his eyes widen in surprise. "Keep trying to sneak it in unwrapped, and I'll cut you off for a month."

He lands on his back with a grunt as I climb off the bed and walk toward the bathroom. I'm not angry at him, but myself for wanting it as much as he does.

"Marry me." His words stop me in my tracks.

"Excuse me?" I say turning to face him.

"If we're married then you can't object when I sink into you bare." I haven't a clue if he's being serious, but leave it to a damn man to offer something so sacred just to fuck without a condom.

"You're an idiot," I say walking into the bathroom.

"I'm *your* idiot," he corrects.

I turn on the shower, gazing into the mirror while the water heats. My almost-sexed cheeks are flushed, and the tingle in my core reminds me, not so gently, that I've been left unsated. I quickly remind myself that my body doesn't rule my brain.

The bathroom door opens. Still looking into the mirror, my eyes meet his.

"I get it," he says wrapping his arms around my waist. "No condom, no sex."

His cock jerks behind my back as if to argue with him giving in so easy.

"Good. I'm glad we see eye to eye." I break free of his arms and climb into the shower.

"Oh, make no mistake, we aren't seeing eye to eye. I'm not happy about this, but I'll respect your wishes," he says climbing into the shower behind me.

"Kegan," I sigh in frustration.

"Are you mad?" his playful smile drops.

"No."

"You sure?" Before I can reassure him, he's on his knees, and his hot breath is tickling my pussy. "Let me make sure you're not."

His mouth hits me like a bolt of lightning shooting through my entire body. I don't have an ounce of energy left when he brings me to orgasm faster than ever before in my life.

"Kegan, no." I look out the window as we make our way toward his parents' house.

With as often as I have to chastise him, you'd think I was at work.

"What are we doing?" He ignores me and keeps driving. "I'll wait in the truck," I tell him as he turns off the ignition and climbs out.

Seconds later my door is tugged open. He reaches in and unsnaps my seatbelt. "You'll be waiting a while, baby. It's Sunday dinner. Come on; the girls are inside."

My eyes snap to his. "The girls?"

He shrugs. "Just like every Sunday, Lexi. My family has been hounding me to bring you."

"Family? As in all of them? Kegan, look at me." I point down to my clothes, then hold up hands with chipped nail polish. "I look like a homeless person. I can't have dinner with your family."

"You look amazing. It's going to be very difficult for me to keep my hands off of you in there." He tugs my hand and practically drags me out of the truck. "You can walk," he says crouching lower and reaching for me, "or I can carry you." I slap his chest. "You've met every one of them before. It's no big deal."

"This is a terrible idea," I complain as we walk to the front door.

"How about we make a deal?" His breath runs down my neck as he whispers in my ear. My body's response to that is not what I need walking into a house full of Coles. "You do this with a smile on your face, and I'll go to every dinner party with your friends that you want."

I grab his arm, stopping him before he can open the front door. "I don't want you to go to them because you feel like I forced you."

His eyebrow arches and he cuts his eyes to his parents' massive front door.

"You aren't forcing me, Kegan. I just want to make a good impression. Worn jeans and a ratty t-shirt were fine for grocery shopping earlier, but dinner with your family? They'll hate me."

He pecks my lips. "They love you already, Lexi, and you're not forcing me to the dinner parties either. I want to be where you are. If you're at the dinner party, I'm right there beside you."

"Who are you?" I ask cupping his jaw. "Where's the crass, no-filter Kegan Cole."

He laughs and pulls me against his chest. "You know, Kadin asked me the exact same thing a few days ago."

I brush his lips gently with mine as a thank you for just being who he is, a praise for the way our last couple of days have been. Leave it to Kegan to slip his tongue past my lips as his huge hand cups one of my ass cheeks.

"Yuck. Just like Mommy and Daddy."

I pull as far away from Kegan as I can. I don't get far because his arms are still wrapped around me. My cheeks flush when I look over and see Anastyn and Lennox standing in the open doorway. I want to shrink away when I notice London standing behind them with her lip between her teeth trying to keep from laughing.

"Why is everyone standing in the doorway," Kegan's dad says just before his face appears around the door. A smile spreads across his face as he notices me in Kegan's arms. "Thank God," he mutters before turning back inside and yelling at his wife.

I slap at Kegan's chest and continue to try to pull away as Mr. Cole yells, "Karen! Your youngest son brought you an early Christmas present!"

"Is it that new Michael Kors purse?" she asks from somewhere inside. She stops dead when she sees me, and I swear a tear pools in her eye. "Oh, this is so much better than a purse."

"See?" Kegan whispers in my ear. "You have nothing to worry about."

After the shock of my presence wears off, we eventually make it inside. Less than ten minutes later, Kegan has disappeared with his dad, and I've been pulled into the kitchen with all of the other women.

I answer questions that Mrs. Cole is firing off at me with ease as she finishes working on the main course. I'm dicing vegetables for the salad as Anastyn and Lennox tear the lettuce into manageable pieces.

London is sitting on a stool holding Easton while he drinks a bottle. Kegan's family is so laid back; I don't know why I was so worried.

I'm rinsing my hands in the sink when Mrs. Cole looks over her shoulder and speaks to London. "Can you go tell Kevin and the boys that dinner is almost ready?"

London passes Easton off to me to go get the guys. It's exactly how Kegan finds me, standing in the kitchen cooing at the adorable little-redheaded boy.

"You know," Kegan says in my ear, "if I went bare we could end up with one of those. Easton is pretty hard to beat, but I bet ours would be cuter."

My spine stiffens. How can he possibly go from zero to asking for marriage and a baby in a matter of weeks? How can he jump from not wanting to hang out with my friends to bringing me to his weekly family dinner? He hasn't gone backward like I've expected him to do, but barreling forward at a million miles an hour is freaking me out. You know those warning signs? The ones that give you hope but at the same time make you want to run for the hills? Yeah, that's where I'm at right now.

"Excuse me," I say placing the smiling baby in his arms. I make my way to the bathroom down the hall, planning to hide out until the dinner is over.

Chapter 33
Kegan

Waking up with Lexi in my arms feels different this morning than it did yesterday. If I let myself worry enough, I know things have been different since dinner last night. I'm still in her bed, so that's a plus. She'd complained of a headache shortly after the meal was finished and once we got back, she shut down all advances I made to help her heal her pain naturally. But seriously, I read an article that said orgasms help with headaches. I was only trying to help her out.

She didn't make me leave, which I'm grateful for. Holding her all night, even though she wouldn't tell me what was wrong, eased some of the fear that she was gearing up to leave me. Knowing I could lose her so easily turned my stomach all night, preventing me from getting much sleep.

I've been lying here awake listening to her breathe for an hour before her alarm went off. Once the shrill sound echoes off the walls for a few seconds, I turn it off and hold her closer, unwilling to let her go just yet.

"I have to get ready for work," she mumbles against my chest.

"We have time," I insist, refusing to let her crawl out of my arms. If changing her alarm to give us thirty extra minutes this morning after her saddened mood last night makes me an asshole, well, I guess I'm an asshole.

"How's your head?"

"Better." Her hand roves down my stomach as she stretches out her muscles. She sighs loudly against my chest. "I hate mornings," she complains.

"All mornings?"

I feel her grin against my skin. "Any one that starts before nine."

"I'll make you love morning time," I promise sliding out from underneath her and pulling her nipple into my mouth.

As much as I'd love to spend the day in bed with her, we both have to work, and the last thing she needs is more trouble where that's concerned.

My mouth trails kisses back up to hers. "I'm wet for you," she confesses against my lips. "I had amazing dreams last night."

I'm glad her night was better than mine.

Her words have me scrambling for the drawer in the side table and making quick work of getting the condom rolled down my eager cock.

I check her for readiness, and my cock jumps when my fingers glide through her slick desire.

After licking them clean, I line up and glide slowly into her. I want to pump in and out of her, build her up and back off until she's begging me to let her come, but we don't have time for that. I quicken my pace and bite my lip at the pleasure I feel when her fingernails dig into my back.

"Harder," she begs.

"Over," I command pulling from her. She scrambles to her knees and elbows, hissing loudly when I thrust back in.

Her cries are caught by the pillow stuffed against her face, but her muffled moans make me fuck her harder. My hands clamp her hips, but I'm merely holding on as she slams her body back repeatedly. Even in this position, she's the one fucking me. I love every single grip of her tight pussy as she brings both of us to rapid orgasm.

The grunt as my cock explodes is animalistic and spontaneous. I can't control it; I don't even want to.

The "Thanks, Doll," and quick slap on the ass isn't as well received.

"It was a joke!" I yell at her back as she closes *and locks* the bathroom door.

"What did you say to her, Kegan?"

I'm trying to explain to Kadin about the pushback that is rolling off of Lexi in waves, and this is the shit he asks me? I know he's asking because he knows me so well.

"Which time?" I mumble into the phone as I walk across Lexi's yard toward the job site. "Hey," I say realizing what Kadin's implying. "What makes you think it was something I said?"

An audible sigh comes through the phone. "It's always something you say, Kegan."

"She makes me wear rubbers," I complain.

"As you should." My own brother is siding against me.

"Well," I groan, "I can't seem to let it go."

"What. Did. You. Say?"

I scrub my hand over my face. "The first time I just grumbled. The second time I argued a little bit. She's on fucking birth control, Kadin. I don't see the big deal."

"And the third time?" he asks without missing a beat.

"I, ummm... I asked her to marry me."

The phone goes silent, and I wait impatiently for Kadin to laugh at me and call me an idiot, much like Lexi did yesterday morning.

"As a joke?" he finally asks.

"Yeah, of course."

"You're the biggest fucking idiot in the world. You don't say shit like that in jest, man. Don't you know a damn thing about women?"

"Apparently not." I look around the job site and as much as I love getting my hands dirty and turning piles of wood into a beautiful house, I'm just not feeling it today.

"Is that the last time the condom issue came up?" If he was confrontive about the proposal, he's definitely not going to like this.

"She was holding Easton yesterday at dinner," I begin.

"Oh God," he mutters, but silences so I can finish digging my grave.

"I might have mentioned that if she wasn't so adverse to me going bare that our baby would look even cuter."

"First off, not possible. Easton is the cutest baby in the world. That level of adorable can't be beaten, not even by you, little brother. Secondly, and I repeat myself. You are the *biggest* fucking idiot in the world."

"I'm getting that now. I'm surprised she even let me stay last night."

"If she did, then there's hope for you yet. And this morning?"

"Well..."

"God damnit, Kegan! There's more?" I can hear the frustration in Kadin's voice, but this is my first serious relationship as a grown man. Yes, I remember Rhonda, but I was not even close to being the man I thought I was back then. My point is, with this being my first, I'm bound to fuck this up.

"I didn't even push the subject this morning. I strapped up like a good boy."

"Good. You may be in the clear." His voice is calmer.

"I thought so too, but then I smacked her ass and said..."

"Thanks, Doll?! Please, for fuck's sake, Kegan. Please tell me you didn't do the same thing to her you've been doing to women for the last ten plus years?" I remain silent for a long moment.

"I fucked up."

"You fucked up," he agrees. "You better fix this shit. After you guys left last night, mom got out the Neiman Marcus catalog."

"Tell her I want blue on the china," I mutter before hanging up on him.

"I expected at least a smile on your face when I saw you walking this way." Leave it to Tony to call me out. "If spending the night with that beautiful girl puts you in this kind of mood, maybe you should go home at night."

"Can we get to work rather than standing here grabbing each other's asses?"

I walk past him toward the house that is now framed out. This is going to be one long-ass day.

I text Lexi off and on all day, but she never responds. I vowed, after getting off the phone with Kadin earlier that I was going to do my best to fix whatever it is that I've messed up with my stupid mouth.

It's going to be hard to do if she's ignoring me. It took all my power not to drop what I was doing at work to go to the school and make her speak to me. Thankfully, I had plenty of things to keep me busy, and I only wanted to kill Tony once when he brought up my sour-ass mood.

The guys call it a day, and I head back over to Lexi's. When she asked me to lock the door when I headed to work, I thought she'd be home by the time I wrapped up my day. She isn't.

I head to my condo for a quick shower. I also pack a bag because if I go back to Lexi's and she's home, I don't plan on leaving. If she's still mad at me, I'll sleep on the damn porch if I have to. Anything to be close to her.

Even after several more text messages, my phone remains silent. It seems I can't hold onto this girl for more than a few days at a time. Since I never want to let her go in the first place, I'm seriously struggling right now.

The sun has already set by the time I make it out of my parking garage. Knowing I can't show up and grovel empty handed, I head to the grocery store. What woman can resist an apology when I have chocolate and wine in my hands? Seems simple enough.

Chapter 34
Lexi

Don't get me wrong; I love some of the stupid things that come out of Kegan's mouth. He's honest, playful, and most days, funny. I seriously think he thinks he's funnier than he actually is. He has to. I know the shit he's said lately isn't coming from a mean place, but that doesn't abate the sting any more.

He knows my history of losing the baby. I've even told him I don't want children. I know what you're thinking, but it's not a lie. I can't imagine going through the loss of another child, so I don't even want to risk it. For him to just throw shit out there like *marry me* and *ours will be even cuter* cuts deep. Those aren't jokes. That's not something you just throw out there to get a laugh.

Thanks, Doll.

That sure as hell isn't something you play with. He pulled that shit the first time he fucked me against the window. Yes, he fucked me so thoroughly that it didn't even compute until after he left, but after I had the chance to think about it, his words twisted my gut. I expected that from him the first time. This morning? He made me feel like he cared for me only to ruin it minutes later with that damn mouth of his.

I'm so over it; I can't even focus on my class the way they deserve. I've ignored Kegan's texts all day. I'm angry, and my feelings are hurt. I don't want to respond until I have a chance to work through that. My day quickly goes down the drain when I find a note in my box during my conference period to see Amelia DuPont after school.

I only have to worry about what the evil headmistress is going to throw my way for one more class period. Fifty minutes of stomach turning worry. I find myself dragging my feet and speaking longer to parents this afternoon just to put off the inevitable.

I knew she wasn't done after that little confrontation in the supply closet. I knew she was too vindictive to let it go, but it has been weeks without a word about it. Yes, there have been snide remarks, but the closet was never brought up again.

A trembling hand reaches for the door to the front office. I eye the exit and for a split second think about just walking out and pretending that I never received the note in my box, but I know it's only putting off whatever is happening today.

The front office is empty and so is Amelia's office, but I follow a group of voices to the conference room around the corner. A sheen of sweat covers the back of my neck causing my hair to stick to my nape. It makes me feel dirty and in desperate need of a shower.

The back of a man's head comes into view as I walk closer to the conference room, and my gut twists further. Amelia, noticing me walk up, gives me a concerned look, one of almost pity or disappointment. It's a contradiction to the sneer that usually covers her face when she sees me.

"Ms. Carter, please have a seat," she says pointing to a chair on the opposite side of the table. Ms. Carter? This isn't going to be good at all.

Further entry into the large conference room reveals several others at the long table. I recognize several of them from the school's website. She has convened the school board for this occasion. My job is gone, and that knowledge is causing the burn of tears behind my eyes. I clear my throat in an attempt to remove the lump that is trying to close it.

A small ounce of gratefulness hits me when I notice that the room is void of a police officer. With any luck, I'll make it out of here without criminal charges.

I take the seat as directed and do my best to keep my spine straight and professional, when all my body wants to do is fold in on itself. My muscles begin to ache as I fight the urge to vomit.

"You know why you're here," Amelia says barely hiding the contempt in her voice. I can hear the edge of derision, but as I look across the table, it seems the board members haven't picked up on it. Either that, or they feel exactly the same way she does.

I lift my chin and ignore her attempt to rile me. I know it may come off as defiant, but with this show of force I know there's no way to keep my job, and I'll be damned if Amelia DuPont is going to make me beg.

"Have it your way," Amelia says lifting a folder and sliding it in front of me. "We're here to talk about your extracurricular activities."

I ignore the folder. I don't have to open it to know the discipline report for the closet incident and my termination papers are inside.

"Open it," she urges with a little too much excitement in her voice.

I wring my hands together in my lap trying to calm my nerves before flipping the folder open. One look at the paper on top and I slam the folder shut again. My blood runs cold. I vow off alcohol, all social situations, and as much as I don't want to, Kegan Cole.

"The board hasn't seen these yet, Ms. Carter, but I think for them to fully understand why we're here today it's imperative that they see."

Amelia reaches out for the folder, and my hand slams on top of it. "That's fine," she says with a sugary voice that makes me want to snap her neck. "I've made copies for everyone."

I watch in horror as she hands folders to each one of the board members. Their audible gasps and grunts will live in infamy, echoing in my head for years to come.

The man across from me looks up at me. If knowing what he's holding in his hands isn't bad enough, the way his eyes roam my body and the disgusting swipe of his tongue over his bottom lip makes things ten times worse.

"What's in your mouth?" the only female on the board asks holding up the picture.

Yep. There I am, in all my half-drunk glory, getting nailed by Kegan Cole in the hallway of the club.

"Her underwear," Amelia informs the group.

The woman drops the picture to the table as if she's going to somehow get infected with an STD by touching a photograph. The disgusting man across from me grunts again and shifts his weight in his chair. My skin crawls knowing he's pretty much getting off on this.

Amelia, digging the knife deeper, spreads the other photos out on the table. I fight the urge to look at them. The club picture is enough to get me fired, but my need to know everything she has against me wins out. I look down and see a handful of pictures of Kegan and me together.

In one, we're at breakfast. The next one is me going into his condo and one of him leaving my house. There's even one of us in the front yard when he came over to talk about the lies I told about my mother. They're all pretty innocuous until my eyes land on the one from the arcade. I'm standing at a pinball machine and Kegan's flush against my back with his arms around me. His fingers are dangerously close to my breasts, and I can remember this exact moment. He was grinding his thick cock against my ass and telling me exactly what he planned to do to me once we were alone.

The picture itself isn't bad. We're clothed, but it's the little boy standing in the background staring at us with his mouth open like he's just come across internet porn for the first time that makes it bad. *Really bad.*

"These are clear violations of Edgewood's morality clause," the female board member says. She closes her folder and shoves it away, disgust marking every inch of her over-botoxed face. "You did read your contract before signing it, didn't you, Ms. Carter."

I nod. I knew the clause was in there, but it was the furthest thing from my mind when Kegan was slamming into me in the very public club.

"Where was this at?" Creeper asks holding up the club picture.

I look away from him, unable to handle the misplaced desire in his eyes. These people are worried about me working around children? This guy is probably a registered sex offender.

"*SWEAT,*" I answer him with my eyes down at the table. I'm certain he wants to know because he's hoping he can catch other couples fucking in the hallway.

"That's over an hour away. She wasn't even in this community," he says causing my eyes to snap up to him. Who knew Creeper would come to my defense. The idea of him thinking I owed him something makes my skin crawl, but I'll take what I can get right now.

"She's fornicating in a public place, Reginald. It doesn't matter what town it's in." I'm beginning to hate the judgmental bitch sitting across from me.

"Oh come on, Florence. Haven't you ever lost your mind over a good looking man? Think back fifty years to before you became a prude." I'm liking Reginald more and more.

Florence gasps and clutches at the pearls around her neck. Clearly, she's been scandalized by his words.

"I'm only forty-eight you pompous ass," she hisses. One of the other men at the table chuckles but tries to cover it with a cough. Here I thought she was upset that anyone would consider her the type of person to get dirty in a hallway, when she's really upset because someone thinks she's older than she is. *Typical.*

"The man in all of these pictures is Kegan Cole," Amelia says interrupting the board members' back and forth. They all turn their heads to Amelia. Clearly, the Cole name is an important one in their circles. "He's the uncle of two of our students. We have a fraternization clause for a reason."

This was the main thing I was worried about, Kegan's relationship to Anastyn and Lennox. There's no way around this.

I look up to Creeper with an apologetic smirk. He's the only one who seems like an ally in this room, and for some unknown reason, I'm clinging to that. He winks at me, and suddenly I'm wishing I hadn't offered up the half smile.

"Kegan Cole is the students' guardian?" Reginald asks.

"On occasion," Amelia says with shaken confidence.

Reginald's eyes turn to me. "Do the students live with Mr. Cole?"

"No, sir," I manage with a weak voice. "They live with their parents. Mr. Cole was helping out with them recently when their youngest child was sick."

"You're splitting hairs with the fraternization accusation, Ms. DuPont. The rule for fraternization clearly states that a teacher shall not engage in outside relationships with guardians of the students. Mr. Cole babysitting for a little bit does not make him their guardian." No matter how today turns out, Reginald is getting a gift basket for Christmas.

I'm surprised that Mrs. Botox has piped up again, but she and the other members of the board grew quiet once Amelia announced who the man in the pictures was.

"We have some discussing to do," Reginald says. "You will be on paid administrative leave until a decision is made."

"It's clear what the decision is, Mr. Reese," Amelia says with a hiss. "I don't see the point in prolonging the inevitable."

"Ms. DuPont," Reginald Reese begins, "we appreciate you bringing this to our attention, but the decision in this matter is the board's, not yours." He holds up a hand to halt her rebuttal. He turns his eyes back to me. "As the President of the board, I will personally let you know what that decision is by the end of the week."

Feeling thoroughly dismissed, I stand from my seat, leaving the folder with some of my most intimate moments lying on the desk. They've seen it all, so there's no point in taking my copies. I feel Mr. Reese's eyes on me every step out of the room, and I can't help but cringe when I think about what he's going to do with his copies.

On my drive home, I run through the meeting. Amelia didn't once bring up the closet incident. In doing so, she ran the risk of me bringing up the fact that she was briefly involved with Kegan. The reminder makes my hackles rise. She planned this all out. She's been pretty much stalking us for weeks, finding ways to get me fired without having to call her own delinquencies into question.

Sneaky bitch.

Chapter 35

Kegan

By the time I make it back over to Lexi's house, thankfully, she's there. I grab my packed bag from the passenger seat and lock up my truck.

I'm damn near giddy as I walk up her front steps and knock on the door. Today was a long day, but I'd live every one just like today if it means spending my nights with her. My fingers tingle in anticipation of touching her.

After several long minutes, the door finally pulls open. I expect to see her in a towel or with wet hair due to how long it took her to open the door. Anger hits my chest when I realize her face is the only thing that's wet. Tear tracks stain her beautiful face.

"Baby, what's wrong?" I take a step closer to her, but she holds a hand up to prevent me from making contact.

"I need you to go," she says through her tears.

"No." I shake my head emphatically. "I'm not leaving you while you're like this. Tell me what's wrong so I can fix it."

"You're what's wrong," she says weakly.

"Me?" Panic nearly crushes me. "I know the whole 'thanks, doll' thing was out of line this morning, but I swear it was a joke."

Her eyes dart to mine. "You think I'm this upset," she says pointing to her face, "over some misplaced joke?"

"It's all I have to go on, Lexi. I fucked up, and I know you're getting tired of hearing me say I'm sorry, but I am. I'm sorry I keep saying shit I shouldn't."

I take a step closer; she takes a step back and looks over my shoulder as if she expects someone to be standing there.

"They have pictures of us," she finally admits.

"They?" I'm so confused.

"Amelia and the school board. They have pictures of you here, me at your place. They have one of us at the arcade." Her tears continue to fall, and as much as I want to wrap my arms around her in comfort, I respect when a woman says no.

"I don't see the big deal with us dating, Lexi. They shouldn't either. My family donates a shit ton of money to that school. Surely they can overlook this."

"The club," she says weakly.

"What about it?"

Her eyes meet mine again. "They have a picture of you fucking me against the wall! Amelia was nice enough to answer the board member's question as to what was stuffed in my mouth!"

I recoil at her anger and the fact that a moment I was certain we were able to keep between us was breached. I take a step back, creating even more unwanted distance between us.

"Someone is following you?" The look over my shoulder makes sense now and causes me to look back as well.

"Us. They're following us. Every one of the pictures was of us together." She swipes at the tears hanging from her chin and looks down at the porch.

"Did they fire you?"

She shakes her head. "Not yet, but I'm sure it will happen by week's end."

"I can fix this." My words are a plea. She's closing down on me, and the pain of losing her over something so fucking stupid is surreal. I have enough trouble holding on to this gorgeous woman on my own, knowing any stupid thing could come out of my mouth and end us. Having outside forces working against me? We'll never get this relationship off of the ground if I have to fight against them too.

"You can't. It's already done." Her hand reaches for the open door as she takes another step back. "I shouldn't have let you in."

I want to point out the obvious, that she hasn't let me in. I'm still standing on the front porch. Then, it dawns on me. At first, I think she's talking about not letting me into her body. When her free hand covers her chest, I know she's talking about her heart.

"Goodbye, Kegan," she whispers on a quiet sob and closes the door in my face.

I lean my head against the cool glass of her front door. "Please, Lexi." My palm comes up and rests flat beside my head. "Please don't walk away from me."

"They're following her, Kadin!" My voice echoes through my truck as I drive back to my condo.

"Why the hell would they do that? Why would they even suspect anything is going on?"

"Amelia," I mutter. She's the one behind this whole damn thing. I put her in her place in the closet and now this her way of being a vindictive bitch.

"The headmistress?" Confusion marks his voice, and I know that's my fault. I tried explaining to him what was going on, but in my haste I've left out several very important key details.

"Amelia DuPont caught Lexi and me in the supply closet at the school."

"Jesus, Kegan. Now you're fucking women at my kids' school? What's next, the confessional at church?"

"I didn't fuck Lexi at the school. And if I hadn't fucked Amelia there, this wouldn't even be an issue."

"I'm so goddamned disappointed in you. With the way you were acting with Lexi, bringing her to Sunday dinner, I seriously thought you'd changed. Being a playboy is one thing, Kegan, but leading her on is a new low."

"Leading her… what the hell are you talking about?" I'm so angry I decide to pull my truck over. Getting into an accident before I have the chance to fix all of this shit wouldn't help anyone.

"Don't you see what's happened? One plaything found out about the other, and she's gone crazy."

I scrub my hands over my face. "One, Lexi isn't a goddamned plaything, so I suggest you don't say shit like that about her. Two, there's nothing going on between Amelia and me. We messed around a few times this past summer, but that's all it was. We both knew it. There was no way lines got crossed. I wasn't even on her radar anymore until she found Lexi and me in the closet."

His sigh is loud through my hands-free speakers. "You sure do know how to make a damn mess."

"I know, and I'm asking for help before it blows up any bigger."

"You mentioned they have pictures."

"Yes. From like four different occasions. One was," I pause not too proud to have to admit this to my brother who already thinks I'm a complete fuck up. "One was intimate. We were at a club, and I didn't think anyone was around. I wouldn't be surprised if someone wasn't lurking outside her house a while ago snapping more of me on her porch."

I rest my head against the steering wheel. "The look on her face. I've never seen her so upset. She was so resigned, like it was breaking her heart to turn me away, but it was the only choice she had."

"What can I do?" There's no longer a hint of frustration in his voice. It's no longer tainted with disappointment, and for that I'm grateful. I'm beating myself up enough for the both of us.

"Fuck, I don't know. Dig something up on her? I need some ammunition, anything to make her back off."

"Kegan, you said the entire board was there. She's not the only one you have to worry about. It's bigger than just a woman upset over not getting Cole dick anymore."

"Please, just look into her," I beg. "Maybe she's fucking everyone on the board, and we can blackmail them."

"You mentioned one picture being intimate. Does that mean what I think it means?"

"If you're thinking it's a picture of me fucking her against the wall with her panties in her mouth, then yes it's what you're thinking."

He sighs again. "You can't make anything easy can you?"

"Look, it's not that bad. We were both dressed, mostly. I can admit it was a stupid decision, Kadin."

"Stupid or not, that's going to be an issue. Teachers, especially ones working at private academies are held to an insanely high standard. It doesn't matter if this is some kind of vindication from one of your scorned lovers. You've given them plenty of ammunition to fire her." There's a long silence, one in which I'm sure he's picturing his hands around my throat. "Let me have my guy do some digging. Maybe she's got some skeletons in her closet. Her family has more money than ours, and you know rich people always have something hidden in their closet."

"I owe you, Kadin." If I weren't all the way across town, I'd drive to his house and hug him.

"Don't thank me yet. This is a complete cluster fuck. I'll call you when I have something. You need to stay away from her until we can figure something out." There's a warning in his voice.

"That's not... I can't do that Kadin. I need her." Truths are coming from all sides today it seems.

"I get that more than you probably realize, Kegan, but if she has someone watching her, it's only going to make things worse. I'll let my guy know to make this his top priority, but you have to do your part as well."

"Okay. I'll stay away from her. Thanks, man." I'm met with silence.

He may be willing to help, but I know he's not happy with being in a situation where he has to. His guy better work fast as hell because I'm already itching to head back over to her. Instead, I put the truck in drive and go home, praying every second that Amelia has some kind of sick fetish that will help us help Lexi keep her job. Besides, any woman who lets you fuck her in the ass within the first hour of meeting her has to be down with some kinky shit.

Chapter 36
Lexi

The shattering of my heart coincides with the soft click of my front door. I never should've given in to him. I never should've crossed that line because I knew it would come to this. I knew I'd get in trouble at work, and I'd end up with my heart broken. Yet, I didn't put up much of a fight did I?

I don't blame him for any of this. I was a willing, active participant. I had an amazing time while it lasted. As far as regrets, there's always regrets aren't there?

I may never be able to work as a teacher again. Once word gets around that the kindergarten teacher likes to be screwed in public, every door that may have once been open will slam shut. Edgewood is the only teaching position I have on my resume, and I can't even imagine the venom Amelia would spread if someone called for a reference. Hell, she could tell the truth, and it would still leave me unemployed. I messed up big time.

As much as I hate what I'm going through, I can't find even a sliver of regret for Kegan. I regret our public dalliances. I regret getting caught with him in the closet, which is no doubt the catalyst for Amelia's ire. But, I just can't find the strength to regret him.

The time we've spent together here, the time we spent at his condo were some of the greatest moments of my life. I'm not just talking about the phenomenal sex, but that doesn't hurt his case either. He held me to him as if he never wanted to let me go. His embrace became something I never thought I'd get from him, especially after the first time we had sex.

He would share glimpses of the man he worked so hard not to let anyone else see. He became vulnerable if only for a few seconds. He let me in; he allowed me to share that with him.

Closing that door on him was one of the hardest things I've ever done, coming in second only to burying my grandparents and Ella. As much as I wanted him to stay, I swore years ago that I wouldn't let another man factor into decisions that will alter my life.

Unable to stay in the house alone, I call Jillian and pray she's available. It's Monday evening, but knowing her, she's at a club drinking and dancing her obsession with Hawke away.

Surprisingly she answers on the second ring. "Hey girl, what's up?" Her bubbly voice brings a faint smile to my face.

I clear my throat, doing my best to hide my raw emotions. "Can I come over?"

"You don't ever have to ask. You know that." Is her response.

I huff a humorous laugh. "I don't show up unannounced. I showed up early once and got an eye full."

"I don't have a man here. I'm not tied up. The coast is clear," she says sarcastically. "I am out of wine, so if that's where your head's at you need to stop by the store."

"Okay, see you in a few."

I head to the bathroom to wash my face. One look at myself in the mirror has me wincing and ducking my head. I look like a troll with makeup all down my face. Red blotches dot my skin. No wonder Kegan didn't put up much of a fight on the porch earlier.

"Listen," Jillian says with a consoling voice. "I know you're upset. I get that, but what I'm saying is the damage is already done. So I'm confused as to why you sent him away. There's nothing more they can do to you. You're sitting here in pain, when you could be in his arms. It doesn't seem that complicated to me."

Leave it to the flighty friend to make complete sense after the fact.

"You're not listening to the whole story, Jillian." I sigh and fill my wine glass again. "I told you about Mr. Reese, the school board president. He may have been bordering on sexual harassment with the way he was looking at me during the meeting, but I felt like he was sort of on my side. He contested each one of the violation complaints against me."

"What's your point?" Jillian sits back further on the couch, clearly frustrated with my side of the argument.

"That Mr. Reese seems to be fighting for me. If he is, I may be able to keep my job. I sent Kegan away because I know people are following me, and if I want to keep my job continuing to see him after being confronted by the board won't allow that to happen."

"So what?" she asks with narrowed eyes. "You're just going to walk away from him?"

"What other choice do I have? I have to keep my job."

"You can find another job, Lexi. You know that as much as I do." She leans forward and places her half full wine glass on the table. I'm in for it now. Jillian never sets down a glass that still has alcohol in it.

"And just who would I use a reference from Edgewood? Amelia would probably forward the picture from the club as her response if she was called."

"Sounds like Mr. Reese would be perfect for a reference."

She catches the pillow I throw at her head with ease. "Will you be serious? We are literally talking about my future here."

She shrugs. "You should've just kept Kegan, job be damned. He's loaded, Lex. You stay with him, and you wouldn't have to work."

"Is that seriously your stance? Mooch off the rich guy?"

I fill my glass once again with wine. Maybe the more I drink, the more I'll like her ideas.

"I'm just trying to think of a way where you can keep the guy. You've clearly fallen for him. Why are you fighting it so much?"

"I do want him. I can admit that, but I have no idea where his head is at. I can't take a gamble on my future if he's just sticking around for a little fun." This is the truth. Hunter, while I was in that situation, seemed like he was all in. He said the right words, made me feel like the only woman on the planet. Hindsight is always a twisted bitch. After stepping away, I could see just how messed up that relationship was. I could analyze every single angle, and what I found was less than desirable. I'm terrified it's the same thing with Kegan.

"Did you bother to ask him?" She knows my answer by the look on my face. "Of course you didn't. That would be crazy. Nothing more foolish than refusing to ask the questions you need answers to."

I came over here for support from her, and this is what I'm getting? I get it, tough love and all that, but shit, talk about being kicked while you're down.

"I'm terrified of his answers, Jillian! If I walk away, then that's on me. I can handle that. But rejection? If he told me we weren't worth fighting for, it would break me more than closing that door on him did this evening."

"He's not Hunter, Lexi."

"I know that." My voice is edgy, annoyed, and near the breaking point all at once. I'm not annoyed at Jillian, per se, rather, this entire situation. Nothing in my life is easy. I just want a damn break from the challenges. Every day it seems to be something new.

"I had asked Hunter to pick our family. I remember the day I stood before him, resigned to begging him to be a part of my life, our baby's life. He blew me off as if I'd asked if he wanted to grab a pizza after class. It was that simple for him. No discussion, no making plans. No. That was his one word, emphatic answer. Then he walked away, wrapped his arm around the nearest girl, kissed her cheek, and whispered in her ear as if I didn't exist, as if his daughter wasn't growing inside of me." I fall back into my chair with a puff of air.

That kind of pain stays with you for a while. That's the kind of pain you'd do anything in your power to avoid again. "That's why I didn't ask the questions I wanted answers to as far as Kegan is concerned."

"From what you've told me about him, he's nothing like Hunter." She just won't give up.

"Right now, he's nothing like Hunter was at the end. Hunter wasn't that way until I told him about the baby. I've never seen someone turn a one-eighty as fast as he did that day."

"And if you had the answers? If Kegan told you before today that he wanted you and only you?"

Our bed.

Was that his way of making a declaration?

"If I was a hundred percent sure that Kegan was as invested in me as I want to be in him?"

She nods. "If you had no doubts about owning his heart."

"If I was certain he was in it for the long haul, I would have quit my job yesterday. I wouldn't need plans if I knew Kegan was going to be beside me, fighting with me."

"Nothing in life is a certainty, Lexi. You know that."

"I know." I drop my head and watch my hands. "I just don't want the heartbreak."

"Lexi," Jillian says practically climbing in my lap. "You're breaking your own heart right now."

Chapter 37

Kegan

I've texted Lexi every damn day this week, multiple times. She hasn't responded once. It means she's either ignoring me or has already moved past annoyance and has blocked my number completely.

I've been at the job site early each morning. I've left small gifts on her front porch. The box of chocolates, bottle of wine and stuffed bear she wanted from the arcade that I wasn't able to win for her while we were there, are still sitting against her front door.

From the looks of it, she hasn't been home in days. I have no idea where she is. As far as I know, she doesn't have any family other than her mother, and I know she would never leave town to go to her. As much as she's hurting herself right now pushing me away, I know she'd never willingly submit herself to that kind of torture.

Three days is my max capacity for not knowing where she is. It would've been less if finding out where she was didn't include...

"Bland and Pratt," a sweet voice says through the phone.

"Justin Pratt, please." As much as I despise making this phone call, that poor office assistant doesn't deserve my frustration.

"May I ask who's calling?"

"Kegan Cole."

"One moment."

Shitty elevator music blasts in my ear for several minutes before the call is answered.

"I'm surprised it took you this long to call." As if I wasn't mad enough just by having to make this damn call in the first place, Justin's voice pisses me off even more. "A real man would've called the first day she didn't come back home."

I growl into the phone; he chuckles. If teleporting was a real thing, I'd jump through this phone and break his damn neck. At least I'd be able to see Lexi at the funeral.

"She pushed me away, Justin. Are you telling me that I should have pushed back and refused to leave? Is that the kind of man you want your cousin dealing with?"

"Good point," he concedes.

"Where is she?"

"She doesn't want to see you." His voice is softer than I would expect. Almost as if he realizes she's making a mistake.

"Is she okay?"

"She's... safe." His sigh makes me wonder if she's as torn up as I am. I don't wish her pain, but I pray she's miserable without me. It's the only way I'll have a chance to get her back.

"What does that mean, Justin?"

"She's her own worst enemy, Kegan."

"Don't I know it," I mutter. "Has the school made a decision yet?"

"Not yet. They told her by the end of the week, but she hasn't heard from them as of this morning."

My phone beeps with an incoming call. I pull it from my ear to see that Kadin is calling.

"I have another call coming in. Tell her I miss her?"

"I will."

The phone beeps again, and I switch over to my brother.

"What did they find?"

"Embezzlement." Well, that's a little more complicated than voyeuristic sex in a BDSM club, but I think it will work in our favor.

"So we can use this against her, so Lexi can keep her job?"

Kadin sighs, and I realize the sound is really starting to grate on my nerves today. "It's not that simple, Kegan. It's a federal offense. It had to be reported."

"So Amelia will be arrested, and Lexi can go back to work."

Silence on his end of the phone is deafening.

"Tell me the Feds have already taken her into custody."

"Her father is a Senator, Kegan. You know how this shit works." He pulls the phone away and gives a direction to someone in his office.

"So nothing happens because daddy has some pull? That's bullshit, Kadin. We never played those political games, why would we start now?"

"This isn't Cole International. This is whoever is in control of these types of things on the federal level. It's out of our hands. We did our due diligence by reporting what was found. It's in their hands."

"Then how did you know it was over?" I'm grasping at straws. If Kadin says nothing is going to happen to her, then I trust him. I just don't like the answer I'm being given. True to my 'baby in the family' form I can ask questions all day long hoping that the answer will eventually change. It won't get me anywhere, but I feel better for the effort.

"I was informed by a clandestine phone call from federal agents that it goes further than just Amelia DuPont, and I was asked to not speak another word of it."

It's my turn to sigh.

"I was told that Amelia will be removed and replaced at Edgewood, but I don't know if that makes any difference in Lexi's case."

That tidbit of information gives me a little shred of hope, that even if we're not together, she'll have her job. I know it's important to her. Keeping her job doesn't help my case any because the fraternization clause will still be in effect no matter who's running the school.

"Well," I say trying to keep the frustration from my voice. "I guess it's better than finding nothing on her. Maybe this way she'll still have a chance."

"You do realize I would've never been okay with blackmailing Amelia, even if we found something on her, right?"

I can't help but laugh. "I know that stuff is above you, but that doesn't mean that we have the same level of morals."

"Jackass," he mutters into the phone before hanging up.

I know exactly what I want to do, but I refrain from calling the private investigator back and hunting Lexi down by the GPS on her phone. As much as I want to go to her, my heart knows that she needs to come to me. I've been the one chasing this whole time. She sent me away, and without her coming to me, I'll always wonder if she's actually in this.

My greatest fear, however, is that she's made her choice, and I don't have one single say in any of it.

Work today wasn't even an option. I threw myself a pity party last night. Seems my closest friends Jim and Jack are jerks, but it was finding out how much of an asshole that Jose can be, that really did me in.

I spent the better part of an hour over the toilet in my en-suite and another with my back against the tub waiting to get sick again. I know using alcohol to help solve my problems creates a problem of its own, but the bottles lined up on the bar were just too much to resist.

I stopped texting Lexi after I spoke with Justin. If she doesn't want to be found, I won't continue to look, hence my little party last night.

Missing work is a shit thing to do. My guys don't deserve it. According to Tony when I spoke with him this morning, I just get in the way as it is. Me not being there is a break for the guys. He guarantees they'll be able to get twice as much done today. I called him an asshole and hung up on him. Can't keep a woman and my guys don't even find me useful? Like I said, *pity party table for one.*

Hanging out on the couch, feeling sorry for myself, and binge watching The Walking Dead are the only things on my agenda today. Tomorrow isn't looking much better either.

I turned off my cell phone, even as much as it worried me I'd miss a call from Lexi, I know she won't call. I wouldn't have had to turn the phone off if Kadin hadn't been sending me depressing memes all morning with captions like "love is a bitch," "forever alone," and my favorite— a link to a relationship test.

Pretty fucked up, right?

The crazy thing is, before Lexi, these would be the things I would find hilarious. I never understood the pain of losing someone who wasn't related by blood. Lexi and I have only been seeing each other for weeks; I can't imagine what he went through when he lost Savannah or when London walked away. I don't know which one would be worse: losing your wife, knowing she's gone forever or the woman who walked away while carrying your child.

It's that over analyzation that kept me from telling him to go fuck himself and the horse I bought for his daughter. I know what I'm going through right now with Lexi is nothing compared to what he's gone through, but shit, give me a break.

I force myself to drink water the rest of the day, but there's no telling what my night is going to look like. I yell at the TV every time a 'walker' catches someone off guard, realizing matters of the heart are exactly like The Walking Dead. You don't realize you fucked up until it's too late and not many make it out alive.

Chapter 38
Lexi

Three and a half days at Jillian's and I've already become *persona non grata*. Apparently, the heartbroken best friend really puts a damper on her sex life. I'm not the one who told her to change anything about her routine, but she doesn't feel like she can be herself with company in her condo.

I have to go home at some point, so it might as well be today. I'm supposed to hear from the school by the end of the week, and since it's Thursday afternoon, that call can happen at any time. I'd rather be at home when the final part of my heart breaks officially losing my job.

I have no clue where Jillian is. She left this morning after another round of "Get off my couch and fight for him" didn't end with me, in fact, getting off the couch. Her tough love has continued since the first evening I arrived. Last night, she resorted to name calling, but even being called a masochist didn't change anything. I analyzed that just like I have everything she's said. It may appear that I'm hurting myself, but I know how much pain comes once you let your heart commit one hundred percent to another person. If I stuck around and let that happen, that would be the true definition of a masochist.

I leave her a short note on the counter and go home. I walk quickly to the front door, ignoring the chocolate, wine, and teddy bear sitting near the door and sneak inside as quickly as I can so Kegan doesn't see me. I don't even allow myself to look over at the job site. Seeing his truck over there would break my resolve, which I have to admit has been waning a little each day.

My intentions for staying at Jillian's were to work on getting over him, getting past the urge to run to him and let him follow through on his promise to fix it like he said he would. I had to stay gone because I knew if he was just a handful of yards away, I couldn't stop myself from going over to him. I knew for damn sure if he came over here I would give in. Staying away hasn't had the effect I was aiming for, if anything it made me miss him even more.

My head perks up at the rumble of a truck's engine, but I realize it's just someone driving by. I busy myself cleaning until I find one of his discarded shirts on the floor of my closet. I forgo straightening up my room and allow myself to fall into bed with his shirt against my nose while the fabric catches my tears.

I don't realize I fell asleep until the ringing of my phone pulls me from slumber. My heart rate increases as I allow myself to hope that it's Kegan calling me. He hasn't texted since yesterday morning, and I was beginning to accept he was done trying.

I swallow down bile when the school's phone number lights up on my screen. I must be a masochist because I answer the phone rather than letting my termination happen through voice mail.

"Hello?"

"Lexi Carter?" Not Amelia's voice asks through the phone.

"Y-yes," I stammer.

"This is Chantel Moreau at Edgewood Academy. I'm the new acting headmistress."

"Yes, ma'am. How can I help you?" See how polite I can be even when I'm about to get terminated for awful morality clause violations?

"I was wondering if you could come to the school for a meeting." She shuffles some papers around.

I'd rather not, can't this be done over the phone? "Yes," I reply. "When would you like me there?"

"Four would be great."

"See you then." I hang up the phone as dread settles in my gut.

An hour later, I'm pulling up outside of the school. I went ahead and brought a handful of boxes, hoping they at least give me the opportunity to clear out my classroom.

Leaving the boxes in my car, I hold my head high as I walk into the school. The final bell rang thirty minutes ago and the parking lot is all but clear except for a few cars I recognize as the teachers'.

I smile at the tall, middle-aged woman standing at the counter.

"Ms. Moreau?" I ask holding my hand out.

"Ms. Carter?" I nod. "Chantel, please," she says clasping my hand in hers. I notice how warm it is and smile softly at the comforting feeling it gives me.

"Let's chat in my office," she says turning around and heading back to the office that Amelia DuPont has chastised me in more than once.

Mr. Reese's head turns to take me in from head to toe as I enter. The comforting feeling I had at Chantel's introduction are now gone. I take the seat across from the desk next to Mr. Reese, trying to be nonchalant about scooting my chair a few inches further away from him.

"You know why you're here," Chantel says as she lowers herself into her chair.

Sweat mists my skin as she says the exact same words Amelia said at the meeting earlier this week.

"Yes, ma'am."

I wait rather impatiently as she begins to shuffle some papers on her desk. I take the opportunity to look around her office. She may not have been here long, but the office walls already have her diplomas, and there are several personal touches on the desk and shelves.

"I have had numerous conversations this week with parents worried about their children because you've been out." I inwardly smile at her news. "That being said, we have a few issues to discuss."

"Yes, ma'am." I tangle my fingers in my lap as a means to release nervous energy. I have the urge to beg, plead, and fight for my job. I love it here. I love it even more now that Amelia is gone, and I have no idea how this new woman is, but it can only be an improvement over what we've been forced to deal with.

She places a calm hand over a folder I recognize as one of the ones Amelia prepared for the board. I cringe at the sight of it.

"Two things of concern to discuss. First, the elicit behavior in public."

I swallow roughly as I try my best to force down the bile that's attempting to crawl up my throat. Thankfully, she doesn't open the folder and flash the pictures. That would be more than I could bare.

"Edgewood Academy, is a very prestigious school. Teachers all over the state look to us for a position." She gives me a chastising look. "I will not tolerate this type of public behavior from my teachers. I don't imagine a public school would allow this sort of thing either."

I hold my head in shame. Kegan Cole and alcohol, although a heady mix, is still no excuse for public sex. I know that now. Hell, I knew it then too.

"If you were caught and charged, you'd be out of a job, Ms. Carter."

My head snaps up to her gaze.

"This will be your only reprimand for this particular situation. If there is ever a next time, you'll be terminated immediately. I understand that you're young Ms. Carter, but you're not some horny teenager who can't hold off until you're in private for such actions." I can't one hundred percent read the glint her eyes, amusement maybe.

"You won't have to worry about anything like this ever happening again, Ms. Moreau." I give her a tight smile when all I want to do is jump up and down, thankful I get to keep my job. My face falls when I think about Kegan. "The man in the picture," I begin.

"Mr. Kegan Cole?"

"Yes, ma'am. We're dating." At least we were dating.

"Mr. Reese," she says angling her head to the man I'd forgotten was sitting beside me, "has explained all about Mr. Cole. He's not a guardian of any children at this school. The fraternization policy is very black and white in that sense. It is not a violation for you to be in a *private* relationship with him." I want to smirk at her emphasis on the one word, but I know now is not the time nor the place.

"Thank you," I say quietly.

"Now, it goes without saying that I expect you to be entirely professional with those girls. No special attention, favors, or allowances," Ms. Moreau stresses.

"Of course not." I bite my lip, unsure if I should ask about Amelia, but curiosity wins. "What happened with Ms. DuPont?"

She frowns at me which tells me she thinks it's none of my business.

"It was discovered that Ms. DuPont has been stealing money from the school," Mr. Reese says.

I snap my head to him so fast my neck aches. "Amelia?" I mean she was a straight up bitch, but embezzlement? She's loaded, it doesn't make any sense.

He nods.

"That explains all of the cutbacks, lack of supplies, and the, dismal at best, refreshments at Open House were dismal at best." I look back to Ms. Moreau. "The gym teacher has been coming in on the weekends to take care of the lawn."

"It's unfortunate," Ms. Moreau adds. "Her family is paying the school back immediately, so those things will no longer be an issue. Supplies will be stocked and Edgewood Academy will be returned to its previous glory."

"What's going to happen to her?" They both remain silent. "Nothing is going to happen to her."

"These types of things are out of our hands," Mr. Reese says apologetically.

I'm fuming mad as my fingers begin to ache from twisting them in my lap.

"Listen, Ms. Carter. It's clear from the way this situation was brought to light that Amelia DuPont had some sort of personal vendetta with you. I want you to know that it's over, and you no longer have anything to worry about so long as these types of behaviors cease. No one from the school is following you, you are not in any harm, and we hope to see you bright and early on Monday morning." Ms. Moreau stands from her desk, holding out her hand. "We do have a staff meeting at seven in the auditorium Monday, right before school."

"Thank you," I say standing from my chair and turning my body so my backend isn't right in Mr. Reese's face, although I'm certain he wouldn't mind. "I'll be there," I reply softly.

I walk out of the school before either of them can change their minds.

I know I was just complaining about everything hitting me at once. I know I should be leery of any good news I get considering the events of last week, but that doesn't stop me from hoping that I can have my job and Kegan too. My luck has probably run out with Kegan, but I was honestly ready to turn down the job at Edgewood if Ms. Moreau had said there would be an issue with me having a relationship with him.

You may not realize this, but that is huge for me. Epic even!

It's almost like a blind person walking into traffic without a seeing eye dog or walking stick. The amount of faith this kind of leap takes is immeasurable. I've never been this person. Since college, I've never put more than one egg in a basket. I've never had the courage to take a chance on an outcome I wasn't one hundred percent sure would go my way.

Finding myself at Kegan's door an hour later, after my texts to him have gone unanswered, makes every atom in my being stand on edge. Terrified he'll be gone or worse yet finding out he's here with someone else keeps me in the hallway without my knuckle making contact with his door for over ten minutes.

I pace back and forth, arguing with myself about being a coward. I call myself every name that Jillian called me during her three-day tough love session. None of it helps, not one personal chastisement gives me the courage I felt all the way over here to take that final step.

It isn't until a neighbor opens their door and insist I either knock or leave that I make my decision. The fact that she threatened to call the cops because some random stalker-woman is wearing a hole in the carpet outside of her condo, also helped in my decision-making process.

My first knock is weak, and I know can't be heard through the condo. I'd wager that even with him standing a few feet away, the thickness of the door masks my attempt. Knowing this, I lower my hand and walk back toward the elevator.

You have to fight for him.

My brain would pick this very moment to remind me of my best friend's words from this morning.

Would you think any different of her if you knew that it was followed by: *Quit being a fucking pussy?*

Believe it or not, it's the second part of her urging that makes me turn back from the elevator and bang loudly on his door. I do this three times with no answer. My bravado falls as more heartache and disappointment settles in my soul. I drop my head and begin to turn around, defeat covering my body when the door is pulled open.

I turn back to find Kegan standing in his doorway with a look of disbelief on his gorgeous face. Even though he needs to trim his beard and his hair is a complete mess, he's still the most gorgeous man I've ever set my eyes on. My heart begins to pound uncontrollably in my chest.

Chapter 39
Kegan

"You're not Chinese food." I'm standing in my doorway seeing this perfect woman for the first time in days, and that comes out of my mouth. At least the 'I'd still like to eat you' stays in my head rather than cresting my lips.

Silence crackles between us and my eyes drift to her flexing fingertips. She wants to touch me as much as I want my hands on her. Looking at her, I'm rendered breathless. I didn't know how much my heart needed her until just now.

"I love you," I blurt. Fire burns in her eyes at my words. "I didn't truly realize it until just now."

She grins at me. "I know that if you knew before now, you would've divulged that information sooner." She takes a step closer. "You have a tendency to speak before you think."

I shrug. "Character flaw."

"It's working for you right now." She walks past me into the living room. "I'm here to apologize." I have the urge to wipe the tear that is silently rolling down her cheek. "I shouldn't have pushed you away."

I swallow roughly. The words I've wanted to hear all week have a greater effect on me than I had anticipated.

"It's over," she whispers.

My heart stops. This can't be the end. She's not the type of person to rub salt into an open wound by showing up here just to verbalize something she's already said.

"The issues at school are over," she explains.

The amount of relief that washes over me nearly brings me to my knees. "I know," is all I can manage to say.

Her eyes flash to mine. "You know?" Anger marks her tone. "You knew I didn't lose my job, and you're here ordering Chinese food? You should have come to me."

I shake my head. How do I explain that it has taken every ounce of power I have not to go to her? I can't formulate words powerful enough to explain the loss I've felt this week.

"I've been coming to you for weeks, Lexi. I needed you to come back to me this time." I take a step toward her, and she takes a step back.

The hurt in her eyes is palpable, and I feel like an asshole all over again for being the cause of that pain.

"A test? This was some sort of test?" Her voice has grown shaky, and the amount of tears on her face has tripled.

"No, baby. Not a test. But if I went to you, I'd spend my life wondering if you were in this because you felt obligated, or if you were with me because you honestly wanted to be. Staying away has been the hardest thing I've ever done." When I step forward, this time, she doesn't shrink away.

"If I knew how you felt, I would've been here a lot sooner. For a man who can't control his mouth, you sure kept your feelings under lock and key." She sighs into my chest when I pull her close. "I would have told Amelia to shove that job if I'd known..."

With gentle hands wrapped around her forearms, I pull her from my chest. "What are you saying, Lexi?"

A soft hand reaches up to touch my cheek; instinctively my head tilts to increase the pressure. "I'm saying, I love you, too."

Am I a pussy right now or is the tear rolling down my damn cheek endearing? I lean my head down, slanting my mouth over hers. The connection, although it rips through my body like the first line of coke I took-don't judge, college was filled with tons of experimenting after Rhonda-it goes off with way less fanfare than it deserves.

I love her; she loves me. That necessitates fireworks, a live band, and the obligatory plane flying over with a hundred foot banner trailing behind. Instead, I get a moan and the texture of gooseflesh under the tips of my fingers. I'll be damned if that isn't better than the pyrotechnic show at the Beijing Olympics.

"Say it again," I mouth against her lips.

She smiles and, even though I can see her mouth, I feel her lips turn up at my request. "I love you," she says.

"I'm going to take you to our bed and make love to you all night. And by make love, I mean I'm going to fuck you hard and dirty, just how you like it."

"Knock, knock." A throat clears behind me, near the front door I inadvertently forgot to close.

Lexi chuckles when my head drops and I have to adjust my cock in my sweats. There is no way to turn around and deal with the delivery guy without embarrassing everyone in the room. There's no way to hide my arousal in the thin cotton, and I guarantee the issue isn't going away anytime soon.

"Don't worry, big fella. I got it." She pats my chest and walks past me to the front door.

A few minutes later the front door shuts and Lexi is walking back into the living room. "You hungry?" She's riffling through the bag. "Oh! They threw in extra fortunes. You want a cookie?" She asks holding up the plastic-wrapped treat.

I turn wicked eyes on her and close the distance between us. I pull the food from her hands and place it roughly on the living room table. "Oh, I want a cookie alright. I'm going to be eating cookie all night if I have anything to say about it," I growl in her ear, lifting her off her feet and tossing her over my shoulder.

Her laugh is a balm to my injured soul. "That's the corniest damn thing I've ever heard."

"Stick around, baby," I say as I lower her to my bed. "I'm sure there's bound to be even dumber things that will slip out."

Her eyes grow soft and warm. "I'm sticking around, Kegan." Her palm nearly burns my chest as she places her hand over my heart. Her mouth inches closer to mine. "I'm yours."

I know I promised hard and dirty, but it doesn't feel right at this moment. Declarations of love and the promise of forever should be sealed with actions that will reflect the way we'll treat each other every day from now on. Attentive hands slowly remove her clothes. Soft fingertips brush over my abdomen as she lifts my t-shirt, her mouth quickly replacing the fabric against my skin.

Sweats and blue jeans pile rapidly on the floor as eager hands grip, caress, and search every inch of our bodies. I almost feel like I'm violating her with my rough hands, but the moans my calloused fingers elicit as they scrape over her most delicate flesh tell me not to worry.

My mouth is like a heat seeking missile, quickly searching out and finding the hottest part of her body. My tongue lashes at her center as two fingers seek entrance to her body. The sound of my sheet's resilience being tested as she grips them in her hands, urges me to work harder.

Before long, her body is quivering under my mouth, and her core is pulsing around my fingers. Demanding attention, my cock jumps only finding the cold mattress for relief. Giving her clit one final swipe of my tongue, I inch my way up planting kisses on her skin.

Lexi is moaning, panting, and squirming under me; the orgasm I just gave her only a precursor to the love we'll make tonight. She's as desperate for me as I am for her, mindless in her need.

A hand presses against my chest as I tease her clit with the glistening head of my cock.

"Condom," she whispers. Well, not as mindless as I'd hoped she was.

"Are they in your purse?" I ask shifting my hips back, readying myself to get off the bed.

Her eyes squeeze shut, and her exasperated groan isn't what I want to hear. In an attempt to keep her in the moment with me, I sweep my thumb over her clit and work the tiny bud with slow circles. Heavy, hooded eyes open as her gaze analyzes my face.

"I didn't bring my purse." Nothing like a bucket of ice cold water being dumped on this moment. "No condom."

I lick my thumb and shift my weight off of the bed. "I'll go get some," I say reaching down for my sweats and trying to figure out how to convince the lady at the CVS drive-thru to let me buy rubbers without going inside, for the sake of decency of course.

"No condom," she says again reaching for me.

"Baby, just hold tight. Fifteen minutes max. I'll get the jumbo box; we're going to need it."

Her grip on my arm doesn't loosen, forcing me to look back at her rather than rip myself from her grasp. Her fingers trail seductively down her stomach and circle around her wet entrance. "No condom," she repeats for the third time as she slowly draws her tongue across her top teeth.

I drop the sweats in my hand. "Do you mean...?" She slowly nods and bites her lip.

I practically jump on the bed. "Having my baby doesn't scare you?" Surprisingly it doesn't scare me either. I can't be one hundred percent sure this is how I actually feel, or if the sex fog is so thick it's clouding my judgment.

She grins up at me as if I've said another stupid thing. "It means I'm on birth control, and I'm taking a gamble that you don't have STDs."

I swipe my thumb back over her clit, her moans causing goose flesh to race down my spine. "I'll take what I can get."

"Like this," she says pushing on my chest until I'm sitting up with my back against the headboard. "Let me take care of you."

I flex my thighs when she straddles me and takes my cock in her hand. Our breaths mingle as she rests her forehead against mine. Two pairs of eyes focus on our imminent connection. Hers flutter closed as my crest disappears inside of her. The first hot inch of her core wraps around me. I feel my eyes grow heavy, but they remain glued to where our bodies are joining.

I wrap my arms up her back and hold on to the tops of her shoulders as she slowly sinks down on me. I hate knowing I'm not the only one to be inside of her bare, but the realization that she's my first is overwhelming. I realize, if I have any control over my destiny, that this is the very last woman I will ever slide into. That knowledge is beyond powerful, and not one single piece of fear comes with the realization that she's it for me. I only regret that I didn't find her sooner.

Chapter 40
Lexi

"I can't believe how much I missed you," I whisper against Kegan's chest. The slow graze of his fingers up my spine set my nerve endings on fire.

We've been in this bed for hours showing each other with our bodies what our hearts feel.

"It can't possibly be more than I missed you," he says with assuredness. "For the first time in my life, I want to spend every second of every day with one person, almost like nothing else matters. That should scare the shit out of me, but I only feel... calm." His body shifts until he can meet my eyes. "How did you become my everything?" he implores.

I cup his cheek with my hand and nuzzle my nose against his neck. "You've got it bad, Cole. Are you sure you don't want to have your head evaluated?"

"I'm serious, Lexi. I don't want to spend another night away from you. I don't want to wake up wondering where you are or what your heart is feeling. I want you with me, in our bed." He swallows hard and shifts his weight between my legs. He's already grown hard again, an amazing feat considering how many times we've already made love this evening. "Move in with me?"

I shake my head, and his face falls. "I'm not giving up my house, Kegan."

"I need to be where you are." His eyes search mine, begging me to change my mind.

"Sounds like you're moving into my place then."

He scoffs and backs away slightly. "Live off a woman? My ego and manliness can't take another hit without being called into questions."

"Don't get all alpha male on me. And you sure as hell won't be living off of me. You're going to pay half of the bills. And do the yard work. And maintain the property. All sorts of manly things to help with that overinflated ego of yours."

His body relaxes.

"We can try it out," I offer. "You can come stay for a while and see if it works out."

"Is there any way I can convince you to move in here?"

I shake my head.

"Then my condo is gone. I won't keep it a minute longer. As far as your 'see if it works,' that's not even an option. Not working out isn't in my vocabulary, Lexi, and you need to remove it from yours, too."

His insistence is heartfelt, and I can't help but smile up at him. "So you're moving in?"

"I'm moving in," he whispers against my mouth. "But first I need to move into something else."

I moan when his hips thrust forward, and he penetrates me fully. "I love your cock."

"My cock loves you."

Those are the last words spoken for several more hours.

"I don't get why it's such a damn big deal," Kegan says crossing his arms over his chest and pouting like a petulant child.

I pinch the bridge of my nose and give myself a second to calm down. Who knew moving in together was going to be such a chore? "We've been over this, Kegan. You're thirty-three years old. The air hockey table isn't coming to my house."

"Please?" He slides his body against mine, not caring that movers are all around us gathering boxes.

"You have to grow up at some point."

"Baby," he whispers, the heat of his breath causing my arousal to spike. "I'm grown where it counts." His hips rotate against mine, and although he's not fully erect, I can't help but agree with him. "You know that thing I do with my tongue that you like so much?" I nod against his neck as my hands find and grip handfuls of hair. "Let me keep it and I'll do that for hours tonight with you spread out on that air hockey table. Imagine the tickle of the air teasing your skin while my mouth does dirty things to your body."

"Jesus," I pant. "You drive a hard bargain."

"*Hard*, being the operative word here." Another rotation of his hips, and yep he's fully erect now.

"You guys need a minute or are the movers going to get a free show?" Justin walks past with a chuckle. "I know you guys are into the whole voyeuristic thing, but the youngest guy on the crew walked into a wall with that expensive vase when he couldn't take his eyes off of you." He makes his way closer to us and whispers. "You'll live in his spank bank for years to come."

Kegan takes a step away, and I block his view from the others as he adjusts his jeans.

"Ma'am?" one of the workers says grabbing my attention from across the room. "The air hockey table?"

My cheeks flush immediately. "Load it up."

I watch for several more minutes as the guys carry armfuls of boxes out to the waiting moving van.

"You sure grabbed a great one," Justin says tilting his head to the side when Kegan squats down to pick up a box from the floor. His eyes follow his ass as he stands.

I slap him on the chest. "You're not being very discrete."

Hearing my words, Kegan turns back and looks at me. Justin in his perusal doesn't have enough time to school his face before Kegan notices. His brows furrow until realization dawns in his eyes. His smirk as he walks out of the condo with the box is all knowing.

"Lucky bitch," Justin mumbles before walking away.

"You've got to be kidding me," Kegan says a few minutes later after giving the moving crew the address for my house. "Justin really wasn't into London after all, not in a traditional sense anyway."

I turn on him. "He cared for her. He could have made her happy. He could make any woman happy, minus the whole sex thing."

"I didn't even realize," he says running his hand over his beard.

"Not many people know." I turn toward him making sure he can see the seriousness in my eyes. "You can't tell anyone, Kegan."

He holds his hands up in surrender. "Not my story to tell, baby." He walks away, and I think the conversation is over, but of course this is Kegan. He turns back and winks at me. "Tell him he has great taste in men."

This man; what in the hell have I gotten myself into?

Epilogue
3 YEARS LATER
Kegan

Sunday dinner remains a Cole family tradition. Not much has changed in the last three years. As much as I wish I could say Anastyn's mouthiness has improved, it hasn't. Her vocabulary is much larger, though. I still can't keep my hands off of Lexi. She's gotten used to the attention around my family. If anything, it's just par for the course. Kadin and my dad are just as attentive to their loves as I am with her. I've been led by a fine example.

Tonight's dinner is even more special. As a family, we're celebrating forty-five years of marriage for my parents. Needless to say, love is thick in the air, and it makes it even harder for any of us to keep our hands to ourselves. It's not weird, like orgy town or anything. Keep it together; there are children present.

Easton, having fully recovered from his illness has grown incredibly fast. He's built like a miniature linebacker, and he's even gotten pretty good at running a few drills. So long as a grasshopper doesn't come along and redirect his attention, he's pretty focused on learning. I mean, as much as an almost four-year-old kid can be.

Lennox always has a book in her hand. I'm certain she gets that from her mom because Kadin is more interested in reading blue prints than anything with actual sentences on it.

I cut my eyes to nine-year-old Anastyn and watch in horror as she applies chapstick to her lips in a tiny mirror as if she's preparing for the red carpet. Kadin is going to have his hands full with that one. She's as beautiful as her mother, but also has the exotic red tint to her hair that Kadin had as a baby. I don't envy him at all. Shotguns, death threats, and a possible prison sentence are in his future when she's old enough to date.

Lexi shifting beside me in her seat pulls me from admiring my brother's family. "I told you," I hiss in her ear. "If you keep wiggling like that, I'm going to take you into the bathroom and fuck you against the door."

She glares back at me. "I told you to let me come in the truck. It's your fault for getting me all worked up and leaving me unsatisfied."

I huff a quick laugh. "Do I ever leave you unsatisfied, baby?"

"You may call it delayed gratification, but in my book it's torture."

"Go into the bathroom and take care of yourself. I can't have you wiggling like a horny worm in front of my family. It's embarrassing."

Her glare grows. "I embarrass you." She smacks me hard on the chest. "You say random shit. You," she says jabbing a finger into my stomach. "You embarrass me daily with the shit that just pops out of your mouth."

She's frustrated as she pushes her chair back. The calm with which she places her cloth napkin beside her wine glass makes me fidget.

"Marry me," I say to her retreating back.

She stiffens and her hands clench. "That's not... funny," she spits turning around to face me.

Her eyes suddenly tear up, and her chin begins to quiver when she finds me on one knee with a tiny velvet box in my hand.

My mom squeals and "about fucking time," comes from my dad. Those reactions mix with London's "Holy shit, hell has frozen over" and Kadin's "atta boy."

Her face softens, the anger suddenly washing away.

"Those are the best words I've ever heard you say," she whispers with her hands to her chest.

I rise from my knee and walk toward her. "I thought the 'I love you' was pretty good."

"Meh," she says playfully with a shrug.

"Is that a yes?" I can read the answer in her eyes, but my heart needs the words.

"Yes," she whispers against my mouth as I slip the solitaire on her finger.

I pull her to my chest and plant my face in the crook of her neck, breathing her in, absorbing my future.

"I still need to come," she says quietly.

I can't get her out of that house fast enough.

"Marriage," Lexi says looking down at the rock shining on her finger. "Are you sure?"

I crinkle my brow. "I wouldn't have asked if I wasn't sure."

She cocks an eyebrow at me. "Okay. I wouldn't have asked *this time* if I wasn't sure."

I lick my way up her body and grab a condom from the bedside table. I wish I could say that she allowed the 'no condom' thing to continue past that one night, but she didn't. I got to spend one blissful night bare inside of the woman I love; then she crushed my heart the next day when she insisted I go back to using them.

"We have a lot to talk about, Lexi." I kiss her lips softly but bite her lower one as I pull away. Soft *and* hard has always been our thing. "I'm not getting any younger."

"Thirty –six next month," she confirms.

"I want babies," I confess. Her eyes shine with unshed tears. "I want you to have my babies."

"I want that too," she says surprising me.

"Really?" She nods with a small smile. "You're sure?"

She wraps her legs around my hips and urges me inside of her. I groan just like I've done the ten million times I've slid inside of her over the years.

"I'm sure," she breathes into my neck.

I pull back so I can look in her eyes. "Full disclosure," I say not knowing how she's going to respond. "I poked holes in all of these condoms last week."

Her cheeks flush red, and I prepare for her to throw me and my ring across the room. "I stopped taking birth control last month," she says with a devious smirk.

I roll my lips between my teeth to keep from laughing as I pull out of her, slip the useless condom off, and sink back in.

More From Marie James
Marie James Facebook: Marie James
Author Group: Author Marie James All Hale Fans
Twitter: @AuthrMarieJame
Instagram: author_marie_james

Hale Series
Coming to Hale

The only time she trusted someone with her heart, she was just a girl; he betrayed her and left her humiliated. Since then, Lorali Bennett has let that moment in time dictate her life.

Ian Hale, sexy as sin business mogul, has never had more than a passing interest in any particular woman, until a chance encounter with Lorali, leaves a lasting mark on him.

Their fast-paced romance is one for the record books, but what will happen when Ian's secrets come to light? Especially when those secrets will cost her everything she spent years trying to rebuild.

Begging for Hale

Alexa Warner, an easy going, free spirit, has never had a problem with jumping from one man to the next. She likes to party and have a good time; if the night ends in steamy sex that's a bonus. She's always sought pleasure first and never found a man that turned her down; until Garrett Hale. Never in her life was she forced to pursue a man, but his rejection doesn't sit well with her. Alexa aches for Garrett, his rejection festering in her gut. The yearning for him escalating until she is able to seduce him, taste him.

Garrett Hale, a private man with muted emotions, has no interest in serious relationships. Having his heart ripped out by his first love, he now leaves a trail of one night stands in his wake. Mutually satisfying sex without commitment is his newly adopted lifestyle. Alexa's constant temptation has his restraint wavering. The aftermath of giving into her would be messy; she is after all the best friend of his cousin's girlfriend, which guarantees future run-ins, not something that's supposed to happen with a one night stand.

Yet, the allure of having his mouth on her is almost more than he can bear. With hearts on the line, and ever increasing desire burning through them both, will one night be enough for either of them?

Hot as Hale

Innocent Joselyne Bennett loves her quiet life. As an elementary teacher, her days include teaching kids then going home to research fun science projects to add to her lesson plan. Her only excitement is living vicariously through her sister Lorali and friend Alexa Warner. Incredibly gorgeous police detective Kaleb Perez was going through the motions of life. His position on the force as a narcotics detective forced him to cross paths with Josie after a shooting involving her friend. On more than one occasion Kaleb discretely tried to catch Josie's eye. On every occasion, he was ignored but when her hand is forced after a break-in at her apartment Josie and Kaleb are on a collision course with each other.

Formerly timid Josie is coaxed out of her shell by the sexy-as-sin Kaleb, who nurtures her inner sex-kitten in the most seductive ways, and replaces her inexperience with passionate need. The small group has overcome so much in such a short period of time, and just when they think they can settle back into their lives, they are forced back into the unknown.

Can Kaleb protect Josie from further tragedy? Can she let him go once the threat of danger is gone?

To Hale and Back

Just when things seem like they're getting back to normal and everyone is safe, drugs, money, and vengeance lead a rogue group into action, culminating in a series of events that leave one man dead and another in jail for a wide range of crimes, none of which he is guilty of.

This incredibly strong and close-knit group of six will be pushed to their limits when they are thrown into adversity. But can they come out unscathed? The situation turns dire when friendships and bonds are tested past the breaking point. Allegiances are questioned, and relationships may crumble.

Hale Series Box Set
Love Me Like That

Two strangers trapped together in a blizzard. One running from the past; one with no future. Two destinies collide.

London Sykes is on her own for the first time in her life after a sequence of betrayal and abuse. One man rescues her only to destroy her himself. An unfortunate accident lands her in a ditch only to be rescued by the most closed-off man she's ever met, albeit undeniably handsome.

Kadin Cole is at the cabin in the woods for the very first and the very last time. Since his grief doesn't allow for him to return home to a life he's no longer able to live alone, he's finally made what has been the hardest decision of his life. His plans change drastically when a beautiful woman in a little red car crashes into his life. How can she trust another man? How could he ever love again? Will happenstance and ensuing sexual attraction be enough to heal two hearts enough that they can see in themselves what the other sees?

Teach Me Like That

Thirty-three, single, and loving life.

Construction worker by day and playboy by night. Kegan Cole has what many men can only dream about. A great job, incredible family, and more women fawning over him than he can count. What more could he ask for?

Lexi Carter spends her days teaching at a private school. Struggling to rebuild her life after tragedy nearly destroyed her, she doesn't have the time or energy to invest in any arrangement that could lead to heartbreak. That includes the enigmatic Kegan Cole whose arrogance and sex appeal arrive long before he enters a room.

It doesn't matter how witty, charming, and incredibly sexy he is. She plays games all day with her students and has no room in her life for games when it comes to men, and Kegan Cole has *'love them and leave them'* written all over his handsome bearded face.

When Lexi doesn't fall at his feet like every other woman before her, Kegan is forced off-script to pursue her because not convincing her to give in isn't an option.

How can a man who hates lies be compatible with a woman who has more secrets than she can count?

Can a man set in his playboy ways become the man Lexi needs? More importantly, does he even want to?

This is a full-length novel that has adult language and descriptive sex scenes. It is NOT a student/teacher book. Both main characters are consenting adults.

Cerberus MC

Kincaid Book 1

I am Emmalyn Mikaelson.

My husband, in a rage, hit me in front of the wrong person. Diego, or Kincaid to most, beat the hell out of him for it. I left with Diego anyway. Even though he could turn on me just like my husband did, I knew I had a better chance of survival with Diego. That was until I realized Kincaid could hurt me so much worse than my husband ever could. Physical pain pales in comparison to troubles of the heart.

I am Diego "Kincaid" Anderson.

She was a waitress at a bar in a bad situation. I brought her to my clubhouse because I knew her husband would kill her if I didn't. Now she has my protection and that of the Cerberus MC. I never expected her to become something more to me. I was in more trouble than I've ever been in before, and that's saying a lot considering I served eight years in the Marine Corps with Special Forces.

SINdicate Book 1.5 (BT Urruela FanFiction)

BT Urruela is former military with scars from war that forever changed his life. He attends an acting class, is a personal trainer at an elite facility in Tampa, and is your typical warm-blooded male. Life is pretty easy-going for BT... then Aviana Maguire catches his eye. Aviana attends the same acting class as BT, but does her best to stay under the radar. She's the product of a broken family and a less than desirable childhood. She's riddled with emotional scars and has extreme trust issues with men and all relationships in general.

Life was hard for Aviana as she struggled daily to just stay afloat. Just when she thought life couldn't get more difficult, she's snatched away from her home as retribution for someone else's mistakes.

Underworlds, debts, and an obsession for justice could change everything for them both. BT may rescue the girl he tracked into the dark recesses of Las Vegas, but will she ever be the same? Or will BT become so deeply involved in SIN, that he becomes the one needing to be rescued?

Kid: Cerberus MC Book 2

Khloe When Khloe Devaro's best friend and fiancé is lost to the war in Iraq, she's beyond distraught. Her intentions of joining him in the afterlife are thwarted by a Cerberus Motorcycle club member. Too young to do anything on her own, the only alternative she has now is to take Kid up on his offer to stay at the MC Clubhouse. As if that's not a disaster waiting to happen, but anything is better than returning to the foster home she's been forced to live in the last three years.

"Kid" Dustin "Kid" Andrews spent four years as a Marine; training, fighting, and learning how to survive the most horrendous of conditions. He never imagined that holding a BBQ fundraiser for a local fallen soldier would end up as the catalyst that turns his world upside down. Resisting his attraction for a girl he's not even certain is of legal age was easy, until he's forced to intervene when her intentions become clear. All his training is wasted as far as he's concerned, since none of that will help him when it comes to Khloe. Will the self-proclaimed man-whore sleep with a woman in every country he visits as planned, or will the beautiful, yet feisty girl living down the hall throw a wrench in his plan?

Shadow: Cerberus MC Book 3

Morrison "Shadow" Griggs, VP of the Cerberus MC, is a force to be reckoned with. Women fall at his feet, willing to do almost anything for a night with him.

Misty Bowen is the exception. She's young and impressionable, but with her religious upbringing, she's able to resist Shadow's advances... for a while at least.

Never one to look back on past conquests, Shadow is surprised that he's intrigued by Misty, which only grows more when she seems to be done with him without a word.

Being ghosted by a twenty-one-year-old is not the norm where he's concerned, and the rejection doesn't sit right with him.

Life goes on, however, until Misty shows up on the doorstep of the Cerberus MC clubhouse with a surprise that rocks his entire world off of its axis.

With only the clothes on her back and the consequences of her lies and deceit, Misty needs help now more than she ever has. Alone in the world and desperate for help, she turns to the one man she thought she'd never see again.

Shadow would never turn his back on a woman in need, but his inability to forgive has always been his main character flaw. Unintended circumstances have cast Misty into his life, but will he have the ability to keep his distance when her situation necessitates a closeness he's never dreamed of having with a woman?

Psychosis
Matthew Hosea FanFiction Novella
Co-write with Gina Sevani

Louisiana-born – Tennessee-raised, sweet talking country boy Matthew Hosea is now the new panty-melting heartthrob model of the Author World. He steals many hearts with his sexy voice and muscular body. Matthew spends his days staying extremely busy between being Active Duty Navy, a Nutrition Sales Representative, and a part-time Bouncer at the local bar. Not to mention the two-a-day gym visits. He has no time for women to take permanent residence in his life. The last thing he needs on top of such a crazy ass schedule is drama.

Leia Walker has had nothing but a troubled chaotic life. Sometimes it's hard for her to stick to reality when fantasy is much more pleasurable. Besides, it's easier to control. Temptation is hard for Leia to fight; it's constantly dangling right in front of her. She spends her time hanging out in the shadows waiting for the perfect man; her eyes are set on Matthew Hosea, the new, inked model taking the world by storm. The connection she feels is undeniable. Matthew's the perfect man for her; he just doesn't know it yet. It's a dangerous and wild game that's being played. What will Leia do to get what she wants? Just how far is she willing to go?

Acknowledgements

Just so you know, this book wasn't supposed to exist. Love Me Like That, in my mind was a standalone, but the insistence of fans (and outrageous demands from my PA Brittney Crabtree) forced me into action. I hope you enjoyed Book 2 in the LMLT series, apparently... according to my writing schedule there will be two more...

As always I have to thank my BETA team... Brittney, Laura, Brenda, Diane, Shannon, Tammy, Sadie, and Jessica for going through this book, not only looking for errors but keeping me in line when I stray off course!!

Super shout out to Brittney and Laura for all of their help behind the scenes! I wouldn't get anywhere without these fabulous ladies!!

My lovely husband JA Essen (Mr. Marie James) did an awesome job on the cover and kept me sane with tons of moral support, all while acting as a sounding board for my plot. Thank you, babe!

Give Me Books, once again has blown me away with their promo services!! Thank you ladies!! You ROCK!!

Jim Cauthen did the photo shoot for this cover and the amazing teasers and I couldn't be happier with the interactions I've had with him! Come home safe, soldier.

Readers!! You are AMAZING! Thank you so much for the support. I cannot even believe how blessed I have been!!

Last, but never least, Justin James Cadwell!! You, Mr. Handsome Cover model are the epitome of class and professionalism. Hell, if Brittney had her way you'd be on every cover, and if I could find a way to make it work... I promise you'd be it!! Thank you so much for another fabulous shoot (the videos of you getting wet weren't too shabby either!)

Made in the USA
Monee, IL
15 September 2021